THE DUCHESS HUNT

"Has no gentleman ever kissed you, other than that lad when you were eight?"

Glancing away, she shifted her stance slightly, and he was beginning to realize she did that when she was striving to determine exactly how much to reveal. So maybe there had once been a man for whom she'd considered giving up everything.

"When I was sixteen," she began before meeting his gaze, "a lad kissed me. I recall it being quite awkward. We bumped noses, then chins. Eventually, his lips landed on mine and lingered for a bit. To be honest, I didn't understand what all the fuss was about."

"A boy and a young, callow lad. Would you like to know what it is to be kissed by a man?"

By Lorraine Heath

THE DUCHESS HUNT

A ONCE UPON A DUKEDOM NOVEL

LORRAINE HEATH

AVONBOOKS

An Imprint of HarperCollinsPublishers

THE DUCHESS HUNT. Copyright © 2021 by Jan Nowasky. All rights reserved. Printed in the United States of America. No part of this book may be used or reproduced in any manner whatsoever without written permission except in the case of brief quotations embodied in critical articles and reviews. For information, address HarperCollins Publishers, 195 Broadway, New York, NY 10007.

First Avon Books mass market printing: October 2021

Print Edition ISBN: 978-0-06-295201-1
Digital Edition ISBN: 978-0-06-295200-4

Cover design by Amy Halperin
Cover illustration by Victor Gadino

Avon, Avon & logo, and Avon Books & logo are registered trademarks of HarperCollins Publishers in the United States of America and other countries.

HarperCollins is a registered trademark of HarperCollins Publishers in the United States of America and other countries.

FIRST EDITION

21 22 23 24 25   CWM   10 9 8 7 6 5 4 3 2 1

For Barbara Dombrowski
Who has been there from the beginning—
Critique partner and collector of obscure facts
But most of all, cherished friend

THE
DUCHESS
HUNT

CHAPTER 1

London
July 2, 1874
Six weeks until the Kingsland ball

IF THERE EXISTED a more unpleasant task in the world than selecting the woman who was to marry the man you loved, Penelope Pettypeace certainly couldn't imagine what it might be. But then, during the eight years she had been secretary to the Duke of Kingsland, she had been beset with unpleasant tasks. She should be accustomed to them by now. The latest, however, was beyond the pale.

Sitting at the desk in her small office in his London residence, using the green-marble-handled letter knife he'd given her one Christmas, she efficiently and quickly sliced open another envelope, preferring to keep the wax seal intact, withdrew and unfolded the heavy parchment, adjusted the position of her spectacles, and began scouring the words some young, naive unmarried miss had meticulously and with unbridled hope penned in response to the duke's recent incisive advert seeking a noble lady of marriageable and procreational age to become his duchess. He'd done the same last year, with disastrous results.

He'd made the selection himself, announcing his choice during a ball within this very residence, one she had arranged and overseen. She'd hovered in the shadows as the clang of the magnificent gong echoing to the far corners indicated he was on the verge of revealing his choice. She hadn't known with whom he'd gone until all of London heard her name pass his lips: Lady Kathryn Lambert.

For nearly a year, he'd courted the woman, but in the end, she'd turned him away in favor of a rapscallion with no title and a heritage that included a treasonous father. Kingsland should have learned his lesson then and there: one couldn't take such an impersonal approach to obtaining a suitable wife.

But no. A mere two days after the lady had rejected his proposal, he'd placed another advert in the *Times*, seeking an easy solution to a complicated issue: securing a woman with whom he could be content. Without even deigning to slit open any of the nearly seven dozen envelopes received and giving the carefully worded missives a read, he'd handed the task over to her.

In spite of her upset with the chore, she took her duty seriously and had created a grid on butcher's paper that nearly covered the entire top of her oak desk. She had a column in which she wrote the la- dies' names and one for each attribute she was rather certain the duke wanted in a wife, even though he hadn't bothered with specific requirements other than the most pressing one: "I require a quiet duch- ess, one who is there when I need her and absent when I don't."

And every woman wanted a man who was there when she didn't realize she needed him. A man of charm and grace and insight. A man who didn't mind being bothered when a woman simply wanted someone near to reassure her that she was of value.

Hugh Brinsley-Norton, ninth Duke of Kingsland, was most certainly not that man.

Yet Penelope Pettypeace had managed to fall in love with him all the same. Drat her impractical heart.

He'd never encouraged her deeper affections, and she hadn't realized she harbored them until he'd called out another lady's name, and the words had struck her like a blow to the chest. As a mat- ter of fact, it had been somewhat of a surprise to realize her depth of feelings for the man. Perhaps it was the trust he placed in her to see to his busi- ness affairs when he was away. He often traveled in pursuit of investment opportunities, a singular purpose to his life that left him with little time for other endeavors—such as a proper courtship. He was responsible for four estates—the dukedom, two earldoms, and a viscounty—as well as the wel- fare of those who were dependent upon them for their livelihood. Until she'd come to work for him, she'd always considered the aristocracy a spoiled and lazy lot, but he had shown her the truth of the matter: their obligations often fell heavy upon them. Her respect for him knew no bounds, and her heart had followed.

"Miss Pettypeace?"

"What the devil is it?" She jerked up her head to glare at the poor footman who had interrupted her. Then she felt contrite for having done so because his eyes had widened in astonishment and reflected a touch of horror, like someone who had come upon a large, hideous spider and realized too late that it had taken exception to being disturbed while weaving its web. "My apologies, Harry. How may I be of assistance?"

"His Grace just rang for you from the library."

"Thank you. I'll be there in a tick."

"Very good, miss."

As he immediately and quietly took his leave, she set aside the letter that had listed a host of talents: playing the pianoforte, singing, croquet, and fencing—*that* was a skill no one else had claimed thus far, would require the addition of another column, and might result in injury to the duke when the woman discovered he had no time to enjoy any of her proficiencies. Snatching up a paperweight of black marble upon which had been carved and embossed in gold, "The early bird catches the worm"—a gift from the duke after she'd been with him for a year—she set it on top of the letter to indicate she had not yet finished considering its author as a potential duchess.

After shoving back her chair, she stood, patting

her hair as she did so to ensure no wisps had escaped the no-nonsense bun. She made complete use of every minute of every day, doing a multitude of things concurrently whenever possible. Satisfied with her appearance, without even going to the trouble to look in a mirror, she began marching toward her destination, along the corridor that led to the kitchens, past the wall upon which hung the parallel line of bells—one for the regular staff, one for her—marking the rooms in which a bellpull had been tugged, past the staircase leading to her small bedchamber in the servants' quarters. Then onward along another hallway to the weathered stairs used by footmen to serve a meal, the butler to answer the front door, the maid who saw to the needs of the dowager duchess when she was in residence, and the valet who tended to the duke. Stairs she was allowed to traverse to the main portion of the residence because she also tended to the duke, although not in a manner as personal as the valet. Still, she would argue her duties were much more important. As would the entire household staff, no doubt, because her presence kept things sailing on an even keel. Not once had the butler objected to her handling the duke when His Grace was in a foul mood.

She'd have preferred her study nearer to where he worked, but he'd never asked her preference. Unfortunately, he would probably never do the same of his wife either. His focus was narrow, seldom venturing beyond the empire he'd built. The man cared about little more than making money and securing success at any cost. But the shrewdness, skill, and ruthlessness with which he managed his business affairs had often left her quite breathless. It was a sight to behold, and she had learned a great deal from him, enough that she had managed, like many women, to invest her income in private businesses and government securities with astounding success. Never again would she be forced to do the unthinkable in order to survive.

As she neared the library, a liveried footman standing at the door gave her a quick nod of acknowledgment before opening it. With her shoulders pulled back, her spine straight, her emotions girded, she strode in without giving the barest hint of how much the mere sight of His Grace always weakened her knees. It wasn't his devilishly gorgeous features. She'd known handsome men aplenty. It was the confidence in his bearing, the directness in his steady gaze, the power and influence he wielded with ease. It was the manner in which he looked at her with no lasciviousness whatsoever. He viewed her as he might a man he respected, a man whose opinion he valued. And for her, who had never known any of that before him, it was an aphrodisiac.

His dark hair, half an inch longer than fashionable—she would have to take up the matter with his valet—called to her deft fingers to brush aside the forelock that forever seemed to be in a state of rebellion, falling over his obsidian eyes as he came to his feet, unfolding that long, lithe body that any clothing would be fortunate to drape. That his tailor painstakingly ensured each stitch was perfect only served to make the duke more dashing.

She'd seen him at breakfast, of course. He insisted she join him because ideas, musings, and things to be researched often entered his mind as he slept or upon first awakening, and they sometimes dictated how she spent her day. She was also prone to fits of stirring from slumber when solutions came to her regarding problems they were striving to solve, and she'd share them with him as they took their repast. It was a lovely way to begin her day, even when they had nothing to say and simply read the separate newspapers the butler ironed and set beside each of their places. The duke believed it to his advantage for her to be as informed as possible.

"Pettypeace, splendid, you've arrived." His deep, smooth voice created warmth in her belly like the brandy she enjoyed before retiring. "Allow me to introduce Mr. Lancaster."

She nodded toward the gentleman in the ill-fitting tweed jacket. "Sir."

"Lancaster, Miss Pettypeace, my secretary."

"A pleasure, miss."

She'd put him a couple of years past her own of twenty-eight. He had a hunger about him, an eagerness in his gray eyes as though he knew he was on the cusp of making a fortune, but she also sensed a wariness because he understood all hopes could be torn asunder with two small words from the duke: *not interested*.

"Miss Pettypeace will be taking notes so I can

consider the matter more fully later. I like to ruminate over investment possibilities, you see."

A polite way of saying he would be digging into Mr. Lancaster's life until he knew the precise day and time and with whom the man had lost his virginity and, ages before that, how long he might have nursed at his mother's teat.

As unobtrusively as possible, she removed from her skirt pocket the pencil and small leather-bound notebook she always carried with her, slid over to a winged chair at the edge of the sitting area, adjusted her spectacles on the bridge of her nose, and sat. Both gentlemen took their chairs.

"Right then, Lancaster, impress me with this scheme of yours that is guaranteed to make me wealthier than I already am."

KING HAD THE enviable skill of concentrating on more than one thing at a time, so as Lancaster waxed on about his invention—a clock that would emit an alarm at a particular time designated by its owner—he appeared to be giving his full attention to the inventor while out of the corner of his eye, he admired Pettypeace's new frock. It was dark blue. Of course it was dark blue. She only ever wore dark blue. However, because he also possessed a gift for memory, he knew in spite of it not daring to reveal so much as the dip of her collarbones, it had two fewer buttons than any of her other frocks, the sleeves running all the way to her wrists were a slightly closer fit, and the bustle smaller. He wondered when she'd had time to have it sewn, but then, she was a paragon of efficiency. He'd once asked her why she always wore dark blue instead of a cheerier color, and she'd immediately taken offense. "Do you ask your solicitor why he doesn't strut about in brighter jackets like a peacock?"

Of course he didn't. He didn't give a damn about Beckwith's attire, but she'd made her point. She took her position seriously and wore nothing to give the impression she was flighty by nature. Still, he thought a hunter green would accomplish the same result while also serving to bring out the green shade of her eyes, sharp eyes, clever eyes. They were the reason he'd employed her.

A dozen men had applied for the position when he'd announced it. She'd been the only woman. She'd also been the only one to meet his gaze straight on, to never look away, to never flinch—not even when she'd lied. If she was a vicar's daughter, he was a beggar's son.

He'd hired the best investigators, detectives, spies—and they'd been unable to discover a single thing about her. It was as though she'd not existed until the moment she walked into his office for her interview.

He of the shrewd mind, who considered odds, was willing to suffer a loss for a larger gain, and weighed risks, had taken a hell of a big one with her—and given her the position. Without knowing anything about her other than what she'd shared that long-ago afternoon. And he had yet to regret it.

She was a marvel. Quite possibly the most intelligent person he'd ever known. That, too, had been reflected in those emerald eyes of hers.

Now they were concentrating on what she was scribbling as Lancaster spoke. She had perfect penmanship, no matter how quickly she wrote. Although at the moment, he knew she was using something she referred to as the Pitman method, a series of curls, slashes, and dots that made no sense whatsoever to him, but then they didn't have to. She would translate it all and write it out later for his records. He seldom forgot anything but preferred to have the reminders all the same. Besides, she often caught the smallest of details that he might have overlooked or decided at the time had no bearing—only to discover later they were crucial. They were a team, she and he. Other than his three best mates from Oxford, he trusted no one more.

Although he wasn't certain she could say the same of him. Otherwise, why had she shared nothing else of her past, other than what she had that first afternoon? On the one hand, he felt he knew her as well as he knew himself. Yet he couldn't deny the gaping holes that seemed to yawn wider with the passage of time. He told himself her past was of no consequence. She did what was asked of her and she did it flawlessly.

Besides, she had a right to keep her secrets. After all, he was damned good at keeping his.

But still, he sometimes wondered . . .

He became acutely aware of the expectant silence looming around him. Uncharacteristically, he'd stopped listening intently, but he had the gist of what Lancaster was proposing. "Interesting. Your invention would put knocker-uppers out of business." Those paid to tap on windows to awaken workers at certain hours. Lancaster appeared stricken by the notion, as though he'd not considered all the ramifications of his invention. "That said, all progress results in someone losing. Look at the railroads. Coach services are used less frequently, and inns along well-worn paths have fewer customers. But opportunities open elsewhere. People can more easily travel to seaside resorts, which are thriving as a result. So you'll need a factory. That's what you're seeking from me as an investor, I take it."

"Yes, Your Grace."

"I shall consider it, Mr. Lancaster, but will need to do some research of my own first. Within a fortnight, we'll meet again, in my London office." He preferred its austere businesslike setting when the possibility of negotiations loomed. "I shall have an answer for you then." As he came to his feet, he extended a card to the man as he also rose. "Leave your own card with Miss Pettypeace. She'll be in touch regarding the exact date and time for our next appointment."

"Thank you, Your Grace."

He rushed over to King's secretary and gave her his card. She smiled. "Well done, sir."

Her response gave King no hint as to what she was truly thinking, because she said the same words, in that cheerful tone, to anyone who pitched him an idea, no matter how atrocious or ridiculous it might be. It was as though she knew what it was to never be encouraged, as though she wanted to provide hope in a world without any.

Once Lancaster was gone, King dropped back

into his chair, met his secretary's gaze, and settled in to enjoy his favorite part of any investment opportunity. "What are your thoughts on the matter, Pettypeace?"

As always when she shared her initial impressions, she removed her spectacles to gently massage the bridge of her nose. A few blond strands had attached themselves to the wire frames and managed to escape the prison of her severely secured bun, so they now dangled loosely along her temple and the edge of her jawline. They caught his attention because it was seldom any aspect of her was unruly. It made her an excellent employee, but suddenly he found himself wondering if she was done up with such precision after she retired for the evening or on her day off. Was what he saw every day merely a facade, or was it her true self? No nonsense whatsoever. He approved, and yet it bothered him to realize he didn't know the sound of her laughter.

"You will need to find a way to make them cheaply. Those who would benefit from this contraption will have few coins to spare for what most will no doubt view as a luxury item." She settled her spectacles into place.

"I quite agree, was thinking along those same lines." He placed his elbow on the arm of his chair and his chin in his palm. Slowly, he rubbed his finger along his bottom lip. "I've seen something similar in France, but it can be set only to blare noisily at a particular hour, on the dot."

"Whereas Mr. Lancaster's invention allows the alarm to go off at a precise moment of a particular hour, so someone who didn't *need* to awaken until half six could sleep for half an hour more."

"When have you ever not arisen at the top of the hour, Pettypeace? When have you ever slept late?"

Her mouth curled up slightly. "I always have a lie-in on Christmas morning, a gift to myself."

His stomach knotted up so tightly as to be almost painful. He hadn't known that. Christ, was he so desperate for any hidden nugget of information concerning her that his body would react as though she'd stood up and stripped bare before him? Or was it because he'd immediately been hit with the image of her in bed, snuggled beneath the covers . . . waking, stretching, remembering it was a holiday, rolling onto her side, and drifting back off, a contented smile on her face? Or was it that her gift to herself was something so simple, something she could experience any day of the year, but denied herself because, like him, she was driven to accomplish great things, no matter the personal sacrifice? That thought led him to wondering what the devil drove her.

"You're too stingy with yourself, Pettypeace. You should purchase something extravagant for Christmas."

"The best gifts usually cost nothing at all." Her smile was winsome, as though she was lost in memories, and he was tempted to ask her what the best gift she'd ever received was. Devil take him, but he wanted to know who had given it to her.

Through his mind paraded all the gifts with which he'd graced her, items one gave a secretary so she could better see to her duties or at least enjoy them more: a gold-nibbed pen, a crystal inkwell, the small leather notebook she'd used earlier, and so much more. But nothing of a personal nature. He had no idea what she liked for herself, what would make her smile in the same warm manner she'd smiled at Lancaster. Suddenly, it seemed imperative to give her something that would be met with more than a "Thank you, Your Grace. I shall put it to good use."

He wanted to present her with something that wasn't useful in the least.

Her mouth abruptly returned to business as she stood. The manners drilled into him since he was placed in a cradle forced him to rise, even though he wouldn't have were she a man employed to assist him with his business.

"I'll write up the notes and present them to you this afternoon. Shall I send word to your usual sleuths and get them on the scent of Mr. Lancaster?" She held up the man's card. Numerous reasons existed for his having Lancaster hand over his card. Some of the men he employed would be able to tell him exactly where the inventor had it printed.

"Most certainly."

"Did you want to move ahead and obtain quotes from factories to compare against the cost of building your own?"

"You know me so well, Pettypeace."

She almost smiled at that. He saw her lips twitch.

"Is there anything else, Your Grace?"

"Yes. We'll be dining tonight at the club with the Chessmen."

"*We*, sir?"

"I'll need you there. Bishop has some scheme or other to present, and I'll want you to take notes."

"But it is a club for men only."

"I've secured a private dining room with a private entrance. Have the coach brought round at half seven."

She gave a curt nod. "Yes, sir."

She turned to go.

"Pettypeace?"

Before she'd stopped to face him, he'd already begun moving toward her. It took him only six strides to reach her. She didn't have the length in her legs that he did. She wasn't so much as a quarter of an inch over five feet. Gingerly, he gathered up the few silken blond strands that had been caressing her check and tucked them behind her ear. "We will all be dressed rather formally. If you have something less . . . staid, feel free to wear it."

She blinked, swallowed, nodded. "But it *is* business."

"Of course, without question."

She patted her hair, then smiled. Warm and bright. "I'm quite looking forward to seeing the inside of a gentlemen's club."

As she left, he was hit with the unexpected realization that he would willingly pay a fortune to keep that tantalizing smile on her face.

CHAPTER 2

GOOD LORD. DINNER at the club with the Chessmen. Known for their mastery of strategy and their ruthlessness when it came to tactical investment and business maneuvers, they had earned their moniker while at Oxford, and it had carried through to the present.

Penelope could hardly believe her good fortune. She'd dined with them before, here at the residence as well as at the ducal country estate. But at the club . . . well, it was unprecedented. None were admitted into their inner circle, and while she wouldn't be in it, she would be at the edge of it, breathing the same air as they did. Even if she was going as a secretary with the specific duty of taking notes, she still felt empowered.

When it came to formal attire, her wardrobe was somewhat lacking. She usually ate her evening meal with the servants, but on the rare occasion the duke invited her to join him and his guests, it had always been an informal affair. Even when the dowager duchess was in town and deigned to have Penelope at the table, it had been with the understanding that it was because of the older woman's generosity, and Penelope was expected to still look the part of staff, so she always wore one of her dark blue frocks.

Within her wardrobe, the only clothing that came remotely close to being formal was the pale green gown she'd worn to oversee last year's ball so she wouldn't look too out of place wandering among the guests as she ensured everything was being managed as it should. Still, it was rather understated, with a square neckline that revealed her collarbones and perhaps an inch and a half of skin below them, but certainly no cleavage, no swells, no hint of forbidden flesh. The sleeves were narrow puffy caps that rested off her shoulders and barely covered the top curve of her arms. The bustle was modest. The skirt was without ribbons, although it did have additional fabric that draped in a few tiers down to the floor. As for her hair—

"Lucy, I simply can't express how much I appreciate this."

The chambermaid smiled, the cheval glass catching her reflection. "Don't be daft, Penn. I enjoy doing your hair. It's incredibly manageable. I'd do it for you every morning if you asked."

Only she wasn't going to ask. Lucy Smithers had enough to see to, looking after all the upstairs chambers. Even when only one was occupied, she had to ensure all the others were dusted, swept, and ready to go at a minute's notice. Still, as Penelope studied her coiffure in the mirror, the manner in which Lucy had pinned up her hair but created curls that floated down her back, she couldn't help but wish that femininity wasn't a detriment to being taken seriously. The pearl comb hiding the pins, helping to keep everything in place, was a nice touch. Penelope had purchased it for last year's ball—an extravagance, but it was something her mum had always longed to possess, and so she'd justified the expense as a tribute to her departed mother.

"You look as fancy as any lady I've ever seen. I daresay the duke won't half change his mind about using that advert when he catches sight of you."

Her heart pounded so hard she was surprised she didn't see the bodice of her gown throb in the mirror. Turning away from her reflection, she walked to the bed, picked up a white silk glove from where she'd set it earlier, and began to tug it on. "Don't be ridiculous. He comes from too storied a family to settle for a commoner." Especially one with beginnings such as hers.

"You never know. He wouldn't be the first duke to do such a thing."

If she could get to a betting book, she'd wager all her yearly earnings that he'd do no such thing. Unlike Lucy, who had a romantic bent, Penelope was moored in reality. As was Kingsland. The man hadn't a romantic bone in his body. She knew because whenever he'd had to be absent for any length of time while courting Lady Kathryn Lambert, he'd instructed Penelope to "Send her flowers or something every few days so she knows I'm thinking of her."

Which meant he hadn't thought about her at all. Out of sight, out of mind. She needed to find a wife for him who didn't cling, didn't need to have her hand held constantly, and was strong enough to see to herself. A woman with her own interests, her own goals, who had the ability to take hold of her role as wife to the Duke of Kingsland and make it her own. An independent sort, a woman much like herself, who knew her worth was not measured by the man in her life but by her own accomplishments. Thus far in their letters, the ladies had listed books they'd read, tunes to which they enjoyed dancing, instruments mastered. The ability to manage a household. How did one go about judging a woman's strengths based on reading words on paper? She might have to actually meet the most promising candidates.

If the woman she selected eventually rejected his suit, the failure would rest on her shoulders, but Society would place it on his—and that outcome she would not tolerate. While he hadn't seemed to mind the recent debacle, the Duke of Kingsland was accustomed to enjoying success. Another fiasco, one delivered by her hands, might see her losing her position.

However, could she carry on, seeing him day in and day out, night in and night out, with another woman? He'd always been so discreet with his affairs that sometimes she wasn't even certain if he'd had any. But a man as virile as he couldn't go long without seeing to his sexual needs.

She picked up her reticule. It contained her notebook and pencil, since the gown was flawed and possessed no pocket. In spite of her requesting the modiste include two, the woman had failed to do so, citing something about them ruining the lines. Lines were not more important than pockets, but she'd had no time to have another gown sewn before it was needed. So here she was with a defective gown, but taking another quick glance in the mirror, she had to admit she looked quite well turned out in it.

"Wake me when you get in," Lucy said as she followed her into the hallway. "I want to hear all about your evening and the gaming hell— whatever bit of it you can see."

"I can't imagine we'll be out so late that you'll be abed by the time we return." She headed down the stairs. When she reached the bottom of them, a couple of footmen stopped to grin stupidly at her as though she wasn't the woman who often scolded them for being so loud she could hear them in her office and barely concentrate. "Off with you. Haven't you work to do?"

"You look quite lovely, Miss Pettypeace," Harry said.

She feared she was blushing, couldn't remember the last time she had—although it was possible it might have happened that morning when the duke tucked her wayward strands of hair behind her ear. He'd never performed such an intimate service for her before, and it had taken nearly an hour to get her lungs to behave properly again. "Thank you, Harry."

"Enjoy your evening."

"I shall."

"Remember," Lucy said, "to come tell me everything."

"All right. Although I doubt there will be anything of significance to report." After all, it was merely dinner, and she was to take notes. Nothing out of the ordinary from her regular duties, except for the location. Then she grinned as stupidly as the footmen had. She was going to a gentlemen's club.

As King descended the stairs, he wasn't at all surprised to see Pettypeace standing in the foyer. The woman was never tardy. She was a breath of fresh air after spending a good bit of his adult life waiting on his mother whenever he accompanied her anywhere. The duchess considered the time for departure to be a mere suggestion, not a goal to be achieved. But for Pettypeace, everything was a marker to be steadfastly met and exceeded whenever possible. Fairly certain she'd already been waiting several minutes, he was enraptured by the excitement shimmering off her, an excitement he remembered experiencing himself when he was a young buck on the cusp of entering his first gentlemen's club. As he neared, he realized he'd judged correctly how her wearing green would bring out the shade of her eyes.

But it was more than that. The shade enhanced the glow of her skin, made her hair look as though it had been spun from moonbeams. Or perhaps it was simply the way the silken strands were pulled away to dangle down her back with a few curling wisps framing her face, making her appear younger, free of cares or burdens. He had an urge to rub the tresses between his thumb and forefinger, to give them more attention than he had that morning.

"Pettypeace," he acknowledged briskly, striving to give the impression he wasn't finding it deuced difficult at that moment to think of her as his secretary. His butler, Keating, handed him his hat and walking stick.

"Your Grace," she said.

"I like that frock. Green suits you."

Pink tinged her cheeks, only the second time since their association that she'd blushed in front of him. He didn't particularly like how much the reaction pleased him, or how much more intriguing it made her. The swath of color seemed out of place on a woman as no-nonsense as she. Another thing not in character for her was that she seemed to be without words. He'd never known her not to have an opinion and express it.

"It's not a practical shade," she finally managed.

"Still." He kept his voice cool, hoping to imply it was no more than a gentlemanly compliment that carried little weight, when in truth he took far more pleasure from the sight of her in it than he should. "Shall we?"

Keating beat him to the door and opened it, leaving King to follow in Pettypeace's wake, tugging on his gloves as they went.

"Are you certain you won't get into trouble, having me at the gentlemen's club?"

An image of the sort of trouble he could get into with her between the sheets—

He shut down those inappropriate thoughts. She was not for bedding. To do anything at all that might result in her resigning her post would be foolhardy on his part. He'd never find anyone as accomplished as she at handling her duties. "I should like to see them try to take issue with anything I do."

Her chuckle was light, demure, and he had a desire to witness her laughing uproariously, full-throatedly. Did she ever lose control and allow laughter to simply spill out of her?

Once they were settled on the squabs, sitting opposite each other, and the coach was on its way, she said, "I notice your valet took shears to your hair."

"At your behest, as I understand it. Apparently, you noted I was beginning to look a bit scraggly."

"Only a bit."

"Whatever would I do without you, Pettypeace?"

"I shall hope you never have to find out."

So did he, more than was wise. What if she had a suitor? What if she married and her husband didn't wish for her to remain employed? Was there someone she fancied? Had she worn that gown for another outing, one with another man? He couldn't imagine she hadn't drawn someone's attention. "I don't believe I've seen that gown before."

"I wore it at last year's ball."

Had she? She was so very skilled at blending in with the woodwork, of handling matters unobtrusively, drawing little or no attention to herself. It was often easy to overlook her, especially when he was occupied with other matters. She seemed to prefer not to stand out, and yet this evening, he was unable to tear his gaze from her. "Ah, yes. We shan't discuss that one. But how are the plans for this year's soiree coming?" It would be held in August, during the final night of the Season.

"Swimmingly. I believe it shall be an even grander success. Will your mother be coming in from the country for it?"

"Yes, but a couple of days afterward she'll be leaving for the Continent with some friends."

"Your mother enjoys her traveling."

"It makes her happy. She deserves all the happiness she can find."

"You spoil her."

He tried. "My father didn't love her. I think he had no further use for her once she provided him with an heir and a spare."

"Will the same be said of your wife?"

"Unfortunately, I inherited my father's heart, which is to say I have no heart at all. But I shall seek to ensure she always feels appreciated." Something his father had never done for his wife.

"With flowers, trinkets, and baubles?"

"With expensive trinkets, diamonds, and pearls."

She glanced out the window, and he was left with the impression he'd said something wrong. He had a strange sort of honest relationship with his secretary. Had never hesitated to tell her anything. "You disapprove."

Her attention shifted back to him. "I think she will be very fortunate to have you, but being fortunate does not always guarantee happiness."

A sad pall seemed to fall over her. "Are you happy, Pettypeace?"

"I have no reason not to be."

"That is hardly an answer."

"Certainly, there are times when I long for more . . . but I do not believe I am destined to acquire those things."

"I believe you can obtain anything to which you set your mind."

She gave him a small, tentative smile. "I appreciate your faith in me."

"It is well deserved. I would be a poorer man if I'd not hired you." And damn if he wasn't referring to the coins in his coffers but rather an aspect to his life that was impossible to measure, which included her. When he returned from a trip, she was always there to reassure him that matters were well in hand. His burdens and worries were less with her at the helm, leaving him free to pursue his obsession of rebuilding what his father had fairly destroyed. He'd long ago surpassed his goals but had continued the pursuit because the achievement had not seemed enough.

Then they were both glancing out the window as though they'd suddenly stepped on a path they'd not before, and neither was quite certain of where it might lead or if it should even be traveled.

CHAPTER 3

*P*ENELOPE HAD ALWAYS enjoyed being in the company of the Chessmen. Kingsland sat to her left, at the head of the table. Across from her was Rook. Knight had taken up position at the foot of the table, and Bishop sat beside her. They were a handsome lot, but it was the beauty of their minds that she truly appreciated, the manner in which they strategized, the ease with which they shared information with each other, the mystery of them. Other than *King*, she had no idea where their monikers had come from or their true names. In every encounter she'd had with them, they only referred to themselves as the particular chess piece they each represented. It didn't strike her as an odd thing. Rather, it seemed to suit them.

They were indulging in their second bottle of Bordeaux and beginning a course of beef filet smothered in a glazed sauce. She certainly found no fault with the chef who managed the kitchens of Dodger's Drawing Room.

"I say, King, I suppose you've heard the news that your former fiancée is soon to marry Mr. Griffith Stanwick," Knight said.

She sensed a subtle drop in temperature at the table as Kingsland sliced his filet while the other gents reached for their wineglasses, their attention homed in on him.

"To be clear, we were never betrothed. She was merely a woman I courted. I wish her naught but the best."

"Well, she's already lost out on that, hasn't she, old boy?" Rook asked. "After all, she turned you down."

"She'd have never been happy with me."

"Will any woman be?" Knight asked.

"One whose heart remains in her keeping, I should think."

Penelope made a mental note to ask after a lady's heart when she began holding her interviews, to discover if it belonged to someone else. Yet if Kingsland had no heart to give, as he claimed, was it fair to ask a woman to deny herself, even for a short while, the joy to be found in falling in love with another? But if she loved another, would she have written to him? However, a title, prestige, influence, and wealth were strong motivators for some, more important than love for a few. If parents were particularly overbearing, all choice was taken away. Few young ladies could afford to be rebellious. She knew that well enough, regretted the one time she had rebelled herself, because it had cost her family dearly.

"I hear Stanwick's club is doing quite well," Bishop said. "Are you familiar with it, Pettypeace?"

She had always liked that the duke's friends had quickly adopted his practice of dispensing with the *Miss* portion when addressing her, as though they recognized she was equal to them, at least when it came to the business aspect of their lives. "I've heard some rumors regarding it."

It was a scandalous place where the unmarried went to seek companionship for an evening. No chaperones were allowed. Women with no reputation to worry over or no hope of marriage frequented the place. Men in want of something other than a business arrangement that concluded with an impersonal bedding spent an evening at the club.

"You're not a member?"

"Certainly not." That wasn't to say she hadn't considered it. She wondered if these chaps were members.

"What is it called again?" Rook asked.

"The Fair Ladies' and Spare Gentlemen's Club," Kingsland answered as though irritated by the name. "Firstborn sons who are to inherit a title are not allowed. Although I'm given to understand that firstborn sons of commoners are welcomed. And there is an age restriction on women. They must be at least five-and-twenty to gain membership."

"Quite on the shelf then," Bishop mused.

"I find it ridiculous that ladies are put out to pasture at such a tender age when men are never considered on the shelf," she dared to say out loud.

"I agree," Kingsland said. "Women tend to get interesting only after they've had some seasoning to them."

She glanced over to find him studying her steadfastly, his thumb and forefinger slowly stroking the stem of his wineglass, and she fought against imagining him stroking aspects of her person just as leisurely, savoring the texture of her skin, finding portions of it silkier. "But *interesting* is not a criterion you specified you wanted in your duchess."

"It's not."

"Then I need not eliminate those who are unseasoned."

"No."

"Good God," Bishop exclaimed. "Pray, do tell us you've not given the task of finding you a wife to Pettypeace."

Kingsland shrugged a shoulder the gods had designed for carrying heavy burdens. "I botched it royally the last time. Besides, I found it a tedious undertaking, and the whole point of my method is to save me some bother."

"Therefore, you give the task to a woman who is as skilled as any of us at detecting a worthy investment?"

She was rather glad she'd not worn one of her serviceable frocks, because the buttons down the front would have popped off with the swelling of her chest at the compliment, at being considered as skilled as these men who were recognized as being without match when it came to identifying sound ventures.

"I employ Pettypeace to handle the unpleasant tasks."

Bishop scoffed and grumbled beneath his breath, "More fool you." Then he winked at her. "If you're ever of a mind to secure a position where you wish to encounter only the more pleasurable aspects, let me know. I'll hire you on the spot."

"Pettypeace is mine. Attempt to steal her from me and I'll see you destroyed."

Her breath caught at the growled words. Surely, Kingsland was jesting, although the tautness of his jaw and the ticking of a muscle in his cheek made him appear deadly serious.

"I would expect no less," Bishop said casually, calmly, and she was surprised his hand wasn't shaking when he picked up his wineglass, but his gaze remained steadfastly on Kingsland, almost daring him to come at him, then and there.

The tension at the table suddenly seemed quite thick. A few shifting in chairs and clearing of throats ensued, and she wasn't at all certain the others weren't anticipating the two men coming to blows. Should she announce she would never leave him, never abandon him? But even as she had the thought, she knew it was dangerous to make a promise that might cause the fates to laugh and seek to prove her wrong. If he ever learned the truth of her past . . . it did not bear thinking about. And if she discovered she could not live with the torment of seeing him with his wife—well, she certainly wouldn't take Bishop up on his offer. She would need to go far away, where she would never have the opportunity to see

Kingsland thriving in the marriage that she had arranged for him.

"I say, Bishop," Knight began cautiously, "weren't you going to share with us some investment opportunity?"

"Ah, yes, as a matter of fact, I did have something I thought we might find as enticing as Pettypeace."

Enticing? Her? He was jesting now because she was no great beauty, and yet his words reflected kindness, not a mocking tone, as though he admired her. She did hope they would attribute the heightening color scalding her cheeks to the wine.

Penelope leaned down for her reticule that she'd placed on the floor beside her chair earlier so she'd have easy access to it, set it on the table, and reached inside for her notebook. She had it halfway out when Kingsland's hand landed on hers, nearly smothering it. His was so large and incredibly warm. Fascinatingly intoxicating. Never before had he touched her so solidly, and for several heartbeats she stared at his long, thick fingers, his smoothly buffed nails, the raised tendons and veins that reflected power. When she finished her thorough perusal and lifted her astonished gaze, she discovered him intensely studying the joining as though he couldn't quite determine how it had happened. Or perhaps he was contemplating how best to extricate himself from the situation without drawing attention to it.

Finally, he said with a hushed whisper that she imagined he used with his lovers, "You don't require your notebook."

"I thought I was here to take notes." The words

came out breathless and soft, surprising her by the intimacy they seemed to weave between them.

He gave his head a small shake before meeting her gaze. In his eyes, she saw what she'd never before seen there: a hint of confusion. This bold, robust man always knew his mind, his path. Even when he sought her opinion, she understood it was a courtesy and nothing more. His decision was already made. "It's not necessary. Enjoy the remainder of your dinner while concentrating on what he says. I'm certain you'll remember it all."

Slowly, he moved his hand away, and she wondered why it made her feel bereft, as though she'd lost something grand, formidable, and precious that could never be regained. Her hand longed to reach across the short expanse and rejoin with his. Instead, she balled it tightly and nodded quickly. "Yes, all right then."

As Bishop began to wax on about some mining operation somewhere, she doubted very much she was going to be able to recall a single word he spoke, because she seemed incapable of focusing on anything except how wonderful it had felt to have Kingsland's hand resting over hers.

⁋IT WAS THE longest, most interminable dinner in which he'd ever partaken. Usually he greatly enjoyed spending time with his fellow investors and discussing business opportunities. For some reason, tonight he was anxious to be rid of them. Perhaps it was the way they made her smile or laugh softly or offer her thoughts. No, it was Bishop's damn wink, as though he shared a secret with her. King had very nearly stood in order to advance on him and throw a punch that would have blackened that bloody irritating eye.

His possessive reaction had taken him by surprise, and he seemed unable to shake off a need to strike something. Pettypeace often shared meals with them at the residence, and his temper never flared. Why should it be different at the club?

While he and the Chessmen usually gathered round in comfortable chairs and enjoyed a bit of port after dinner, he made their excuses and escorted Pettypeace to the coach that was waiting nearby. Once he handed her safely inside, he stepped back.

"Aren't you coming with me?" she asked.

"No, I have another matter that needs attending to. The driver and footman will see you safely home."

"Do you not require the coach?"

"I'll hire a cab."

He hated the way her brow furrowed, and her eyes searched him as though she thought something was wrong, as though she could discover it if she looked hard enough and long enough. "Did I do something to upset you?"

He offered her a small—what he hoped was a reassuring—smile. "Absolutely not. I should have mentioned earlier I'd not be returning with you. But nothing is amiss."

"Thank you for dinner. I'll write up what I remember regarding the mining opportunity."

"It's not necessary." He'd expected relief, not a

further falling of her face into worry. "I have little interest in those mines." *Especially after Bishop winked at you. Because Bishop had the audacity to wink at you.* Whatever was wrong with him? He never allowed petty matters to influence his decisions when it came to investments, and yet that bloody wink did not seem a petty matter.

"I hardly blame you. Based on the information he shared with us, the mines seem rather played out to me."

Strange how her siding with him over Bishop did wonders to improve his sour mood. "I'll see you at breakfast." With that he shut the door, shouted up at his driver to be off, and watched as the coach rattled over the cobblestones and carried her away.

Deciding against hiring a cab, he began striding up the street, easily working his way around those searching for entertainment, food, or something nefarious. His destination was not far, and he needed to work off the tension plaguing him, tension that had struck like a blow to the chest when he'd laid his hand over hers. Tugging off his glove, he made a fist as though he could recapture the feel of her silken skin against his palm. For a moment there, it had seemed she'd become part of him. He wondered if all of her was as soft, as smooth, as creamy . . . as tantalizing.

With a groan, he shoved his hand back into his glove. She was Pettypeace. His secretary. Competent. Able to manage any task. Who always wore dark blue, but in green rivaled the beauty found in the artwork created by the Masters. Her bared shoulders called to a man's lips to travel over them. The slope of her neck, the delicate collarbones served as a lure for questing fingers. Not the sort of inappropriate thoughts he'd ever had about her before, and certainly shouldn't have now.

It was those tantalizing little wisps of rebellious strands of her hair that he'd tucked behind her ear that morning. They'd made her appear feminine and soft in a way she never had before, and made him aware of her as a woman. Dangerous thing indeed. He was her employer, needed to keep his distance. Should never act in an untoward manner or cause her to believe he expected anything of her other than what he would expect of a male secretary.

Placing her on equal footing with the Chessmen, he valued her opinion, the sharpness of her mind. But of a sudden, he wanted to value the softness of her body. It wasn't as though he'd never noticed she was female. It was simply that he'd acknowledged her gender in the same straightforward manner he noted a bird was a bird or a rose a rose. An identifier. Except tonight more had bombarded his musings. A beautiful bird, or a soft, perfectly formed petal. An incredibly intriguing Pettypeace.

Thank God his destination finally loomed before him. He jogged up the terrace house steps and tapped the knocker. Waited, his body tightening with anticipation.

The door swung open and the dark-haired beauty stood before him. "King, what a pleasant surprise. You haven't come to see me since you made that silly announcement at that ball of yours last Season."

It hadn't seemed appropriate to call upon her when he'd begun courting another. Good Lord, had it been at least a year since he'd been intimate with a woman? No wonder his muscles and nerves had reacted with intense anticipation when he'd touched Pettypeace's hand. It hadn't been her specifically that had caused sexual need to overwhelm him. It had been simple male lust and primal desire. "Hello, Margaret. Have you company this evening?"

She gave him a seductive smile. "I have now. Do come in."

He strode over the threshold into the familiar foyer that opened into a parlor on one side and a hallway at the far end that led to stairs he'd ascended to her bedchamber numerous times. After relieving him of his hat and walking stick, Margaret placed them on a nearby table.

"I should be put out with you," she said. He removed his gloves. She set them beside his hat and turned to him. "But I'm not so petty as to do myself a disservice and turn away the glorious pleasure you'll bestow upon me."

Like a wraith, she glided over to him, pressed herself against him, and wound her arms around his neck as his circled her waist, pulling her in close. She lifted her mouth, and he took it, falling into the familiar, into the—

Her fragrance was all wrong. Had she changed her perfume, whatever she put in her bathwater?

She pulled slightly away. "Did you just sniff me?"

"Pardon? No. Don't be ridiculous." Drawing her back in, he was determined to make good on the promise his arrival at her door had signaled. The ardor and passion she expected, deserved. But the manner in which she fit in his arms was different, somewhat awkward . . . not as pleasing as it had once been. They no longer seemed to match in places where they had before.

Once more she pulled back. "What's her name?"

"I beg your pardon?"

Her smile was laced with drollness, melancholy, and . . . was that pity? Not directed at herself but at him. He was not accustomed to being pitied. It irked, pricked his considerable pride, made him wish he hadn't decided to pay her a visit.

She skirted beyond his reach. "Usually you'd have had me against a wall by now."

She disappeared into the parlor. Like a fool, he followed. "Margaret, I apologize. It's been a rather long day, but I do want you."

"Don't insult me, darling." After pouring scotch into two glasses, she handed him one. "You're here because you can't have the woman you want, and I haven't the fortitude to turn you away."

"There is no other woman I want."

She cradled his jaw. "Oh, you poor man. I think you probably believe that. I imagine I can even tell you who she is."

"There is no woman," he emphasized again.

With a secretive smile, she gave him a little pat on his cheek before wandering to the sofa and dropping elegantly onto it, her skirts billowing around her. "Tell me about your rather long day."

He'd not come here to talk about his day, but to whisper naughty words into her ear. To hear her sighs and moans, to groan in return. He fully intended to stalk across the room, pull her up and into his arms, and have his way with her, allow her to have hers with him. And prove he did want her. As a result, he was a bit surprised to find himself walking over to the fireplace, where he leaned a shoulder negligently against the mantel. "Just business."

"And your evening?"

Taking a sip of his scotch, he wondered why all the sexual tension and need radiating through him had dissipated the moment he'd taken her into his arms. She'd once been the mistress of the Duke of Birdwell, and as was often the practice with favorite mistresses, he'd set her up nicely upon his death, leaving her this residence and an annual income that had ensured she could choose her future lovers, if she desired any.

King always enjoyed their time together. Immensely. And she'd spoken true. He should have had her pressed to the wall within minutes of entering the residence. By now, clothes should be scattered over the floor, and the two of them should be on that sofa, lost in the throes of passion. Instead, his ardor had cooled, and he rather wished he'd climbed into the coach and returned home with Pettypeace. "Dinner at the club with the Chessmen."

"That usually doesn't leave you with a foul temper."

"I'm not foul-tempered." But even as the words

spewed forth, he realized he did indeed sound as though he was in an extremely unpleasant mood. And why was his end of the conversation mainly composed of repeating in the negative what she'd said? "I apologize. It was a less than satisfactory meeting."

His relationship with Margaret was not a complicated thing. It involved good sex and pleasing conversation, but nothing that ever delved beneath the surface. So much dwelled beneath his surface that he'd never shared with anyone, and it suddenly seemed a heavy burden.

"How is Miss Pettypeace?"

His heart gave a little lurch at the mention of *her* name, especially with the inclusion of the *Miss*, reflecting her femininity. He'd called her Miss Pettypeace during her interview, but once she came to work for him, she'd simply become Pettypeace. It had seemed to suit her. She'd been twenty at the time. Young and fresh, but not innocent. Her eyes revealed that little fact. They revealed everything he knew about her, which, he was beginning to realize, wasn't much at all. "Efficient as ever."

"I saw your advert in the *Times* indicating you are again accepting applications for the position of duchess." She didn't give the impression she was insulted that he didn't ask for her hand. Early on she'd admitted to being unable to bear children, which made her promiscuity safe, meant she had no need to concern herself with bringing by-blows into the world. But it also limited her marriage prospects, at least among the aristocracy—as obsessed with heirs and bloodlines as its members were. Not that she'd ever indicated she would welcome a husband in her life. He suspected she rather preferred the freedom of being untethered.

"I require an heir." At four-and-thirty, he was getting a bit long in the tooth. It was time he saw to this aspect of his duties.

"How romantic you are, King. If your handsome features, wealth, and titles don't win a woman over, I expect she'll swoon at your feet when you whisper those sweet words into her ear."

He scowled, not certain if she was serious or teasing. But he knew the truth of the matter. "Pettypeace will not select a swooner."

"You gave the task to that poor girl?"

She wasn't a girl. She was a woman, with curves the green gown had highlighted in a manner the dark blue didn't. With unblemished skin. Why of a sudden was everyone questioning his decision to hand the task over to his secretary? It was deuced irritating, especially when he was unaccustomed to having his decisions doubted. "I trust no one more."

"In this matter, is it not better to trust your own heart?"

"You trusted your heart, and look where it got you."

Her eyes softened, and her smile turned wistful. "Almost a dozen years of happiness. I couldn't have him always. A duke does not marry a woman such as myself—although I was really just a girl, barely seven-and-ten, when Birdie took me in— but the hours he was able to give me, I wouldn't trade for all the riches in the world. His wife had her lover, and he had his. Not uncommon among the aristocracy. But still, King, is it not better to love the woman you are to wed than merely the woman you may occasionally bed?"

He heaved a heavy sigh. "I seem to have taken us down a melancholy path. I came here with a much more entertaining purpose in mind. But you're correct. My thoughts reside elsewhere, and you are deserving of a man's full attention. I have missed your forthrightness. And I have been remiss in asking after you. How have you been, Margaret?"

"Missing Birdie. It's been five years this month. You would think I would miss him less, but there is something extremely comfortable and comforting about being with someone who knows you so very well. Pleasure is certainly not to be taken for granted, but some of my favorite memories involve the quiet moments when we were together. I hope you have those with your duchess."

He was going to have an abundance of quiet moments with his duchess. It was a requirement he demanded, and his secretary never failed to ensure his requirements were met.

CHAPTER 4

"*Y*OU DIDN'T SEE the exciting part of the club at all?"

Having changed out of her evening attire into her nightdress and wrapper, Penelope sat at the foot of Lucy's bed, with her fingers buried in her cat's black fur. "Not so much as a peek. The door we entered led into a hallway that took us straight to the private dining room. We left the same way." Not *exactly* the same way, at least as far as moods were concerned. Something had been amiss with Kingsland. He'd seemed disgruntled, which was unusual after spending time with his friends.

"That is disappointing." Lucy took a sip of the brandy Penelope had brought her. "I've always wondered what a gentlemen's club looks like, and I don't know why. I suppose because women aren't allowed."

"Eventually we will be."

"Do you really think so?"

"Absolutely. A woman's money spends the same as a man's."

"Mine never seems to. Always spends too quick."

"I wish you would let me help you invest some of it." She suspected people would be incredibly surprised to discover how much of the public works were funded by women investors.

"Investing is too much like gambling. It doesn't always pay off. M'dad liked to gamble, but he never had any luck at it. I could be the same. Just giving my hard-earned coins away, really."

They'd had the discussion a couple of times. Investing was one of the few avenues open to women that allowed them an opportunity to be financially independent. Lucy was skeptical even about the steadfast investments in which widows would place their inheritance to guarantee themselves a steady yearly income. "Well, if you ever change your mind, I can help ensure you're not just giving it away."

"Did the duke compliment your hair?"

Taking a sip of her own brandy, Penelope felt the heat suffuse her cheeks as they shifted the conversation to the topics Lucy preferred to discuss. "He doesn't notice things like that." Although it had surprised, but pleased, her that he'd commented on her gown. When she was younger, she'd drawn the attention of men, had experienced lascivious gazes and, on a couple of occasions, even wandering hands. She'd learned it was best not to dress provocatively or in any manner that might distract a man from focusing on her words or profession-alism. That attitude had served her well as the duke's secretary.

"Harry certainly liked the look of you," Lucy said, and Penelope thought she detected a measure of jealousy in her friend's voice.

"He was being polite. I wouldn't read too much into his comment."

"I think he's rather handsome. Got lovely calves."

All footmen did. It was a requirement of service. "Are you keen on him?"

Lucy shrugged. "What do you think of the new footman, Gerard?"

She thought what she did with each new em-ployee: *Will this be the one to bring me trouble, the one to recognize me, to reveal my past?* When she had sought a way to provide for her family years ago, she hadn't considered how far her choice would ex-tend or that she would never know exactly whom it had reached. It had seemed innocent enough at the time, until she'd discovered she had absolutely no control over the influence of her actions. "Mr. Keating said he came highly recommended."

Lucy laughed. "I'm not asking your opinion on him as a worker, Penn. Do you fancy him as a man at all?"

"In my position, I don't think it's wise to get involved with staff."

"But would you want to?"

"That's beside the point." And if she was to get involved with anyone, she'd rather he be the duke, although she suspected his moral fiber wouldn't allow him to have any sort of personal relationship with someone in his employ. "And I have Sir Purrcival for company."

The cat spent much of his time wandering through the kitchen to ensure it remained free of mice, but he was always on hand for a snuggle when she needed it.

"Don't you ever dream of a gent sweeping you off your feet?"

She gave her friend an indulgent grin. "I'm too practical for such whimsy. I think a love that develops over time would be more reliable." She'd seen Kingsland when he was out of sorts, when he grew impatient with someone who had not delivered what was promised. He didn't gloat when successful, didn't sulk when an investment didn't go his way. While he might not like them, he saw each failure as an opportunity to learn, so he didn't repeat the mistake. She was familiar with every aspect of his character, and so it was unlikely he'd managed to fool her into believing he was someone other than who he was. The same couldn't be said of all the people who had traipsed through her life, which was the reason she never sought out anyone who had known her before she became Penelope Pettypeace.

"I suspect you're right." Lucy set her glass aside, drew her legs up, and hugged them tightly to her chest. "But still, that first blush of awareness should steal your breath."

That had certainly happened the first time Penelope's gaze had fallen on Kingsland. She'd known little about him before she'd walked into his office, had expected she was answering an advert for an ancient duke, not a young, virile one with goals and ambitions he'd needed help keeping organized. She'd been working for a grocer in the East End, helping him keep track of his inventory in between seeing to customers, but she'd noted he'd begun studying her a little too intently. Then her landlord had taken a sudden interest in where she'd lived before letting a room in his boardinghouse, and she'd known it was best to move on. "How many times have you had your breath stolen, Lucy?"

"Too many to count, and it was lovely every time." She yawned. "I should probably turn in. Morning comes early."

As Penelope slid off the bed, Sir Purrcival agilely leapt to the floor. "I should retire as well. I'll see you tomorrow."

When she returned to her room, she settled beneath the covers, stuffed her pillow behind her back, and began reading *A Tale of Two Cities*. But the pages might as well have been blank for their inability to hold her attention. Her mind kept drifting to her dinner at the club and everything she hadn't shared with Lucy.

For the tiniest speck of time, when Kingsland's hand had rested on hers, when he had looked at her as though truly seeing her for the first time, hope had flared within her breast, only to be extinguished when he'd deposited her like a wayward child in the coach so he could enjoy the rest of his evening without her presence intruding upon it. She didn't delude herself into thinking he was going anywhere other than into the arms of a disreputable woman.

He'd had a restlessness about him, the same edginess that had bombarded her as the carriage had rattled through the streets. Her skin had felt too tight, her lungs too small to draw in all the air she needed. Her body had yearned to be stroked, touched, caressed. The secret spot between her legs had fairly screamed for attention. There, within the confines of that vehicle, after drawing the curtains at the windows, she'd seen to her needs. It hadn't been easy with the volume of silk the seamstress had used for her skirt, but Penelope had never been one to shy away from a challenge.

Now it was impossible to concentrate because she kept seeing Kingsland pleasuring a woman. No, not a woman. Just as she'd fantasized in the carriage to bring about her quick release, she saw him pleasuring her. Envisioned his mouth trailing along her throat as he emitted little growls of satisfaction. He would loosen her fastenings and kiss the skin that was being slowly, methodically, exposed. He would taste what no man had ever tasted, would—

With a groan, she threw back the covers. "This is ridiculous, Sir Purrcival." Curled at the foot of the bed, the cat barely opened his eyes. "I shan't be long." She snatched up her wrapper and drew it tightly around her. What she needed was Jane Austen. She'd gone too many nights without reading a romantic tale.

Taking her lamp, she made her way through the various familiar corridors, not at all bothered by the hush of the house. She rather liked it. Except she could sense the emptiness of the residence.

He wasn't yet home. It was odd how different the place seemed with him in it—more alive, more vibrant, more substantial. Even when she wasn't in the same room as he was, she was aware of his presence. It had been like that the moment she began working for him and had only strengthened over the years.

Therefore, she knew she wouldn't be disturbing him or running into him in the library. Not that he objected to her taking books from his domain. Shortly after she'd begun working for him, he'd given her permission to read his entire collection of tomes. She'd never seen the like, all those books in a residence, in a family home. Her father would have been in heaven. As it was, he was likely in hell. Although she didn't want to think about that. But then, she never did.

She walked into the library, set the lamp down on a table near the shelves that housed novels, and wandered along, trailing her fingers over the spines. So many books. She'd never have a chance to read them all and wondered how many might be overlooked by future generations. How many might be added to the collection? At the duke's ancestral estate in Cornwall, the library was three floors high, with a wrought-iron spiral staircase that she'd climbed numerous times. She loved that chamber. This one she merely treasured. Her dream was to have a cottage where every room had a wall of books. The small fortune she was accumulating ensured she'd have it when she was no longer employed by the duke, when they parted ways, when she could no longer pretend her indifference to him.

She spotted the book she sought on a higher shelf. Not that high. Surely, she wouldn't need the ladder stored behind a hidden door, if she just rose up on her toes and reached, reached—

A large hand shot past her, a hand the palm of which she remembered from their encounter earlier in the evening was a little rough, like fine sandpaper. "Which one? *Pride and Prejudice* or *Sense and Sensibility*?"

The low, seductive voice sounded so near her ear that it could have been the whisper of a lover. God help her, but she wished it was.

DEVIL TAKE HIM, but she smelled of the fragrance for which he'd been searching. Jasmine, a little musty warmed by flesh.

She went as still as he did, her hand near his elbow. He wasn't touching her, but the distance between them didn't prevent him from luxuriating in the heat emanating from her.

"*Pride and Prejudice.*"

His gut tightened and shot need straight to his groin because the words were uttered in the rasp of a woman aroused. Or perhaps it was his own arousal influencing what he heard and how it sounded to his ear. So sensual, so inviting. It took everything within him not to do something untoward, not to nibble on her lobe or nip at the soft skin beneath her jaw. Her hair hung in a long plait down the length of her spine, and he was tempted to unravel it, to comb his fingers through it, gather it in his hands. Fighting to give the impression he was completely unaffected by her nearness, he plucked the book off the shelf, took a step back, and held it out to her.

"Thank you," she said in a meek way not at all like her as she took it. And he wondered if she'd been struck by desire as strong as his, desire so potent he wanted her up against that bookcase, the whole of his body pressed against hers. Never before had he felt such a strong urge where she was concerned, and yet it seemed as natural as breathing.

"I don't know why you don't acknowledge how tiny you are, Pettypeace, and retrieve the ladder." He was rather pleased with his neutral tone, his ability to not reveal how her closeness drove him to near madness with want.

Her chin shot up and her eyes blazed. "I could have reached it myself without a ladder."

Ah, the Pettypeace he knew so well had returned in full force, which unfortunately made him want her all the more. "Shall I put the book back then?"

"No, that would be pointless." She clutched the tome to her chest as though it was a shield. "I wasn't expecting you back so early."

His return a few minutes shy of ten was a surprise to him as well, but he and Margaret had quickly run out of topics of conversation. "I finished with my business sooner than anticipated."

He'd never seen her in her nightclothes before. The white lace that ran down the front of her floral wrap surprised him, seemed too frilly and frivolous for her. Perhaps she was a different Pettypeace when alone in her bedchamber. He wondered what else about her might astonish him, might call to whatever he'd been searching for when he'd gone to visit Margaret.

She lifted the book. "I shall say good night then." She started to edge past him.

"Join me in having a bit of scotch before bed."

Her expression brought to mind the image of a hare that had just realized it had been spotted by a cobra. As he was trying to decide if an apology was in order or if he should just laugh off his inappropriate request—a duke did not imbibe with staff or mention doing any activity before retiring—the corners of her mouth eased up slightly. "I prefer brandy, actually."

The relief that washed through him because he'd have a few more minutes in her company and had just uncovered another little tidbit of knowledge about her was disconcerting. "Brandy it is. Settle yourself somewhere comfortable while I see to our glasses."

On his way to the sideboard where the decanters were lined up like little obedient soldiers, he decided he'd forgo the scotch and join her in brandy. He'd stood in the doorway watching as she'd trailed her fingers over the spines and found himself wishing she'd trail them over him—over his stubbled jaw, his chest . . . lower. Even without her in his arms, he'd experienced a powerful yearning that he'd not with Margaret. A hunger no woman had stirred within him in a good long while, if ever. The potency of it nearly dropped him to his knees, and he was a man who never went to his knees, not for anyone.

After putting a splash of brandy in each snifter, he turned, unsurprised to discover she'd drawn aside the draperies and settled in a thickly padded dark brown wingback chair near the window, giving her a view of the garden limned by moonlight. On more than one occasion, as he'd worked into the late hours, he'd looked up from his desk to see her strolling about outside. She never appeared to be a lonely figure, but rather someone who found solace in the path she walked. So much of what he knew about her was based solely on observations, leaving most of her a mystery to be discovered, and he was suddenly of a mood to go exploring.

He strode over to the sitting area and offered her a snifter. She smiled up at him. It was unsettling how much it pleased him to be the recipient of her gladness. As he lowered himself into a chair opposite her, she cradled the snifter, rubbing the glass between her hands. "I like to warm it a bit."

He was a cad to suddenly envision her warming aspects of his person in the same manner. In response he took a rather large swallow of his brandy and realized he hadn't poured himself nearly enough for the length of time he wished to remain in her company. "How did you enjoy Dodger's?"

"Disappointed I didn't get to see the more interesting parts."

"I understand there is a club for ladies. The Elysium." It was owned by Aiden Trewlove, a man with a rather ignominious beginning who had risen above it to become successful enough to marry a widowed duchess. They would no doubt be sent an invitation to the ball where he'd announce his intended.

She glanced out the window. "I'm not a lady."

He hadn't used the term in reference to an aristocratic position, but she'd obviously taken it that way. "It was my impression noble birth wasn't required for membership."

Her gaze slid back to him, and he liked having it there, focused on him. "I don't think I'd really enjoy gambling. I work too hard for my money to risk losing even so much as a tuppence on the turn of a card."

"It sounds as though you have a monster for an employer."

Her light laughter floated toward him and swirled through his soul, creating havoc there. "He has his good qualities."

And his bad. He was well aware he wasn't the easiest of men to get along with, had very exacting standards he expected others to meet. She excelled in that regard. Still, he was amazed she'd stayed with him as long as she had. "How goes the hunt for my duchess?"

She gave a little scoff. "You make it sound as though she's to be your prey."

"Hardly."

"Still, *duchess* sounds so impersonal. Would it not be better to be searching for a wife, a partner . . . a soul mate?"

"Can you imagine what a woman whose soul

mirrored mine would be like?" Cold, haughty, unbearable.

"One of the ladies has claimed she is a master at fencing, but I fear with her you might find yourself skewered."

He laughed darkly. "So you do find me difficult."

After taking a long, slow sip of her brandy, she said, "The servants are terrified of displeasing you."

"Are they?" He knew he was a hard taskmaster, had little patience for mistakes. But *terrified* seemed a bit of an overreaction. "It's not as though I flog them."

She lifted a delicate shoulder. "You're a duke. That alone is unnerving for some."

"You're not afraid of me."

She held his gaze, and he recognized a bit of a dare in those green eyes. "No, but then, I have placed myself in a financial position to be able to walk away without looking back, without worry, should I find myself more than periodically miffed at you or consider myself ill-treated."

Something in her tone, a forced lightness with an undercurrent of warning, caused a fissure of unease to score his gut. Had she been forced to run, to escape, to go into hiding? Was that the reason the men he'd hired had been unable to find any evidence of her existing before she stepped into his office? Once he'd determined he didn't care about her past, he'd never delved into her personal life or asked about anything other than what she'd shared during her interview. He'd relegated their relationship to business only. In his obsession with amassing a fortune, of ensuring he could provide for his family and the estates, he may have been remiss in devoting the proper amount of attention to her. With earnestness, he leaned forward. "Before you came into my employ, did you experience an occasion where you couldn't walk away?"

She glanced back out the window, and he wondered if she was contemplating running now. *Tell me, tell me who you were before you were my secretary.* It suddenly seemed vital to know.

"Don't you think everyone has moments like that?" Her attention landed on him so solidly he felt it like a blow. "Even you. Surely the mantle of duke sometimes feels like a shroud rather than a cloak woven of silken threads."

Sometimes it felt like a coat of iron dragging him down into the mire. Not that he was going to admit that. Admiring her ability to deflect, he settled back and decided to pursue what he sought more subtly. "What part of Kent are you from?" She'd told him at least her county of birth during her interview.

"A little village you would have never heard of."

"Where your father is the vicar."

The corners of her mouth turned up provocatively. He liked this late-into-the-night-sipping-brandy-not-working Pettypeace. "You knew that for the lie it was."

"I did, yes."

"But you hired me anyway."

"If I ever needed you to lie for me, I knew you had the talent for it. Most would have been duped by your forthright delivery, but I have a tendency not to trust the surface of things and to look a little deeper. What was your father's occupation?"

"I was born in Kent, but we moved to London when I was quite small."

Apparently, she didn't want to talk about her father. He rarely spoke of his but suspected they avoided the topic for different reasons. "You know, Pettypeace, you can trust me with your secrets."

"Once told, it's no longer a secret."

He couldn't argue with that assessment. "You do harbor one, then."

"Everyone has secrets. I imagine even you have one or two. You can trust me with yours."

It wasn't a matter of trust but rather of shame. He wondered if the same could be said of hers but wasn't going to press. "This reminds me of a game I played with the stablemaster's daughter when I was four-and-ten: show me yours and I'll show you mine."

Even from this distance, with so little light in the room, he saw the pink hue darken her cheeks, signaling she'd caught his innuendo. Of course she had. Often he didn't have to finish a sentence before she knew where he was going. Quite frequently they were of the same mind. "You are naughty, Your Grace. Do you require naughtiness in a wife?"

A bit of teasing edged her tone, but on this matter, he needed to be honest. "I require a woman who will not come to love me."

She visibly stiffened. "Earlier you claimed to have no heart. Do you not want her to love you because you will be unable to love her in return?"

"Because loving me, eventually, will bring her naught but heartache."

"You're not a particularly jolly sort, but I think perhaps you judge yourself too harshly."

"Trust me, Pettypeace, I do not."

"I find it difficult to believe you would intentionally set out to wound her, to hurt her."

"It would not be intentional, but—"

The unexpected echo of stomping feet drew his attention to the doorway. The servants tended to move about in unobtrusive silence. When King had returned to the residence, he'd dismissed his butler and any lingering footmen for the night, and so he was surprised to find himself with the possibility of guests now, especially as he knew the manor was locked up tight.

Appearing quite disheveled, his brother entered the room, two bruisers lumbering on either side of him. King didn't like the looks of the other fellows. They appeared to be trouble, and he did hope he wasn't going to regret giving his brother a key so he could come and go as he pleased. Setting his snifter aside, King calmly came to his feet, even as every aspect of his being was on excessive alert. Pettypeace rose as well, and he couldn't stop himself from stepping in front of her, providing a barrier between her and the trio making their way across the room toward him and Pettypeace. "Go out through the doors that exit onto the terrace," he quietly ordered her.

"I will not." It took everything within him not to growl at the stubborn wench. "Besides, others could be waiting in the garden. They look the sort who travel in a pack. I feel considerably safer staying where I am."

So he wasn't the only one who recognized miscreants when he saw them. And she had a point regarding the possibility of others lurking about, but he still didn't like her being here, loathed the idea of her coming to any harm. He'd die first.

His unwelcome company came to a halt a short distance away, near enough for him to discern that his brother's lip was swollen and bleeding. He'd wager his sibling was also going to have a nasty-looking blackened eye in the morning. "Lawrence."

"I'm in a spot of bother," his brother said, which was his polite way of informing King he was in need of funds. "Allow me to introduce Mr. Thursday here"—he tipped his head to the right, signifying the larger and beefier of the two—"and Mr. Tuesday."

Tuesday was uglier, resembling a rodent, his feral eyes narrowed, indicating he was the meaner one.

"How might I be of service?" King asked.

"Well, you see, m'lord—" Thursday, obviously the leader of the duo, began.

"Your Grace," Lawrence muttered irritably.

"Wot?"

"My brother is a duke. You address him as 'Your Grace.'"

"Well, then *Yer Grace*, I'm 'ere to collect the two thousand quid your ne'er-do-well 'ere owes me boss."

With a grimace, Lawrence stared at his boots, their scratched appearance no doubt a result of the scuffle that had obviously taken place as a form of persuasion signaling that it was indeed time to pay up. Why hadn't his brother come to him if he needed funds? How had he even found what King, judging by the roughness of these fellows, was certain was a disreputable moneylender? "I see. I'll have the amount owed delivered on the morrow."

Thursday clucked his tongue. "Ain't good 'nuff, I'm afraid. Gots to be tonight or his lordship 'ere might find 'imself meeting the pointed end of a knife."

Christ. "The lady and I will be more than happy to retrieve the funds for you." He had a safe concealed by a painting on the wall behind his desk but wasn't about to reveal it. Another safe was hidden away in her office, and he'd given her the key to the pickproof Chubb lock.

The lasciviousness in the blackguard's eyes as he swept his gaze over Pettypeace had King balling up his fists. "The lady stays. Gives me more leverage, ensures ye don't do somefink ye ought not." He gave his head a jerk to the side, and the rodent stepped toward Pettypeace.

"Touch her," King said with deadly calm that stopped the man in his tracks, "and you will leave here without that hand."

"I gots to 'old 'er so she dun run off."

"I'm not going to run off," Pettypeace said, evenly, flatly, but with heat.

The blighter cracked his knuckles and curled his upper lip into a sneer. "'Cuz ye be scared."

"Of you? Don't be ridiculous. You don't frighten me with your ragged clothing and your grimy hair and your dirty face. But you do need to move beyond reach of my olfactory senses."

"Yer wot?"

"My nose, sir. You have a stench about you that I refuse to tolerate. If you want me to stay here, move back. Otherwise, I shall accompany His Grace when he goes to fetch your money."

"Ye think we won't stop ye?" Thursday asked.

Pettypeace skewered the man with a look. "I'd like to see you try."

The confidence, the challenge, the absolute certainty that she would prevail—all five feet and one quarter inch of her was standing up to these men as though she towered above them. If King had a heart, he'd have fallen a little bit in love with her at that moment. He couldn't be absolutely certain that he hadn't anyway.

Thursday once again jerked his head. "Get back over 'ere, Tuesday. We don't want no trouble. We just come for our blunt, wot's owed."

"The lady can fetch the money," King said, "and I shall remain as your guarantee that she'll get up to no mischief."

"Do I look stupid?" Thursday asked. King refrained from announcing that as a matter of fact, he did. "Once she's out of 'arm's way, ye ain't gonna 'esitate to come for me. You go. And be quick about it. Me patience's wearing thin."

King looked over at Pettypeace, and she gave him a little nod. How could she not be terrified? Most women would have swooned by now. "I'll return in all haste."

To give the impression he remained in control, he exited the room at a sedate clip. He considered detouring by the billiards room to retrieve a broadsword one of his ancestors had wielded in battle that now was displayed on a wall. Instead, when he was no longer in view of the ruffians, he made a mad dash for her office.

WITH COMPLETE FAITH in Kingsland's ability to handle this challenging matter, Penelope held Lawrence's gaze and tried to convey that everything would turn out well in the end, even if at the moment the situation seemed quite dire indeed. She'd had enough encounters with bullies to recognize them when she saw them. They might have taken their fists to Lawrence, but the danger of them was easily dispelled with a tone that signaled who was truly in command. She'd been a tiny little thing when she was younger, so small that other children had often taunted her. "When you stand up to them, never flinch, never back down," her father had told her. "You'll be at their mercy if they spot a weakness."

Like a wounded gazelle to a lion.

"I'm sorry," Lawrence said, his tone filled with contrition. "I knew King usually spent his evenings in here when he's home. I simply didn't expect you."

"You're forgiven." The conversation with Kingsland had been turning a bit too personal, and she'd been close to confessing everything—and would have found herself dismissed. She'd told him true. She did have the means to survive without employment, but her position here gave her life purpose, and she was loath to give it up.

Lawrence sighed. "Don't suppose you chaps would mind if I poured myself a whisky?"

"Just stay where ye are," Thursday said, "'till we got our blunt, and then ye can drink yerself into the gutter."

"My brother is an honest fellow. He said he's gone to get the money and so he has."

"'E's a toff. I don't trust no toffs. I need ye close in case I gots to give 'im cause fer regret."

Out of the corner of her eye, she saw Tuesday reach for a ship nestled inside a bottle, resting on a wooden stand. "Don't touch that," she snapped.

"Wot? Ain't gonna nick it. Jest wanted to look at it good. I ain't no thief."

The fellow who delivered blows for a living was insulted. She almost laughed. "I assume Tuesday is not your real name."

"Nah, boss gives his lads names so's we remember what day it's our turn to deliver the punishments."

"Do a lot of that, do you? Mete out punishment?"

He shrugged. "Lots of blokes borrow from 'im. Then forgets to pay 'im. 'Ow'd they put that little ship inside the bottle?"

"Very carefully, I should imagine."

"Never seen the loike."

She relented. "You may pick it up to study it, but if you break it, then Lord Lawrence's debt is paid in full."

"Don't do it, Tuesday. By the time we get back to the boss, it's gonna be Friday, and ye know Friday. He ain't gonna show ye no mercy, and boss'll let 'im at you 'cuz 'e'll be mad ye ain't got the blunt." Thursday gave Lawrence a pointed look. "Yer lucky we caught up wiv ye today. Friday woulda busted yer jaw, not yer lip. Bloke's got a powerful punch."

"Have you considered another occupation?" Penelope asked.

"What else am I gonna do? Don't read. Don't write. 'Sides. I make good money collectin' on debts owed."

"Here you are." Extending a packet, Kingsland strode into the room. She'd never been more relieved to see him, had worried he might attempt to secure a weapon in order to take these two on by himself.

Thursday opened the packet and quickly counted its contents. "Right-o then. Let's go, Tuesday."

"Lawrence, see them out, and then I want you back in here immediately," Kingsland commanded.

With a long-suffering sigh, his brother nodded. "Of course. I suppose a reckoning is in order."

As soon as the three men quit the room, Kingsland was in front of her, a hand coming to rest reassuringly on her shoulder as his gaze wandered with purpose over her face, as though he was mapping every curve, crease, and plane. "Are you unharmed?"

His thumb was stroking the circle of her shoulder, making it difficult to think. "Yes."

"You were so damned brave."

"Actually, I was angry. I've little tolerance for bullies."

"Remind me never to get on the wrong side of you. I think you terrified that Tuesday fellow."

"I don't believe they meant us any real harm."

"If he'd touched you, I would have killed him." The vehemence of his words seemed to surprise him. He released his hold on her and stepped back. Or perhaps it was the echo of Lawrence's footsteps that had him putting distance between them. It wouldn't do for them to be touching when his brother strode in.

And he did, at that precise moment, heading straight for the sideboard of decanters. "I know you're upset, and I can explain."

Based on the tightening of Kingsland's jaw, things were about to get unpleasant between the brothers.

KING LOVED HIS brother. He had from the moment he came into the world four years after he did. The second son, the spare, the one who would inherit the titles if anything ever happened to King before he provided an heir. But the fury that slithered through him because Lawrence had placed them all in danger threatened to cause him to do something rash and unfortunate—like deliver a punch to the other side of his brother's wounded mouth.

If any harm had come to Pettypeace, he would have gone berserk, like his ancestors, and destroyed those responsible. Would have shed all semblance of civilization. Would have turned barbaric. That realization was both horrifying and terrifying because he was a man who always maintained control of himself, his actions, and his thoughts. He was not accustomed to floundering, to . . . *feeling*.

"May I borrow your handkerchief?"

He wasn't certain what his features reflected, but her tone echoed a reassuring calmness similar to one he used when approaching a skittish horse. She now garnered all his attention. The faint pleat between her brows. The worry in her eyes. Could she sense he was having a difficult time keeping his anger tethered? Without a word, because he wasn't yet ready to unclench his teeth, he handed her that for which she'd asked, and then watched as she glided over to Lawrence, who was now leaning against the wall near the decanters, his gaze on the Aubusson carpet. She dabbed some whisky on King's pristine white linen before turning to Lawrence and gently patting it against the ruined lip that was going to no doubt scar. His brother was so undeserving of her kindness and consideration, and King was considerably irritated she was bestowing such tenderness upon him. "Is there any chance more of the blighters are about?"

"No, only two accosted me. I locked the door after we entered and once I let them out."

At least his brother hadn't been completely irresponsible. "To whom did you owe the money?" he demanded.

Pettypeace lowered her hand. "I shall bid you both a good night."

"You should hear this," King assured her. "His actions placed you in danger."

Lawrence skirted beyond her reach and poured himself more scotch, gulped it down, and added another splash. "The card tables haven't been kind to me of late, so I went to a moneylender."

"Not a legitimate one, I assume."

He shook his head. "I thought it less likely you'd learn of my circumstance."

"Your club wouldn't give you credit?"

Another shake of his head. "I'm afraid I owe considerably there as well. And my reputation precedes me making it impossible to get it elsewhere through more reputable means."

"Why didn't you come to me?"

"I hoped my fortunes would soon change, and you'd never hear of it. Besides, I wasn't in a mood to endure a lecture on my gambling habits."

"I'm not in the mood to have my residence invaded by the likes of those two miscreants. Not to mention that your actions placed Pettypeace in jeopardy. You owe her an apology."

"I already gave her one while you were getting the blunt." Still, he said, "I truly am sorry, Miss Pettypeace."

"No harm done, but I can't fault your brother for being upset by your handling of this matter. What is a lecture when compared with what your face endured?"

With a sigh, he looked at King. "They threatened to break my arm. Otherwise I wouldn't have disturbed your evening."

His brother's words were only adding to his frustration. "It's not the disturbing of my evening, Lawrence, that troubles me, but that you would go this dangerous route. What if I'd not had the money?"

"That wasn't even a consideration. Ever since Father's death, since we realized the dire straits he'd left us in, the cupboard bare, so to speak, you've been obsessed with filling the coffers."

Because they'd been left with almost nothing, and he never again wanted to experience the fear of wondering how they were going to survive. Merchants never hesitated to allow the aristocracy to purchase on credit, often only asking for payment at the end of the year, but what he'd discovered they'd owed when he took over the reins of the dukedom could have bankrupted a small nation. He'd put aside what remained of his youth and anything he considered frivolous in order to ensure his family never went without. "Give me your word that you will not go to moneylenders in the future."

After nodding, Lawrence downed his scotch and poured another. "May I stay here tonight?"

"You are always welcome to a bedchamber here." He was leasing his brother a small terrace house so he could experience some independence, but King suspected his encounter with the ruffians had left him a bit more shaken than he would willingly admit.

"I shall make amends," Lawrence insisted.

He had little doubt his brother would try. He was also rather certain the spare was on his way to getting soused as he filled his tumbler to the brim this time.

"I'll away to bed now," Pettypeace said. "Good night, Lord Lawrence."

He gave her a smile filled with contrition. "Miss Pettypeace, have sweet dreams."

"I'll walk you out." A ridiculous thing to suggest since they knew no reprobates were lurking in the hallways. But still he wanted to reassure himself she wasn't going to have the opposite of what Lawrence had wished her: terrifying dreams.

Once they were in the hallway, he clamped his hands behind his back to stop himself from reaching for her as he strode beside her toward the corridor leading to the stairs that would carry her to the servants' quarters.

"I think he's feeling rather embarrassed by the entire episode," she said. "He told me he wouldn't have brought them here if he'd known I was going to be in the library."

"He shouldn't have placed himself in a position to be threatened. He knows better. I hope only that you will not have nightmares."

"Tonight's drama was not the stuff of nightmares for me."

The words were casually spoken, and yet they echoed the absolute truth. He also heard the admission that something had been, something worse than what she'd faced or been threatened with by the two debt collectors. Doubting she would share the details, he refrained from asking. Besides, it wasn't the time to bring up memories that might make it difficult to sleep. But tonight he'd learned additional information about her. The more he unveiled, the more curious he became. He was desperate to know everything. She'd always been an important part of the business side of his life, but it seemed at some point today a shift had occurred in his world, and he could no longer relegate her to only a portion of it.

"I was afraid you were going to come in swinging the broadsword that hangs in the billiards room," she said lightly.

He chuckled darkly. "It was certainly a consideration. Your calm throughout the ordeal was quite impressive. I find myself wondering what shaped you into the person you are."

They'd reached the door. After placing her hand on the latch, she gave him a desolate smile. "It's best not to know."

"Pettypeace—"

"Good night, Your Grace. Sleep well."

Quickly she made her escape into the servants' realm before he could ask more of her. But he knew he was the one who would not sleep well this night as he contemplated her cryptic words.

By the time he returned to the library, Lawrence was gone, as was the decanter of scotch. King poured himself a brandy, wandered over to the window, and gazed out. His focus should have been on his brother, but his thoughts drifted to Pettypeace.

He remembered the first time he'd seen her, when she'd walked into this very room. While he had offices on Fleet Street, he'd decided to hold his interviews here because the grandeur of the residence could intimidate some, impress others, and he'd believed someone's reaction would provide him with an initial understanding of what they valued, how they adapted to unfamiliar environments. She had marched in as though she owned the place, owned him.

He'd been twenty-six, with too many irons in the fire to keep track of them all. With her ability to organize, she'd quickly made herself indispensable. And in doing so, she'd given him the freedom to travel, to search far and wide for other investment opportunities, to scour the globe. But of a sudden, he was more interested in what was closer to home. In unraveling the mystery of her.

CHAPTER 5

SHE DIDN'T SLEEP. But it certainly wasn't because of any nightmares. It was because of how much she had enjoyed sitting in the library with Kingsland when no business hovered between them to intrude. Then, when the debt collectors had joined them—the manner in which he'd defended her, the feral growl in his throat when he'd threatened the grubby man who had made a move toward her. Never had anyone stood as her champion before. She had been on her own for so long that his defense of her had nearly brought tears to her eyes.

He was a far greater danger to her than those ruffians had been. To love him when he was indifferent to her was relatively harmless, but for him to unintentionally give her hope that more could exist between them, that he could return her affections—

But of course, he couldn't. He'd made that clear.

Last night he'd simply been defending his home and the people within it. Not her specifically. He'd have reacted the same if Lucy had been there instead of her. Wouldn't he?

By the time she strode into the morning dining room for breakfast, she had convinced herself that even if only his butler had been in the library with him, he would have indeed been as fierce.

In a rare occurrence, he had arrived at the table ahead of her. Setting aside his newspaper, he came to his feet. "Pettypeace."

He appeared tired, drawn, as though he hadn't slept either, although she suspected very different reasons had kept him awake. "Good morning, Your Grace."

After retrieving a light repast from the sideboard, she joined him at the table, settling into her usual place to his right. He retook his seat.

She poured herself some tea and, without thought, refilled his cup. It was a far too domesticated thing to do and yet it seemed quite natural, to make note of what he lacked and to see his needs met. "I've been giving some thought to last night."

"Which portion?" An undercurrent of something dark and intimate threaded itself through his tone, and she was tempted to respond with the truth: all of it. But surely, he placed no weight on what had transpired between them before the brutish men arrived.

"The latter, after we were interrupted."

"I'd have never let them hurt you."

She gave her head a little shake. "I know that."

And she did. With every fiber of her being. "I wasn't thinking about the rapscallions but rather Lord Lawrence."

"It seems he's been a rapscallion."

He sounded none too pleased, his brother's troubles still weighing on him. Because she handled the books, she knew the duke was incredibly generous, bestowing upon his brother a yearly allowance that many would envy. "I think he has no purpose in his life."

"His purpose is to replace me should I die."

No one could replace you. Those words hung on the tip of her tongue, desperate to be uttered, inappropriate to be spoken with the heartfelt conviction she held for them. "But that's just it, don't you see? He must feel he is somewhat untethered. He is what? All of thirty? You're hale and hearty and healthy. Soon you'll marry"—*I'm not certain I'll have it within me to remain and watch*—"and obtain your heir. Then what? You provide Lord Lawrence with everything. He needs to provide for himself. I think that's the reason he went to the moneylender. He was trying to be independent, but it . . . well, unfortunately, it didn't go well."

Without taking his gaze from her, he stirred his tea, then took a sip. "You understate it. It was a disaster."

"Next time, it very well could be. Many second sons have occupations. Perhaps you should encourage him, guide him, even find something substantial with which he could assist you. It just mustn't come across as charity or indulgence."

"It's guilt, you know? My spoiling of him, requiring so little of him."

She didn't know, hadn't known, but then, neither had she known he'd rebuilt what his father had almost destroyed. But she didn't say anything. Simply waited because she sensed what was to come next was not easily said.

"When I disappointed my father—and I did on numerous occasions, which I realize is rather difficult to believe—he punished Lawrence. Sometimes I would get so angry at my sire's domineering attitude that I would rebel and behave worse, and Lawrence suffered because of it. I suppose I indulge him now in an attempt to make up for it. Perhaps I've only served to cause more harm."

Her heart was breaking for him and his brother. "I don't think I would have liked the previous duke."

"You would have found him charming. Everyone did. That is the thing about monsters, Pettypeace. They are monsters because they can delude people into believing they aren't."

She knew a thing or two about monsters, but they were dealing with his past, his troubles, not hers, and it was not the time to reveal the hardships she'd endured. Besides, she needed neither sympathy nor understanding because she'd escaped them, and they were unlikely to ever trouble her again. She'd been taking what steps she could to ensure it. He was not as fortunate. The remnants of the suffering remained to haunt him, him and his brother.

"But you might have the right of it. Lawrence

is untethered. In spoiling him, I've done him a disservice."

In his furrowed brow, the distant focus of his gaze, she could see he was working things out. Early in their relationship, she'd noted that when he needed to ponder a situation, he could separate himself from his surroundings until it was only him and his thoughts. She did hope his duchess wouldn't pester him during these moments. Perhaps she needed to provide lessons for his future wife in order to ensure they got along amicably.

"Keating," he suddenly announced, and the butler stepped forward from his post where he'd been keeping watch. "See that Lord Lawrence is immediately stirred from his slumber, bathed, and readied for the day. He is to join me in the library within the hour."

"Yes, Your Grace."

The duke slid his gaze over to her. "I'll need you there as well, Pettypeace."

She was not going to acknowledge how much joy it brought her every time he said he needed her.

KING STOOD AT the window beside the sitting area where he had enjoyed conversing with Pettypeace last night before everything had gone awry. He had yet to feel that he had regained his footing. If he was more himself, he wouldn't have revealed all that he had during breakfast. He'd never told anyone else how the duke had controlled him by punishing Lawrence in his stead. King had been defiant whenever his father took a hand or switch to him, and so the duke had sought to break him. And he did it by inflicting the harsh discipline on his younger son to more effectively penalize the older and bring him to heel. It had always shamed him that he hadn't been able to protect his brother.

Sometimes he had misjudged what his father would view as behavior in need of correction. Becoming friends with a lad whose father had slighted the duke. Dancing with a girl his father thought not pretty enough. Reading a questionable book. Receiving imperfect marks in school. Losing during a tumble with another boy. Losing was never tolerated. So he'd focused his entire being on winning, until nothing else mattered. And he'd learned not to display any emotion when Lawrence was the recipient of King's punishments, because to flinch, to indicate anger, to reveal any reaction at all only served to increase the number of lashings, as though his father enjoyed creating the mental anguish as much as he did the physical pain. King had sometimes wondered if his father was a trifle mad.

As far as King knew, his mother was unaware of how his father had disciplined him. It was a secret he and Lawrence shared. However, now Pettypeace knew. He should have felt vulnerable. Instead, he felt not quite alone. But there was danger in that, in becoming too reliant upon her, in wanting to confess everything, to seek absolution in her eyes, confirmation he was not indeed a monster like his father.

The truth, however, was that he was much worse, and he could not risk giving in to this dangerous desire to bare his soul to her. The wall he'd built between them had threatened to crumble the night before, and he needed to shore it back up. Before he did something completely idiotic and trusted her with everything. The weight of his sins was his and his alone to bear. Bear them he would.

At the echo of footsteps, he turned. Pettypeace was sitting in the chair near his desk that she usually occupied during meetings when she was taking notes. Her gaze was on him, and while he wanted to offer her a smile, he instead slid his attention to the doorway. Lawrence sauntered through looking quite a bit tidier than he had the night before and seemed not to display any ill effects from his imbibing. Perhaps he hadn't finished off the entire bottle. Although he also had a knack for quickly recovering from any overindulgence. King had been right about his eye. It sported a black bruise, his lip not appearing much better. He wouldn't be kissing anyone soon.

"I suppose you've decided to purchase me a commission in the army," Lawrence grumbled as he headed straight for the decanters.

"No, I haven't."

"As someone who enjoys sinning, I'm not fit for the clergy." He lifted a crystal decanter.

"Don't."

Lawrence glanced back. "I could do with some scotch if I'm to endure a lecture."

"It's too early in the day, and you're going to need your wits about you."

His brother studied him for a heartbeat before finally lowering the decanter. "I'm surprised after I botched things so badly last night that you believe me to have any wits at all."

"I see no advantage to dwelling on last night. It's behind us. It's time to move forward." He strode to his desk, picked up a packet, and extended it toward Lawrence. "I require your help with a matter."

Lawrence approached cautiously as though King was presenting him with a black adder. "What is it?"

"A man came to see me yesterday"—good Lord, was it that recently?—"about a wake-up clock he'd invented."

"A wake-up clock?"

"Yes, you turn some knobs, and at a particular time, it makes an atrocious noise to wake you up."

"Why in God's name would anyone want that?"

"Not everyone has the luxury of sleeping late. They have to get to their workplace, preferably by a certain hour. I need you to determine the viability of it as an investment."

"Why me? Isn't that something Pettypeace would research?"

"Her time is better spent finding me a duchess."

Hesitantly, Lawrence took the packet.

"Those are all the notes she took from our meeting with the chap. You'll want to study them, and then determine the cost, advantages, and disadvantages of engaging in such an enterprise. Pettypeace can help you there." He held up a key. "You may use my office on Fleet Street as your headquarters. When you're ready, the three of us will discuss your findings. Then we'll meet with Mr. Lancaster to let him know our decision based upon your recommendation."

Lawrence plowed a hand through his perfectly brushed hair, causing it to look quite mussed. "What if I get it wrong?"

Leaning his hip against his desk, King crossed his arms over his chest. "Why should you do that?"

"I've never done anything like this before."

"It's either that, the army, or the clergy."

His brother released a harsh laugh. "You're mad to put this in my hands."

"You wager, do you not?" Pettypeace asked. "It's not that different. You take the information you know and determine the odds of success."

"As you learned last night, I'm bollocks when it comes to wagering."

With the same encouraging smile she'd offered Lancaster, she rose to her feet. "Everything has an element of risk. The more information you gather, the better able you are to evaluate the probability of success. As the duke pointed out, you're not going to be making the decision by yourself. He has the experience to take the information you provide and guide you in the right direction. I'm rather certain he made mistakes in the beginning, but they didn't destroy him, did they?"

That stung. That she should think he hadn't always judged correctly. He hadn't, but still, he'd have preferred she believe him infallible.

"I don't even know where to begin."

"I made some suggestions," she assured him. "Your brother can offer more."

"All right then." He met King's gaze. "You won't be sorry for trusting me with this."

"It never occurred to me I would be. Now, on to a less pleasant matter. I require a list of your debts so we can get those sorted and they aren't hanging over you."

Pettypeace lowered herself to the chair and began scrawling the names of the places Lawrence— somewhat embarrassedly, thank goodness—recited for her. King should have paid more attention to how his brother was spending his time. Lawrence had been fifteen when King had become duke at nineteen and begun sorting out the mess his father had made of things. He'd wanted Lawrence to have a much easier life, just as he'd wanted his mother not to have a care in the world. But he could see now that a young man did need a purpose other than play.

He could also see the kindness with which Pettypeace repeatedly assured Lawrence that he hadn't mucked things up beyond repair. He wondered why he'd never noticed how soft she could be. With him she was all tart and business and efficiency. He valued that aspect of her. But the gentleness in her . . . he yearned for that as well.

He had business to which he needed to attend, and yet he found it nearly impossible to look away from her, wished she'd remove her spectacles so a few wisps of her hair might escape their bounds. Imagined himself removing the pins until every strand tumbled around her shoulders and down her back.

Whatever was wrong with him to be so drawn to her of late? She wasn't a great beauty, but there was a prettiness to her that began deep within her and flowed outward to the surface. It made her eyes shine and her smile joyous. And that smile made her lips the most kissable-appearing pair he'd ever encountered.

What a mistake that would be. To kiss her. To give any indication at all that he wanted her. It would make matters awkward between them, and she might decide that she couldn't remain in his employ. He couldn't fathom the bleakness of a day without her in it.

CHAPTER 6

$\mathcal{T}$HE ADVANTAGE TO being employed by the Duke of Kingsland was that Penelope had access to all his contacts, including his investigators and spies. So it was with a great deal of ease that she was able to find the location of the Fair Ladies' and Spare Gentlemen's Club, known more intimately as the Fair and Spare. She stood across the street from it now, striving to gather up the courage needed to walk in.

For the past three days, ever since that morning in the library when Kingsland had given his brother a task, the duke had been scarce. He had spent a good part of his time seeing to one matter or another and had gone out each evening to have dinner elsewhere. He'd been uncharacteristically secretive, not bothering to enlighten her regarding his plans. While she had made a trip to his library during the late hours, hoping her path might cross with his and he would once again invite her to have a brandy with him, her hopes were repeatedly dashed when he never appeared. If she didn't know better, she'd think he was sleeping elsewhere.

But each morning he was there at breakfast, discussing what he needed of her for the day, yet something had changed. He seemed done up as tight as a drum. Not a single smile or a chuckle or even an inquiry as to her well-being. While she fully understood that an employee did not become friends with her employer, that one of common birth did not become friends with an aristocrat, she'd allowed herself to believe they shared some sort of personal bond that deepened their relationship and made her slightly more than staff. More fool she.

Well, she'd never been one to feel sorry for herself. She was in charge of her destiny, and if he could seek out companionship, so could she.

Taking a deep breath, she crossed the street and marched up the steps to the behemoth of a man who guarded the door. "Hello, I'm here to inquire about membership."

With a grave nod, he opened the door. "First room to yer right."

That was easier than she'd anticipated. As she entered, she heard a cacophony of laughter and the din of voices coming from down the hallway and up the stairs. The first room to the right resembled a parlor. While a few chairs circled about, no one was waiting in them. A man sat at a small desk in the corner, near the window, but she chose to approach the woman occupying the larger desk in the center of the room. "Good evening. I'd like a membership."

"Name?"

"Penelope Pettypeace."

The woman began riffling through a small stack of cards. Once. Twice. Looked up at Penelope. Riffled again. Set them aside. "I'm not seeing that you've been referred to us."

"Referred?"

"Someone must refer you in order for us to grant you membership. Without a referral, I'm afraid you'll need to remove yourself posthaste."

"A referral is not a very practical means for gaining members."

"Membership is only conferred upon those who someone can vouch are not gossips."

"I assure you I am no gossip."

"Someone else must do it."

What poppycock! She'd never heard the like. Why hadn't the investigator told her that important tidbit of information? "Surely you can make an exception."

"I'm afraid not."

"This is ridiculous."

"You'll have to find someone to recommend you."

"But your membership is secret. How would I even determine whom to ask?"

The irritating woman merely shrugged.

"I'll recommend her, Gertie."

Penelope swung around to find Lawrence grinning broadly. "My lord."

"Miss Pettypeace, I certainly never expected to find you here."

"Nor I, you."

He shrugged. "This place was created by a second son for second sons." He took a step closer to the desk. "I'll vouch for her. She's no gossip, our Miss Pettypeace."

She was surprised he waited patiently while she filled out her membership application, handed over a stipend as her yearly dues, and had the young man at the table draw her likeness on her membership card.

"Simply show that to the man at the door the next time you come," the skilled artist told her.

The man at the door, the fellow she was fairly certain could snap anyone's neck without breaking a sweat.

"May I interest you in joining me for a drink?" Lord Lawrence asked.

"That would be lovely, thank you." But only a drink. She certainly wasn't going to seek out companionship with the duke's brother.

He escorted her along the hallway to a room filled with people, talking and sipping their beverages. A man stood behind a long counter, filling glasses with various libations. After getting them both a red wine, Lawrence guided her across the room to a small table with two chairs. As she took her seat, she noted that most people stood, no doubt because that made it easier to flit about from person to person until interest sparked, took hold, and hinted at commonalities or at least a desire to explore where further conversation might take them.

"It was your idea, wasn't it."

She jerked her attention to Lord Lawrence. He

hadn't asked a question, but rather had issued a statement. He shared his brother's dark hair and eyes, but not the seriousness. His burdens weren't nearly as heavy. "I beg your pardon?"

"Giving me a task. That was your idea."

She took a sip of the excellent wine. "I might have suggested you lacked purpose."

He laughed robustly. "You don't consider gambling a purpose?"

"Not really, no. And you don't appear to be very good at it."

Another laugh before he sobered. "Does he know you're here?"

With a shake of her head, she looked back at the crowd. Few groups contained more than two people, but no one seemed to be permanently engaged, and they moved on easily enough. "I doubt he would care."

"I suspect he would care very much."

She wasn't going to hope he spoke true. The duke would soon be lost to her completely. She gave Lord Lawrence a challenging glower. "What his staff does once the sun retreats is really not his concern."

"You believe you are only staff to him?"

"Of course I am. I'm his secretary, nothing more."

"Ah, Miss Pettypeace, I'd always considered you the smartest among us."

"Granted, I do believe he values me, but only to the extent that I lessen his number of duties by handling the more boring tasks for him."

"He invites all his servants to have a drink with him?"

"That was happenstance. And he certainly hasn't done it since. As a matter of fact, he's rarely about of late. Something—or someone—is occupying his evenings."

"Which left you free to seek companionship tonight."

"I'm eight-and-twenty, my lord. With no family to speak of. Why should it be wrong for me to enjoy the company of a gentleman for a few hours when it is perfectly acceptable for a man to spend time in the company of a woman whom he has no intention of ever marrying?"

"I didn't say it was wrong. Simply unexpected. But you are correct"—he glanced around—"and not alone in your belief. It is more of a challenge for women to arrange assignations with men, I think, which is one of the reasons the club is garnering such success." He finished off his wine and winked at her. "Enjoy the hunt, Miss Pettypeace."

"You as well, my lord."

After he left her, she sat for several minutes savoring her wine, wondering what in the devil she was truly doing here. If only the duke hadn't invited her to join him for brandy in his library, she might never have noticed how extremely empty her evenings were. Oh, she spent some time visiting with Lucy and one or two other servants, but it wasn't as rewarding as spending time in the company of a man she admired. After the work was done, when they were free to delve into secrets. Not that either had revealed any, but still, the potential had been there. Along with the occasional heated look and the pondering of *what if*. What if he wasn't a duke? What if she wasn't charged with finding him a wife? What if she intrigued him as much as he did her?

And if wishes were horses . . . well, she'd have to learn to ride a horse, wouldn't she? Being here tonight was just as challenging because she'd never flirted with a gent before. Had previously avoided seeking out the attention of one, because she'd always worried that actions she'd taken in the past might surface to ruin things. But enough years now separated her from them, so surely she was safe.

After standing and handing her empty glass to a passing footman, she was tempted to claim another but needed her wits about her as she strolled through the throng. Smiling here, nodding there, she wondered how one even began to determine who might appeal.

No gentleman was as handsome as the duke, but then, she'd never been swayed by comely features. It was intelligence, cunning, and inner strength that appealed to her. And kindness, even if it was sometimes masked by a gruffness to disguise the fact it existed at all. She was almost to the door when a man stepped in front of her.

"I don't believe I've seen you here before."

He was a pleasant-enough-looking fellow, his blond hair tidy, his blue eyes alert. His voice polished, but she caught an undercurrent of the street in it.

"I've only just become a member."

"How fortunate for me."

She furrowed her brow. "How is it fortunate for you?"

"It's given me the opportunity to meet you."

"But having just met me, you're a bit hasty in your assessment. It might not be fortunate at all."

He blinked, grinned. "That is indeed true. However, I lean toward optimism. Allow me to introduce myself. George Grenville, at your service."

"What sort of service do you provide?"

He laughed. "You are quite literal."

"I am, yes." She was in over her head. Her life had not allowed for moments like this, striving to be intriguing, to meet someone who was not a matter of business, whom she wished to know better.

"And you are?" he prodded.

"Oh. Penelope Pettypeace." She held out her gloved hand. He took it and brought it to his lips.

"A pleasure, Miss Pettypeace."

She almost commented that he didn't yet know if it was a pleasure, but realized he was only being polite, issuing compliments that were nothing other than a means to fill in the silence. He squinted as though to see her better, and she wondered if he was in need of spectacles and too proud to wear them.

"Although you look vaguely familiar. Have we met before?"

Could he hear the thud of her stomach hitting the floor? No, he wouldn't recognize her, not after all these years. She had changed. Her mien was different. "I think I simply have one of those faces that makes me not very distinguishable from everyone else."

"I doubt that's it. Perhaps we met at a ball or a recital?"

Her stomach returned to its rightful place. "By any chance did you attend the Duke of Kingsland's ball last Season?" It was the only one he'd ever held, the only one she'd ever attended. She had no memory of addressing an invitation to a Mr. George Grenville, but having sent more than two hundred, she couldn't recall all the names. If one had gone to his family, then he might have simply accompanied them.

"I did, as a matter of fact. Spent a good bit of time drying tears after he made his announcement. Were you one of the ladies who wept because she was not chosen?"

"Heavens, no. I was never even on the list for consideration. No, I'm the duke's secretary and oversaw the affair. I was wandering about, ensuring all was as it should be. Perhaps you caught sight of me there."

"Yes, that must be it. What are your impressions thus far?"

"You seem pleasant enough."

He laughed, a relaxed sound that echoed between them, and turned a few heads in their direction. "I was referring to your opinion of the club."

"Oh, my apologies." She did feel rather like a cabbagehead. She was out of her element here and didn't like floundering about. "I've not seen much of the club, but people seem to be enjoying themselves."

"I would be honored to escort you through the various rooms and entertainments."

"I don't wish to monopolize your evening."

"Nonsense. You're the most intriguing woman I've met here since acquiring my membership."

She very much doubted that, suspected he was simply striving to flatter her in order to have his way with her, but she was not one easily seduced. At an early age, she'd learned to be wary of the motives of silver-tongued devils. Still, she accepted his proffered arm and allowed him to lead her up the stairs.

He escorted her to a small ballroom, but she wasn't in the mood for a waltz. They spent a little bit of time playing darts in another room, until he grew weary of losing to her. She seemed to have a natural talent for sending a pointed projectile into the center of a circular board. When she missed, it was only by a hair or two.

"Are you certain you've never played before?" he asked as they went back into the hallway.

"Quite."

In a different room, he taught her to smoke a cheroot. Afterward, her throat felt a bit scratchy, but the aroma surrounding her reminded her of her father smoking his pipe. He'd once allowed her to take a puff on it.

"That's a rather secretive-looking smile," he said as they wandered out of the haze-filled room.

"I was just struck with a pleasant memory of my father. I don't often have those."

"Here I was hoping you were thinking of me."

She released a small laugh. "I'm afraid I'm not very skilled at this flirtation game."

"At least you're honest, and a gent knows precisely where he stands with you."

Except for Kingsland. He didn't know how she truly felt about him. Some matters were best kept to oneself. "Are you always honest with the women you escort through here?"

"I try to be. At this moment, I would very much like to take you up to the next floor."

His voice had gone low and slow, as though he was saying more than he was. "And what is up there?"

"Private rooms . . . for exploring."

"Exploring each other, I presume."

"Indeed." He appeared incredibly pleased by her response. "Would you care to accompany me?"

His hair was the wrong shade, his eyes the wrong color, his jawline not pronounced enough. He was a couple of inches too short. "I don't know you well enough."

"With privacy, we could quickly remedy that."

"I like you, Mr. Grenville, and have enjoyed our time together. However, I apologize if I gave the impression I was here tonight for more than a scouting expedition."

"I completely understand, Miss Pettypeace. A woman needs to exercise caution. To be honest, my esteem for you is greater because of your prudence." Taking her hand, he brought it to his lips. "Perhaps once we get to know each other a bit better you'll realize you need not be so wary. Enjoy the remainder of your evening."

He left her then and approached a woman who was studying a painting of a couple locked in an embrace. Based on the smile his new partner gave him, she suspected they were quite familiar with each other and would no doubt journey up those stairs together.

A couple of other gentlemen introduced themselves, but she didn't spend long speaking with them. Her head had begun aching, no doubt from her time in the smoking parlor. Little wonder it was a separate chamber in most homes. Accustomed to hours working in solitude, she found it rather taxing to spend her evening in the company of so many others, constantly smiling and engaging in conversation with people she didn't know, even if she did consider them interesting and looked forward to becoming better acquainted over time. Still, a weariness soon overtook her. When she left the club a little before midnight, she was glad she'd come, but thought she might need a few lessons on the art of flirtation before she returned.

KING WAS IN a wretchedly foul mood. Pettypeace had not joined him for breakfast. In his effort to put distance between them, it had become his favorite hour of the day, the one time when he didn't have to come up with an excuse to see her. It was their routine. While he could call for her whenever he wanted, he'd begun limiting how many times he yanked on the bellpull in his library, how often he summoned her. But he jerked on it so hard now that he nearly tore it from its mooring.

He required an update on how his brother was making out gathering his information. Lawrence hadn't come to King for any guidance, and while he admired his brother's independence, he also worried that Lawrence might muck things up and an opportunity would slip through their hands.

Besides, he just wanted to spend time in her company. He'd avoided her yesterday after breakfast simply to prove he could go an entire day without sight of her and not suffer for it. Unfortunately, he had suffered. He'd missed her rare smiles, her rarer soft chuckles, her voice. He'd missed the fragrance of her. He'd missed the challenge of her. She forced him to look at things from impossible angles, to consider what he hadn't before.

Because he found himself yearning to sit in his library in the evening on the off chance she came to retrieve a book so he could invite her to join him for a drink, he'd gone out every night. Gone to clubs with the Chessmen, a pleasure garden with Bishop, a gaming hell. Boring, boring, boring. So deuced boring. Every hour away from her.

She constantly haunted his thoughts and confused him. When had she become such an integral part of his life beyond business? It was simply the familiarity of her. Other than his mother, he'd never had a woman in his life as long as he'd had Pettypeace. It was natural that he would have a care for her.

It was also natural that he would spend two hours with a jeweler the day before striving to find a gemstone that mirrored the shade of her eyes. The emeralds had been too dark, lacking the shine for which he searched. The gift would have been inappropriate, and yet he no longer wanted to give her gold-nibbed pens. He wanted to present her with something demonstrating her worth to him could not be measured. Something of a more personal bent.

Keating strode silently into the room. "Your Grace, you rang for Pettypeace."

"I did. Some time ago." She never kept him waiting, and he wasn't going to stand for her doing so now. Just because they'd sat in here in camaraderie and sipped brandy, and he yearned for those moments again, did not give her leave to ignore his summons or to answer it at her leisure.

"She is indisposed."

"Indisposed? In what manner?"

Keating took a step back. Not that King blamed him. He'd unintentionally roared those questions, and they were still echoing through the cavernous chamber. The butler cleared his throat. "She is unwell."

He came up out of the chair with such force that it nearly toppled. He was not a man prone to panic, but if the pounding of his heart was any indication, he'd just taken up the practice. "What precisely do you mean by unwell?"

"She assures me it is nothing to worry over. A bit of fever—"

"Fever? Pettypeace does not get ill." Illness wouldn't have the gall to visit upon her. King was already on the move. "She could be on her deathbed and she'd answer my summons."

But even as he said it, he knew it for a lie, but also knew it was the only thing that would prevent her from coming to him. He'd just passed Keating when he came to a staggering halt and glared at the man as though all of this mayhem was somehow his fault. Especially as King had just realized something of paramount importance. "Where the bloody hell is her chamber?"

"This way, sir."

He followed Keating into the bowels of the servants' area, all the while refraining from shoving the stately man and ordering him to move his feet faster. The butler walked as though there was no need to hurry, as though unaware that even now Pettypeace might be drawing her last breath, would do it without knowing King had come to her.

After passing by the kitchens, they went to a set of stairs. Up they climbed, one step at a time when King wanted to take two or three, as many as possible to shorten the distance between him and his secretary.

Finally, at the top of the stairs, Keating led him to a door and knocked. Even knowing it was an irrational action, King had an urge to kick it in. Instead, when no answer came, he edged his butler out of the way and shoved open the door.

The small windowless room caught him by surprise, as did the sparse furnishings. A bed, a bedside table, a wardrobe, and a wooden straightbacked chair. Was that where she read? No, she would lounge on the tiny bed with the brass headboard. The tiny bed upon which she was presently curled on her side. Near her head, a cat licked its paw and studied him, leaving him with the impression the creature found him lacking. As he wasn't one to visit the servants' areas, he wasn't aware the creature had a home here. Careful not to interfere with its grooming, he crouched beside Pettypeace and cradled her cheek.

Her eyes fluttered. "Your Grace, give me a moment to ready myself."

"You're fevered."

"My throat hurts, but it's nothing to worry over. It's happened before. I'll be on the mend in a day or two."

What if it was something more dire? Tossing aside the covers, he lifted her into his arms.

"What are you doing?" she asked weakly, and it was her not fighting his inappropriate action that terrified him all the more.

"Taking you someplace more comfortable. Keating, send for my physician."

Ignoring the wide-eyed stares of servants and her feeble protests, he carried her through the residence until he reached the hallway that housed his bedchamber. He strode through the open door of the room opposite and settled her into the more comfortable bed.

"I can't stay here," she said.

"Of course you can. It's now your chamber. I'll have your things moved in." He tucked the covers around her. "Sleep until the physician arrives."

With no further protests, she closed her eyes, not stirring when the cat leapt up and made itself at home on the pillow.

"For God's sake, Pettypeace, why didn't you tell me I had you living in a hovel?"

If she heard him, she didn't answer. She appeared so much smaller in that larger bed, smaller and more vulnerable.

He should leave, but he couldn't. Not until he knew she would be all right.

SHE DRIFTED IN and out, kicking off the covers, only to have Lucy put them back into place. During the day her friend forced Penelope to drink warm tea laced with honey and gargle some horrible concoction the physician had given her.

"It's your throat causing the fever," Lucy confirmed for her. "It's festering or something, but the physician says it should all clear up within a few days, and you'll be right as rain."

When night fell and all grew quiet, Lucy would leave her to sleep and then *he* would come. The first night, he looked as awful as she felt. He sat in a chair beside the bed and simply held her hand. Whenever she awoke, it was to find his gaze on her, to watch the corners of his mouth lift slightly. Her name would pass softly and quietly over his lips. "Pettypeace." A benediction and a prayer, as though if he called to her often enough, she would eventually escape the fever.

The second night he read to her. Even when she slept, his voice droned on in her dreams. She wasn't certain the words always came from the book, though, because sometimes when she stirred from slumber he was patting a damp cloth over her face or along her throat. Even as she knew it was inappropriate for him to be with her, she wanted no one else more.

When her fever broke, a fire was built and a bath was readied, and Lucy returned to assist her. As

Penelope luxuriated in the warm water, Lucy told her everything she'd missed.

"He's had all your personal things moved into this room."

She recalled him saying something about doing that, but the activity must have all taken place while she was sleeping.

"He was appalled by your living accommodations."

"But it's common for staff to have plain rooms."

"Apparently, he doesn't consider his secretary *staff*, but something more."

"That can't be sitting well with the rest of the servants."

Lucy shrugged before moving in to help her wash her hair. "You have those who are talking ugly, saying the *more* is sexual favors, but I don't believe that."

"While I appreciate your support, Lucy, what the others believe could cause trouble. I can't stay in this room." No matter how large and beautiful it was. Or how comfortable the bed.

"He has replaced all the wooden chairs in our rooms with plush wingback chairs. I fell asleep in mine last night."

She smiled. "Did you really?"

"I did, yes." Lucy moved around until she could meet Penelope's gaze. "I don't think you should give this room up. I wouldn't."

But when he married . . . to know he and his wife were across the hall—

She shook her head. "It would be entirely inappropriate."

"He's moving your office as well."

A jolt of surprise went through her. "What do you mean he's moving my office?"

"Well, not your office, but the things in it, to what was the duchess's morning parlor, that small room near the library."

She shouldn't be so pleased or feel so warm, as though the fever was once again upon her. "I'll be closer to him."

"Quite." Lucy bit down on her lower lip, her expression one of glee. "Honestly, Penn, you should have seen the way he looked when he came for you. He was a knight on his way to rescue you from a dragon."

She couldn't stop herself from laughing. "Lucy, you read too many fairy tales."

"I promise I am not exaggerating. When he carried you out . . . my heart melted. He was so fierce I knew you wouldn't die."

"I don't think I was ever in any danger of dying. It was just a tender throat. I was plagued with them when I was younger." It had been deuced irritating sensing it might be happening again, after so many years of being dormant. She'd hoped it was just the dryness of the wine or smoke from the cigar.

Lucy glanced around. "I wouldn't care about the gossip, Penn. I wouldn't give up these nice accommodations. Besides, they all think it anyway."

She suddenly felt more ill than she had when she was fevered. "Whatever do you mean?"

"The maids, even some of the footmen. All the nights when you're with him late, I know you're working and I tell them so, but they think you're making a stitch with him."

Making a stitch? Having a casual affair? Bloody gossips. As though any of it was their business. Who were they to judge her life, when she didn't judge theirs? She imagined if they learned about her visit to the Fair and Spare, they'd be gathering kindling to burn her at a stake in the garden. Why shouldn't a woman be able to live as freely as a man?

Besides, he'd never made any untoward advances. That wasn't going to change simply because she was across the hallway from him. He didn't view her in that way, as someone he was drawn to. She wasn't even certain he was aware of her as a woman.

"I am going to keep this room," she suddenly announced in a firm tone, having convinced herself she deserved it and he wouldn't take advantage.

"Jolly good for you," Lucy said. "You work harder for him than anyone. You should have nice things."

CHAPTER 7

Five weeks until the Kingsland ball

"A LITTLE NEARER TO the fireplace," King ordered the two footmen who had brought the elegant rosewood desk into the room. He wouldn't be surprised to learn it had been at least one generation if not two since any furniture in this residence had been moved so much as half an inch. While Pettypeace had been ill, he'd had sofas, chairs, and small tables carted to other areas of the residence to make room for the large desk—the one at which she'd worked in a near dungeon had been too small—and an assortment of larger and more substantial chairs. This chamber had been his mother's domain for much of her marriage, but the furnishings had all been too dainty and frail. His secretary needed a place that more adequately reflected her—all business and no nonsense.

He would, of course, make it clear she was welcome to change anything she wanted, but he was rather certain she would be pleased with the furniture he'd chosen and the manner in which he'd had it all arranged.

"What the devil are you doing?" Lawrence asked from the doorway.

King glanced over his shoulder at his brother. He'd not seen him since he'd given him the clock project. "Establishing this room as a study for Pettypeace."

"Where is her office now?"

"In a place more suited to trolls." When he'd gone to her office to access the safe, he'd failed to notice its inadequacies. It might have served sufficiently for someone else but not for *her*. With a nod to the footmen, he said, "Very good."

With that he dismissed them and began wandering through the room, striving to determine if anything else should be added. He would have the remainder of the items in her office moved in this afternoon, and then all would be set. Now when he had a need for her, it would be only a short walk down the hallway. However, he hadn't designated this room as her office for his convenience, but hers. She was deserving of the finest, and he'd been remiss in seeing to her comfort, her needs.

"Where is she, by the by?" Lawrence asked.

"Recovering from an illness." Her fever had finally broken that morning, but he expected her to rest for a couple of days.

"She's been unwell?"

"Fever, nasty throat. On the mend now."

"I thought she looked a bit poorly at the Fair and Spare."

King swung around to see his brother's eyes had gone wide in horror. "The Fair and Spare?"

"Bollocks. Forget I said anything. We're not supposed to reveal who we see there. They'll take away my membership, they'll—"

He slashed his hand through the air. "I'm not going to tell anyone. But what was she doing there?"

Lawrence shrugged. "What we're all doing there. Striving to ease the loneliness, seeking companionship."

"How often does she go?"

"The other night was her first time. I had to—" He shook his head. "I shouldn't be telling you all this."

He advanced on his brother. "You had to what?"

The strength of Lawrence's sigh could have stirred the leaves in a tree. "Vouch for her so she could gain membership."

"Vouch for her in what way?"

"That she could hold secrets. Ironic, since I obviously can't."

He didn't want to think of her being lonely, of turning to strangers for companionship. Of being desperate enough for company, yearning so much for someone to make her feel treasured, that she would go to a place where first one had to acknowledge their lack of being wanted. She was wanted, wanted by a man who shouldn't want her.

In somewhat of a trance, he walked to the window. Her previous office had no window, but this room had a large, glorious one that gave her a view of the gardens. She could enjoy sun and rain and snow, when they weren't at the estate. What was her office like there? Probably as atrocious as the one in the servants' area. Why had he given no thought to her comfort, to what she deserved? He'd taken her for granted, this woman who was such an important part of his days, who had begun to haunt his dreams. What if she met someone who would show her the appreciation she warranted, someone like Bishop with winks and promises of spoiling her, someone who wanted to take her away from him? Someone she wanted to take her away?

"You won't tell her?" Lawrence asked.

That no matter how he tried to keep himself occupied, her presence invaded every thought? That he wanted to share with her everything he saw or heard when she wasn't with him? That he was constantly speculating on what she was doing? He gave his head a shake. "No."

He realized Lawrence had approached, and King hadn't even heard him, so deep in thought had he become. "I think Pettypeace became ill because I've placed too much of a burden on her, expecting her to do everything, helping you and me. We'll need to hire you a secretary."

"All right."

He was also going to hire an assistant for Pettypeace, to take care of the mundane. She was much too valuable for things that required no thought. "Why are you here?"

"I've gathered enough information that I believe we can make an informed decision regarding Mr. Lancaster's invention."

"Good. When Pettypeace is fully recovered—"

"I'm fully recovered now."

He swung around with such haste that he might have lost his balance if he hadn't a sturdier build. Never in his life had he been so relieved to see someone strolling toward him. In spite of the physician's reassurances she was likely to recover with no ill effects, he had calculated odds using worst-case scenarios. Pettypeace, who always saw the silver lining in the blackest of clouds, would have been appalled by the dark path upon which his fears had journeyed. He couldn't imagine a life in which she wasn't handling his affairs. No, it was more than that. He simply couldn't imagine a world in which a day began without her in it. That she did appear no worse for the wear at the moment, outfitted in her usual dark blue, was of little solace. She'd looked pitifully weak for a time there. "You should have a day of rest."

"I don't require it and have found occupying myself with meaningful tasks usually shakes off any lingering effects. I promise not to overtax myself."

"In that case"—he took several steps toward her before waving his arm in a circle to take in the room—"welcome to your new office."

She glanced around, a ghost of a smile on those lovely lips that had chapped with fever, and to which he'd gently applied a salve in order to prevent them from going so dry they bled. She'd been sleeping at the time, hadn't moved so much as an eyelash under his ministrations, and he wondered if she even knew of his care for her.

Her gaze returned to him, her green eyes filled with a softness that delivered a blow to his solar plexus more powerful than anything that had ever been dealt with a fist. "Thank you."

"You don't have to thank me for something I should have provided long ago." It irritated the devil out of him that she'd not demanded more, that he'd viewed her as a fixture in his life and taken so much about her for granted: that she would always be there, would always be content. That she would never consider that something better, more fulfilling, might reside elsewhere.

"Regarding the bedchamber —"

"Don't even consider returning to that depressing room where you slept before."

"Must I remind you that I am staff?"

"You are not staff, Pettypeace. You are my right hand. Were you a man, as soon as you made yourself invaluable to me, you would have negotiated a separate residence into part and parcel of your yearly earnings. As I cannot in all good conscience be responsible for a woman living alone, you'll have to make do with one of the lavish chambers here. Select one in another wing if you're not comfortable with the one in which I placed you."

"I accept the graciousness of your offer. However, the servants will talk."

"Then they will be let go. You are not deserving of their salacious gossip. I know few ladies who are as above reproach as you are. I've never had any patience for wagging tongues. Which is the reason I like you so well, Pettypeace. You do not traffic in rumors."

The reason? One of the reasons, surely. But it was a minor one. Not that he was going to list all the things about her that he liked and favored. Things he'd only recently begun to parse. His impassioned homily seemed to have left her speechless, because she glanced around the room again, cataloging various aspects of it. "You may, of course, change anything in here to suit you."

"I like it as it is." Her sudden smile radiated through the room. "Shall we test it out and see what Lord Lawrence has to reveal about Mr. Lancaster's invention?"

HE GAVE HER an hour to gather her things from her office belowstairs, with the aid of two footmen, because she wasn't to tax herself. It had been years since anyone had given her so much attention, had cared about her well-being to such a degree. She was finding it a bit overwhelming. After being independent and on her own for so long, she was struggling to determine if she liked having someone take such ardent interest in her welfare. But wasn't that part of the reason she'd gone to the club the other night, to find someone who would appreciate enough about her to want to spend an evening with her? Or several, for that matter?

She had just finished arranging on her desk all the small items the duke had given her over the years when he and his brother strode into the room. Lord Lawrence arrived with his usual swagger, but it contained more confidence now than entitlement. She was glad to see it. As for the duke, he always exuded confidence as though it had been woven into the very fabric of his character.

He stood before her desk, his gaze lighting upon all the various tokens of his appreciation. She felt rather silly that each held a place of honor where it could be easily viewed, and had not been shoved into a drawer. Not even the gold-plated ruler he'd given her one Christmas, which she had recently used to create the grids to help her narrow the selection for wife. The butcher paper she'd written on was now rolled up and resting in a corner. She hadn't wanted it covering the beautiful rosewood desk.

He lifted his eyes, dark and knowing, to hers. She treasured these small gifts. Heat swarmed through her cheeks. Never before had he visited her in her office. When she'd first come to work here, Keating had escorted her to it and to her small bedchamber. She hoped Kingsland attributed the color in her cheeks to her recent illness.

With a nod, he settled into the plush chair. "Right then, Lawrence, share with us what you've learned."

Penelope opened her notebook to begin making notes, only she didn't need to because Lord Lawrence had written out three times everything of importance and handed her and the duke sheaves of paper. She was impressed with his attention to detail, was glad to see he'd taken the task seriously. As he waxed on regarding his findings, without giving the impression she had diverted her attention, she managed to look slyly at the duke—

Shocked to discover his gaze rested squarely on her. It was not as impartial as it had once been, as though her illness had made him reevaluate how easily he might lose her. As though it would matter if he lost her.

She realized what had been lacking at the club: a gentleman who looked at her with such intensity that while he might be focused on her face, she felt his perusal from the roots of her hair to the tips of her toes. She suddenly wished she wasn't in her somber dark blue, but instead was wearing a beautiful gown of green that left skin exposed, that made him want to trail his enticing mouth over her flesh aroused by his attention.

She may have been fevered and feeling rotten, but having him carry her through the residence had been one of the more heartwarming experiences of her life.

"What do you think?" Lord Lawrence asked.

The duke's gaze slid away from her. "I think we should send a message to Mr. Lancaster and have him meet us in your office Monday."

"Do you agree we should invest?"

"I think you've made a sound argument for doing so. I also applaud you recommending the use of an existing factory that can easily shift gears to make this product. What think you, Pettypeace?"

"I agree. I shall be one of the first to purchase a wake-up clock."

Lord Lawrence laughed. "You shall have the first one that comes off the assembly line. God, this is exciting, King. Thank you for trusting me with it."

"It's only the start, Lawrence. Now the real work will begin, but I believe you're up to the task."

"We should celebrate." He glanced around. "I have found a flaw with this office. No spirits whatsoever. I'll fetch us something as we'll want to toast Miss Pettypeace's new accommodations as well."

As Lord Lawrence strode out of the room, Kingsland stood and moved around the edge of the desk until he was able to hitch a hip onto one of the corners on her side. "This desk suits you."

"I feel as though it rather swallows me up, but I do like all the space of it."

He picked up the paperweight with the early bird proverb. "You are the only woman I have ever known who is prompt."

"I see nothing to be gained in being tardy." Did she have to sound as though she had yet to learn how to take a breath?

He set the marble block down exactly where it had been. She wasn't surprised it required no straightening whatsoever, as they both shared an appreciation for precision. "For at least a week, you are not to overly tax yourself. I have decided Lawrence needs his own secretary. Perhaps you can assist him with the interviews, since you are familiar with the duties and skills we require."

"I'm more than happy to do so."

"You should also hire an assistant for yourself."

"Your Grace—"

"Don't look as though I've slapped you, Pettypeace. I find no fault with your work. It's excellent. I rely on you heavily. But you should have someone to take care of the mundane matters."

Where he was concerned, she found everything to be important, but it would be a relief to have some help. "Thank you, Your Grace. I shall begin the search for someone immediately."

"Good." He studied her for what seemed an eternity. "I was surprised to discover you slept with a cat."

"Sir Purrcival. P-U-R-R."

He grinned. "Because he purrs, I assume."

"Quite often, but he's no trouble. I've had him since he was a kitten, and he is quite independent, really."

"Like you. I'm remarkably grateful you recovered."

The statement warmed her in ways it shouldn't, as though it held a deeper meaning, a stronger sentiment, when it couldn't. "As am I, although I don't think I was ever in any danger of not doing so."

"You are incredibly important to me, Pettypeace."

Had he suddenly lifted his backside from the edge of the desk and stripped off his clothes, she'd have been less surprised than she was by the words he'd uttered. Not that he felt that way, but that he'd given voice to them. She hardly knew how to respond.

"I don't know if I've been particularly good at demonstrating my regard for you. You are irreplaceable."

"You are extremely kind to say so."

"Kindness has nothing to do with it. It is fact."

But there were other facts as well, facts that should not be. "You tended to me while I was ill."

"Some, yes."

"You are a duke. A duke shouldn't tend to staff."

His grin was self-effacing. "A duke can do any damn thing he wants."

She released a bubble of laughter. Their gazes held, and she wondered if he could see into her heart, if she should open it fully and allow him to glimpse all the love she held for him. But what good would come of it? To reveal all would serve only to make things awkward between them.

Slowly, ever so slowly, he reached out and tucked a stray wisp of hair behind her ear. Placing an elbow on his thigh, he leaned toward her. "Pettypeace—"

"Here we are," Lord Lawrence announced as he strode back in, two snifters dangling between the fingers of one hand, a third held in the other.

Kingsland slid off the desk. "I was just explaining to Pettypeace that she is not allowed to take ill again."

Is that what he'd been doing? She could have sworn he was on the verge of kissing her.

"Rightfully so." Lord Lawrence set a snifter in front of her and handed another off to the duke while she slowly came to her feet. "My brother would become quite lost without you."

"I shall do all in my power to remain well, then," she said.

Kingsland lifted his glass. "To success with Lawrence's new business venture."

"It's our venture," Lord Lawrence corrected him.

"You did the work. It's yours."

"I wasn't expecting that. Money will be needed—"

"I'll provide it. Reasonable interest."

"What if it fails?"

"My coffers will be poorer for it, but at least I won't come after you with the . . . what did he call it? The pointed end of a knife?"

She could tell the younger brother was over-whelmed. "Well done, Lord Lawrence." He snapped his attention to her. The poor man looked terrified. "I have little doubt you will meet with success. You've too much of your brother in you not to."

With a nod, he visibly swallowed before raising his glass. "To my older brother, who has yet to give up on me."

It was not often that Kingsland showed much in the way of the gentler emotions, so it was with some surprise that Penelope saw the softening in his eyes, the hint of embarrassment that his kindness was being recognized, and yes, the love—visible for the span of only a single heartbeat, and yet so deep and profound that it took her breath. She'd always considered her heart foolish to latch on to him, but oh, it seemed it was far wiser than she'd ever realized, to see the potential of what this man could give from the depths of his soul. He who claimed to have no heart would cause any woman to deem herself fortunate to have it turned her way.

She was going to redouble her efforts to find a woman worthy of his love. It couldn't remain bot-tled inside him but needed to be set free.

"What the devil have you done to my morning parlor?"

With a start, Penelope looked past the two broth-ers to see the formidable dowager Duchess of Kings-land standing just inside the threshold.

CHAPTER 8

"MOTHER, I WASN'T expecting you until August," King said as he crossed the expanse to greet the woman who had birthed him.

The duchess's hair was more silver than black these days, and she walked with a silver cane, although he wasn't quite certain she needed it. He suspected she used it because she believed it gave her an air of regality suitable to her position as a widow. "I'm leaving the country for a bit and wanted to visit with you lads before I left. Lady Sybil invited me to spend some time with her at her villa in Italy. How could I refuse?"

Her friend, the spinster sister of a duke, was no doubt surprising her brother with her own arrival in London. King gave his mother a quick peck on her rosy cheek. "You absolutely could not."

As he stepped back, Lawrence moved in and hugged their mother. His brother had always been better at demonstrating his affections. Or perhaps it was because they shared a common bond, having both suffered at the duke's hands—not that either, as far as he knew, was aware of what the other had endured. After patting Lawrence on the shoulder and giving him a wink, his mother looked past King. "Miss Pettypeace."

As she always did in the duchess's presence, his secretary gave a graceful curtsy. "Your Grace."

Waving her hand around, his mother gave him a pointed look. "What is all this then that you've done here?"

"I've converted the room into an office for Pettypeace. As you prefer to stay in the country or travel, I didn't think you'd miss the morning room."

"Quite right, m'dear. This is a much better use for the chamber. Puts Miss Pettypeace nearer to you. Now, as I will only be here until the morning, we shall all have dinner tonight, shall we?"

It sounded like a question, an invitation, but King knew it was a command. As did Lawrence, who said, "Of course, Mother."

"I'm including you, Miss Pettypeace."

"I'm honored, Your Grace, and look forward to it."

"Splendid." She wove her arm around Lawrence's. "Take a walk through the garden with me. I want to hear about everything you've been up to of late."

After they left, Pettypeace came three steps nearer to him, bringing her jasmine scent with her. "I should sleep in the servants' quarters tonight."

Truly perplexed, he furrowed his brow. "Why?"

"She's going to think I consider myself above my

station to be sleeping in such a glamorous room so near to family."

"You are above your station."

Her lips parted slightly, and she blinked.

"What I meant to say was that my mother thinks highly of you. We both value you as more than a servant. She wasn't at all upset that her favorite room has been converted into an office for you. I can't imagine she'll be the least bit bothered you have nicer accommodations upstairs."

"This was her favorite room," she murmured quietly in the same tone one might use in pronouncing someone guilty.

"She's hardly ever here, Pettypeace."

"Still." She glanced around. "Perhaps I should seek out a different room."

"This one suits you."

She looked over at the window. "I do like it."

Her words shouldn't have pleased him so much, and yet they did. "Then enjoy it."

DINNER TOOK PLACE in the smaller dining room, with Kingsland sitting at the head of the table, his mother at its foot, Penelope and Lord Lawrence positioned between the two and opposite each other. The first time Penelope had been included, her status among the staff had been elevated, although she'd also experienced a few glares and tipped up noses. Being snubbed hadn't bothered her much. She couldn't deny the slight sting but knew how hard she'd worked to make herself indispensable to the duke. That his mother recognized her was a testament to her efforts. She wished her own mother, who in the end had been disappointed and ashamed of her, could see her now, could see how she'd managed to make something of herself.

Conversation flowed easily. The duchess shared the more memorable aspects of her recent trip to Wales. Lord Lawrence regaled his mother with his manufacturing plans. He'd never been so animated. Penelope glanced over at Kingsland. He gave her a small, soft, secretive sort of smile, acknowledging her role in his brother's changed mien. His acknowledgment sent her heart to galloping like mad, and she rather feared the flush taking hold was going to travel all the way up to her hairline and be visible for all to see. Hopefully, if they spotted it, they'd attribute it to the wine. She was grateful her fingers were steady as they wrapped around the stem of her wineglass. She took a healthy swallow of the Bordeaux and didn't object when the footman stepped forward and refilled her glass.

"I say, Miss Pettypeace," the duchess began, "Hugh tells me he has saddled you with the chore of securing him a wife."

"Mother—" Her pointed look cut the duke off.

While it appeared the duchess could easily control her son, Penelope knew it happened only because he allowed it. It was an aspect to him that never failed to warm the cockles of her heart. "Yes, Your Grace, I am seeing to the task."

"How goes it? Will you share the name of the

lady whom you have chosen, or will you torture me by holding her secret until the unveiling?"

"I would never wish to torment you, ma'am, but I'm not yet that far along. I've narrowed the list down to a dozen or so. I hope to narrow it a bit further, and then intend to interview each of the remaining candidates."

"Why is an interview necessary?" Kingsland asked.

"I rather fear the ladies may have only included their best qualities in their letters, and for some, I'm failing to get a true sense of their personality or character. I thought if I were to visit with a lady in her residence, she would be more herself in her natural habitat."

"You're putting a good deal more effort into the process than I did."

"Yes, well." She saw no need to point out that perhaps the lack of securing additional details was one of the reasons his endeavor had failed so miserably. "I want to ensure I select wisely. After all, you will spend the remainder of your life with her. I'd rather your years not be fraught with discontent."

"I daresay I am impressed with your devotion to the task, Miss Pettypeace. I can certainly understand why my son values you so highly. However, if you wish to observe my future daughter-in-law in her *natural habitat*, I suggest you attend a ball. I'm rather certain you'll acquire a more realistic notion regarding her disposition there than while sipping tea in her parlor."

The duchess was no doubt correct on that score.

Following his announcement during last year's ball, she'd seen ladies in tears, in anger, in gracious acceptance. In each letter, the lady had put her best foot forward. She would probably do the same in her parlor, hardly giving an accurate assessment of her character. "While I concede you make a valid point, it would hardly be appropriate for me to make an appearance at a ball to which I've not been invited."

"You'll attend with Hugh, naturally."

Penelope looked at the duke, who stiffly lifted his wineglass as though he might like to hurl it across the room. "I seldom attend balls, Mother."

"Whyever not?"

"I suspect for the same reason you don't. I find them dull and would rather engage in other activities."

"Becoming a widow granted me some liberties. Unfortunately, becoming a duke robbed you of some, but Miss Pettypeace has the right of it. It is imperative you avoid another fiasco when selecting whom you intend to marry. Or people will begin to think the fault lies with you rather than your method—the effectiveness of which I still question. Be that as it may, I believe it is to your good to make an exception and attend one ball so Miss Pettypeace can engage in some espionage and better deduce who is best suited to carrying the title as the Duchess of Kingsland."

Having dinner with him at the club had been one thing, but to have him escort her to a ball—

"Your Grace, people will talk."

"They generally do at balls," the duchess said.

"No, I mean they'll gossip, start rumors, assume something more than a working relationship exists between the duke and I."

"He's made no secret of how crucial you are to the state of his affairs. I can't fathom why anyone would think you accompanying him anywhere was out of place, and if they do, well, then, shame on them."

Her entire body was jumping with nerves because she wanted far more than she should to arrive on his arm at a ball, even if it was all fantasy and had the potential to break her heart when she witnessed him flirting with other women, giving them his attention, smiles, and laughter.

Except Kingsland had no desire to go. She turned her attention to him. "I consider the selection of your duchess to be the most important task you've ever given me. It would behoove me to have all the pertinent information I require to see it justly done." She considered suggesting Lord Lawrence accompany her, although the sight of them together at a ball would certainly cause tongues to wag among those who had seen them speaking at the Fair and Spare.

Kingsland released a put-upon sigh. "Mother no doubt has the right of it. She usually does. I'd be honored to accompany you to a ball."

A spark of joy leapt through her chest at the word *honored*—until reality caught hold and she realized he probably uttered the word out of habit, the proper response drilled into him since he was in short trousers.

"Splendid," the duchess announced. "Now the

matter is settled, following dinner, Miss Petty-peace, you and I will look through the invitations to determine the best ball to attend next week, shall we?"

Although phrased like a question, Penelope knew it was a command she had no choice but to obey. "I've already sent the duke's regrets for any to be held next week."

"A simple letter from me will easily undo it. I'll write it before retiring and have it delivered in the morning. Now, Hugh, darling, tell me how your friends, the Chessmen, are managing these days. Will wedding bells be ringing for them anytime soon?"

WHILE PENELOPE HAD considered the plush wing-back chair near the window to be adequate for her purposes—it balanced the room and she couldn't envision she'd spend much time away from her desk—the duchess had ordered footmen to bring in a second matching chair, small tables to rest beside them, lamps, and two glasses of sherry. Now she sat across from the duchess as the woman rif-fled through the invitations with a practiced hand. Fortunately, Penelope was in the habit of filing them away in order of date held, so it had taken no time at all to retrieve those scheduled for the following week.

"Ah, here we are," the duchess said, smiling with satisfaction and waving the vellum. "The Duchess of Thornley is hosting a ball Wednesday. I like her immensely. No airs about her. She is a wonderful hostess, and a crush of people attend her affairs. Curiosity about the tavern owner who married a duke spurring most of them. Although I suspect a few want to witness her making a faux pas, but she has yet to satisfy them. And that, m'dear, is the reason I believe you'll get a truer sense of the character of the women you are considering if you observe them at a ball. Are they snide in their comments? Do they gossip? Do they spend the evening smiling or frowning?"

"I appreciate your counsel on this matter, Your Grace."

The duchess set the box of invitations on the table beside her, with the chosen one on top, and took her glass of sherry in hand. "You don't consider me interfering?"

"No, not at all."

"Good, because I wish to discuss another matter with you, and I do hope you won't take offense."

Her stomach threatening to knot up at the serious tone, Penelope took a sip of her own sherry and waited.

"You will need a gown to wear to this affair."

A wave of relief washed through her. "I have a gown."

The duchess's lips flattened and her eyes narrowed as though she were attempting to envision it. "The one you wore last year? The pale green?"

"Yes, ma'am."

She gave her head a little shake. "It will not do at all to display yourself in the same gown."

"I doubt anyone noticed me in it last year, or if they did, would even recall it."

"Are you questioning my wisdom?"

"Oh no, Your Grace, absolutely not. 'Tis only that I have so few occasions to wear a gown that I can hardly justify the expense."

As though a fly had suddenly appeared to irritate her, the duchess fluttered her hand. "I'll cover the cost. You'll visit my modiste tomorrow. In the morning, I'll send word to her to expect you."

"But the ball is only a few days away." It had taken a seamstress a couple of weeks to sew the pale green gown.

"Do not concern yourself. She will accommodate our needs. I will pay her well to do so."

Penelope hardly knew what to say. "Your Grace, while I appreciate your generosity, I simply can't accept it. I'm not going to the ball to be noticed, but rather to ferret out the information I need. I am rather certain my current wardrobe will suffice."

"Miss Pettypeace, you have served my son faithfully for some eight years now. Consider it a show of my appreciation for lessening his burdens."

She was a bit surprised to discover the duchess knew precisely how long she had worked for Kingsland.

"Don't allow your pride to prevent my joy in gifting you with this," the duchess added.

Such earnestness in the woman's tone and expression took Penelope off guard. How could not accepting a gift, one that would be costly, make her feel incredibly selfish? Yet it did. And if she were honest, she wanted something a bit more daring than what she already owned. If the gown was pretty enough, drew Kingsland's eyes to her, might he deign to waltz with her once? What a gift that would be. She would hold it close in her memories until the day she drew her last breath. "I would be most honored to visit your modiste, and I appreciate your desire to see me well turned out for this affair."

"Graciously done, Miss Pettypeace." After taking a sip of her sherry, she settled back into her chair and gazed out the window. "Before you, he had a challenge of it keeping a secretary for any length of time. He has such exacting standards, applies them most harshly to himself, I think. His father was not one to condone mistakes, you see, no matter how slight. Hugh tends to hold himself responsible for matters that aren't really his responsibility. My happiness, for example. I hope the woman you select for him will have the ability to make him . . . forget his cares . . . laugh uproariously . . . dance in the rain."

For the life of her, Penelope couldn't envision Kingsland doing any of those things, and yet she couldn't help but wish the same for him. "I want him to be happy, Your Grace."

"I know you do, m'dear. Unfortunately, I don't know if he would recognize the potential for happiness if it stood right in front of him. I fear he focuses so much on the details of the trees that he fails to see the magnificence of the forest."

Sipping his scotch, King stood on the terrace while Lawrence bid farewell to their mother because he wouldn't get a chance to see her in the morning before she left. He had an appointment with the man whose factory he intended to use. King couldn't be more pleased with his brother's enthusiasm and devotion to the project.

Hearing the door leading onto the terrace open and the quiet footsteps, he glanced over his shoulder. "What are you up to, Mother?"

"To whatever are you referring?" she asked innocently as she came near to him.

"A ball?"

"Disagree with my logic, do you?"

That was the hell of it. He couldn't. He avoided soirees because of the various games played, insincere flirtation, and patronizing compliments. It would be an excellent opportunity for Pettypeace to get some insight into the ladies. Rather than answer, he merely took a sip of his scotch.

"I thought not," his mother said gloatingly.

With a huff of a laugh, he leaned down and pressed a kiss to her cheek. "Ah, to be as wise as you."

They stood in amicable silence, simply absorbing the night. After a while, she said, "I don't know if I've ever seen Lawrence exhibit quite so much confidence before. Or excitement. He's quite humbled you trusted him with this endeavor."

"It was Pettypeace's idea. She thought he needed something to anchor him."

"It seems I'm not the only wise woman in your life. What will she do after you marry?"

His mother had never taken a hand to him, but at that moment he felt as though she'd smacked him about his head. What an absurd question, and yet it seemed stunningly significant. Turning, leaning a hip against the low wall, he faced her more squarely. "I don't follow."

"I can't imagine that your wife will be pleased to have another woman who has such a prominent role in your life living within the residence, especially with an office *and* a bedchamber so near to yours."

"Pettypeace will select a woman who will not be bothered by it."

"Mmm."

He didn't particularly like the little mewling sound she emitted, as though he had the wrong of it. "If she is bothered, I shall explain she has no reason to be."

"That will certainly put matters to rights."

"Your sarcastic tone implies you think it will not. What are you hinting at?"

"You must give some thought to ensuring your wife never feels she is the second most important woman in your life."

"Naturally, she'll be second. You hold the place of first."

Laughing, she slapped lightly at his shoulder. "You flatterer." She studied him, gave her head a little shake. "You're not taking my words seriously."

"I think you worry for naught."

"Marriage brings changes, Hugh. You need to be prepared for them."

Why did her words cause an unease to settle in the pit of his stomach? Of course marriage brought changes. He was well aware of that fact. It would bring a wife and, eventually, an heir.

But Pettypeace would schedule his day so he was available to devote some time to his wife and children. "How long will you be at the villa?" he asked, wanting to change the subject.

"I'll return a few days before your ball. But now I must abed as I'll be leaving quite early in the morning. Sleep well, my son."

"Pleasant dreams, Mother."

She left, but her words remained, lingering in his mind. His gaze drifted over to the window where faint light from Pettypeace's new office spilled forth. She hadn't accompanied his mother when she'd joined him and Lawrence in the library. Was she still working?

After draining the last of his scotch, he retrieved from his desk a letter he'd written earlier. He'd intended to mention it to her in the morning but saw no reason not to get the matter out of the way now. He wandered into the hallway. It was late enough that no footman was on duty. When he reached her office, he stood just inside the doorway and watched her, standing at her desk, reading what appeared to be a missive, before making a notation on an incredibly large piece of paper. He suspected even a general gave less attention to mapping out his campaign and determining the position of his army. The glow from the lamp cast a softness over her, and he suddenly had a desire to see her awash in moonlight. It would turn her blond strands silver.

That was the sort of thought he could not have after he married. He couldn't contemplate inviting her to join him for a brandy. Could not be alone with her in a shadowy room after everyone else had retired.

Even from here, he could see the familiar furrow in her brow indicating her intense concentration. For the first time, he wanted to press his thumb to it and smooth it out, reassure her the matter at hand was not so dire as to warrant wrinkles.

"You know," he began, causing her to give a little start and jerk up her head, "this room does contain gas lighting, the use of which would no doubt make it easier for you to see."

Straightening, she removed her spectacles and smiled. "I prefer less lighting. It helps me to block out the rest of the world and focus more intently on the task at hand."

He casually strolled over. "And that task would be?"

"Striving to reduce the number of ladies for consideration. A dozen is too many to spy upon." She slipped on her spectacles, and it took everything within him not to reach out and tuck away the wisps of hair resting along her cheek. "If you'd rather not attend the ball, I can ensure the letter your mother writes to the Duchess of Thornley is not delivered."

After coming into the library, his mother had mentioned the ball they'd selected. "I respect Thornley and his wife, enjoy their company. It will be no burden to attend their affair. Mother has the right of it. You should see these women doing more than sipping tea. After all, one will become mistress of your residence."

For the span of a blink, she looked as though he'd slapped her. "It is not *my* residence, Your Grace."

Now he felt as though he'd been slapped. He had a butler and housekeeper who managed it, and yet he could not help but believe that Pettypeace was the reason everything ran as smoothly as it did. What if a wife interfered or resented his secretary's role in keeping his life in order? Would tensions ensue? Would Pettypeace leave? Were those the changes his mother had been hinting at? He had to ensure that didn't happen. "Of course it's not. A slip of the tongue. But you have a vital role here. It's imperative you select someone with whom you are comfortable and will have an amicable relationship."

Her laugh was soft but brief. "Her suitability for me is hardly a consideration. I am not the one who will marry her."

"You will not select a termagant, surely."

Had her smile always been that beautiful?

"I shall add her not being so as a requirement."

Her smile faded away, and he wondered if she'd given it to any of the gents at the Fair and Spare. He rather hoped she hadn't. Was fairly certain she hadn't. Otherwise, flowers would have been delivered here for her.

"Did you require something of me?" she asked.

"Yes, as a matter of fact. Lady Kathryn Lambert is to marry on Saturday. Would you see that this letter is delivered to her on that day?"

"Yes, of course." She took the envelope from him. "May I ask why you went with her last year?

What did she write that drew you to her? Knowing might assist me in narrowing my list."

He chuckled darkly. "She didn't send me a letter, actually. A gentleman penned one on her behalf, and I thought if she could inspire such devotion in him . . ." He shrugged.

"She would inspire it in you."

"Something like that. I'm giving his letter to her. Since he is to become her husband, it seems she should have it."

That smile again, like the flames of a thousand candles. "I shall see it placed in her hand."

"Splendid." He was reluctant to leave but had no reason to stay. "I should let you get back to your task." Then, damn it, he reached across, gathered up the errant strands of her hair, and slipped them behind her ear, even knowing no one was about to see her in an unruly state. "Don't work too late."

"I shan't."

"Good night, Pettypeace."

"Good night, Your Grace."

With that, he spun on his heel and strode from the room, because he'd have preferred to set all the other strands free.

CHAPTER 9

SATURDAY AFTERNOON, PENELOPE watched the passing countryside as the coach traveled back to London after she had personally delivered the duke's missive to Lady Kathryn. The woman had been jubilant to have her husband at her side. It had been obvious they were besotted with each other. Penelope wanted that for the duke, for the woman she chose to become his wife to openly adore and appreciate him.

However, seeing the newly married couple had served to reinforce how difficult it would be to witness Kingsland showing the same adoration toward his bride. But she wanted that for him as well, to marry a woman who could stir to life all the love that for some reason he had buried within him. From years of observing him interacting with his mother and brother, she knew he loved deeply, in spite of his protests to the contrary. To watch him showering affection on another woman would be difficult at best, which meant she needed to begin giving serious consideration to what she would do with herself when the time came to give her notice. He intended to marry before the year was out. No long courtship this time, no possibility of being cast aside for another.

She could do like the duchess and travel, visit all parts of the world. She certainly had the funds for it, but her family had moved about so much that she was keen for permanence. Never before had she stayed in one place as long as she had since coming to work for the duke. While her time was split between the London and country residences, she still experienced the sameness of routine, of knowing each place, and being comfortable within them.

Therefore, she intended to purchase a cottage, and she would begin by paying more attention to the advertising section of the *Times*. While she could place an advert outlining what she was seeking, her past experiences—before coming to work for the duke—had shown her that so many residences were listed for let and sale that she was fairly certain she could find something suitable without going to the bother of having interested parties contact her. Better to be the one contacting.

She also needed to begin giving some thought to how she would fill her days. The interest and dividends she earned would provide her with a steady income and the freedom to do as she pleased. As much as she enjoyed serving as the duke's secretary, she wanted to have her own business, to guide women toward making safe investments. The most recent law affecting married women's property allowed women to keep ownership of their shares. If handled properly, investing could give wives a measure of independence within the marriage. But it also provided an avenue of security for women before they married or if they never wed. Penelope loved her parents, but through them she had learned the dangers of relying solely on a man to provide even the most basic of necessities.

A need for financial independence had long driven her decisions, and she suspected a good number of women could benefit from what she'd learned.

The coach slowed as it reached the more populated area of London, and she turned her musings from the future to the present. She had visited the duchess's modiste the day before, and the woman had assured her the gown would be ready in time. She had been surprised to discover that in her letter, the duchess had provided a detailed description of the gown as well as the shade and type of material to be used. Not that Penelope had taken offense in having so little say. The woman was purchasing the item, after all, and so her opinion on the matter should carry weight. Based on what the seamstress had shared, it was going to be quite exquisite.

The coachman brought the vehicle to a stop outside the shop Penelope had visited on several occasions. She snatched up her satchel just before the footman opened the door and handed her down. "I should need no more than half an hour."

"Very good, Miss Pettypeace."

Marching forward, she smiled at the sign above the door: Taylor and Taylor. The sisters hired out to arrange and manage Societal affairs. While Penelope had no plans to give up the reins for the Kingsland ball, she had sought the advice of the ladies last year when she'd been charged with arranging her first social function. As this year's event had come about unexpectedly and needed to be assembled in a much shorter time period, she had decided to hire the ladies to assist with the more tedious aspects of the enterprise.

After entering the shop, she walked to the counter behind which the elder sister stood. "Miss Taylor."

The woman smiled. "Miss Pettypeace. It is so good to see you. We've been making considerable progress on getting everything you asked for."

"The orchestra?"

"Yes." Miss Taylor opened a drawer and removed a sheaf of paper. "Here we are. Twenty-four players as requested. The terms for payment as well as a suggestion regarding the tunes to be played. If you are agreeable, you have but to sign it and I shall see the matter taken care of."

Penelope read the contract. Before last year, she'd had no idea how one even went about hiring an orchestra. The sisters had been a fountain of information. "This all looks wonderful." She applied her signature and handed the document back to Miss Taylor. "The invitations?"

"This way." The woman slipped out from behind the counter and escorted Penelope to a desk in the corner, where a gentleman with ink-stained fingers was slowly etching letters on parchment. "Miss Pettypeace, allow me to introduce Mr. Bingham.

He is new to us, but his penmanship is without rival."

The young man rose quickly to his feet and gave Penelope a deferential bow. "Miss Pettypeace."

"It's a pleasure, sir."

He studied her as though arrested by the sight of her. "We've met before."

"I don't think so, sir."

He tilted his head to view her from a different angle. "No, I suppose not. Although you do remind me of someone I once knew."

She'd never met him, she was sure of it, but that didn't mean he didn't know her. He could have seen her before, and later might recall where. Suddenly, she had a strong urge to be done with this task.

"Mr. Bingham, the Kingsland invitations, if you please," Miss Taylor said briskly, obviously aware of the tension her new employee had created.

"Yes, ma'am." He pulled two large boxes from a shelf and placed them on the desk.

Miss Taylor opened a box and slipped out an invitation nestled in an envelope. "They're all addressed as requested."

Penelope had approved the design of the invitation before providing the list of guests who were to be invited and their corresponding addresses. "Very elegant and legible handwriting, sir."

"Thank you."

After the invitation was returned to its place, Penelope picked up both boxes. She'd have several footmen hand-deliver the invitations later that afternoon.

"Mr. Bingham can carry those out for you," Miss Taylor said.

"They're not heavy. I have them." She began walking toward the door, the shop owner in her wake. "I appreciate all your assistance, Miss Taylor."

"It's been a pleasure. If there is anything more we can do, please don't hesitate to call upon us."

"I think everything else is well in hand." Addressing the invitations was the most time-consuming aspect of the event, so she was glad to have avoided doing it herself this year. Even though Mr. Bingham's continued stare was causing the short hairs on the back of her neck to rise.

Miss Taylor opened the door for her, and Penelope crossed the threshold before turning back to her. "Do be sure to send a statement of what is owed for your services."

"I will, and I wish you the best of success with the ball."

"Thank you." As she spun on her heel, she nearly collided with the footman who'd come forward to relieve her of the boxes. She was grateful the coach was waiting. Once she was settled inside and they were on their way, she took a deep, cleansing breath and wondered if a time would ever come when she didn't fear the revealing of her past.

KING HAD NEVER known the days to pass so slowly. They were always filled with reviewing his ventures, analyzing his investments, researching new opportunities, seeing to his duties in the House of Lords, discussing needed changes to the law, drafting bills to bring before Parliament, holding meetings with businessmen, and any number of other tasks. His evenings were seldom free to do as he pleased. Assemblies, dinners, or the occasional lecture graced his time. When nothing was pressing, he would visit his club or spend time with the Chessmen. Busy, always busy, with the hours rushing past like a locomotive.

So it made no sense whatsoever that now the minutes dragged along, ever since his mother had proposed—not *proposed*, insisted—he accompany Pettypeace to a ball.

With his arms crossed over his chest, standing near the window in his office on Fleet Street, he watched her taking meticulous notes as Lawrence and Mr. Lancaster hammered out the details required to guide their association. He'd offered a few suggestions here and there but was determined not to interfere unless he believed his brother to be making a grave error. A small misstep was of no consequence, would provide a lesson best learned from experience. He'd made a number himself in the early days and was better for them.

He could only hope the same would not be true after he attended the Thornley ball. He'd never anticipated nor dreaded attending anything as much but could afford no mistakes where Pettypeace was concerned. Knowing she was going to be there made the upcoming ball—the sort of soiree he'd always considered uninteresting—exciting. Not that she would remain in his company once they arrived. She'd be off doing her research, learning more about his potential duchess, and yet her presence, the possibility of occasionally crossing paths with her, had him eagerly awaiting the arrival of the affair. It was the unheralded strength of his anticipation that had him so unsettled.

During his day, she was commonplace, summoned with the tug of a braided rope. On occasion she was even part of his night, when work kept them huddled together into the late hours. It made no sense whatsoever that he was having a difficult time not thinking about the pleasure he'd experience arriving with her at his side.

As his secretary. Not a woman he was courting or favored. Certainly not a woman he'd begun wondering what it might be like to kiss.

"Have we overlooked anything?" Lawrence asked, interrupting King's musings before he could further contemplate those lips that he could still feel his fingertips gliding over as he applied the salve during her illness. They had somehow branded him.

"Not that I noticed." But then, it was very likely he wouldn't have noticed a volcano suddenly erupting into the room. When he looked at her, he lost his ability to focus on more than one thing at a time. She'd begun taking up the entirety of his attention. How had that happened? Why had it happened?

"I'll deliver this information to the solicitor then," Pettypeace said with her usual succinctness. "We should have an agreement for you to sign within two days, Mr. Lancaster."

"Very good." He stood, as did Lawrence and Pettypeace.

King shoved himself away from the wall, shook the man's hand, and watched him take his leave.

"Pray tell me that you find yourself quaking after an intense meeting such as that," Lawrence said.

"The first time I negotiated a business deal, afterward I cast up my accounts," King admitted. "When the magnitude of what I'd done hit me, when I realized what was at stake if I'd guessed wrong. But eventually I came to understand that no mistake I made couldn't be corrected in one manner or another with a different investment or another scheme. I learned from my mistakes, as will you. But in spite of negotiating becoming a rather regular part of my life now, I have yet to lose the excitement of venturing into something new."

Against his will, his gaze drifted to Pettypeace. She'd once been new to him. After all this time, she should be boringly familiar, but as always, she seemed full of possibilities. Perhaps that was the reason he was so looking forward to the ball. He'd not danced with her at the one she'd arranged for him last year. It had been the talk of London for weeks. He hadn't taken all her hard work for granted, but had rewarded her with a generous stipend for the success of it. Still, she hadn't been ensconced in the middle of the affair, hadn't truly been part of it.

Her words from a lifetime ago echoed through his mind: *The best gifts usually cost nothing at all.* He should have waltzed with her.

"Well,"—she held up her leather-bound notebook—"I'd best get to the solicitor so he can begin work."

"I'll see you delivered there."

"It's not necessary."

She was an independent woman, his secretary, always ensuring she never put him to any bother. His caring for her while she was ill no doubt did not sit well with her. She wouldn't have even wanted the chambermaid looking after her. "It's on my way."

"Actually, Your Grace, I have an appointment for a fitting with your mother's modiste that I must attend to first."

"Indeed."

"She insisted upon purchasing me a gown. I tried to convince her it was unnecessary."

"It is difficult to change my mother's mind once it is made. Still, I'll accompany you."

"I don't wish to delay you in attending to your other matters."

"We'll make it work, Pettypeace. We always do." He clapped his brother on the shoulder. "The hard part is only just beginning."

"I think I'm up to the task."

"I know you are."

Following a few more encouraging words to his brother, he and Pettypeace made their way to the mews, where his coach was waiting. After handing her up, he gave the address to the driver and joined her. "You are very wise, Pettypeace. He needed a purpose."

"Not so wise. We all need a purpose."

"What is yours?"

"Seeing that your needs are met."

Her words were spoken lightly and innocently,

and yet other needs, darker needs, carnal needs, slammed into him as though she'd crossed the short distance separating them and whispered seductively into his ear before tracing her tongue along the shell of it, her hot breath coating his skin in dew. As he shifted uncomfortably on the seat, thinking of her as Pettypeace, his ever-efficient secretary, did nothing to assuage the ache that was making it damned difficult to simply sit there. "You must have higher aspirations than that, surely." Did he have to sound like a garrote had been wrapped about his neck, strangling him?

"Not at the moment."

"But when the moment has passed?" He hoped she knew he wasn't referring to this precise moment but to a time in the future. Of course she knew. She was Pettypeace. Often knowing what he was going to say before he did, providing what he needed before he even recognized what he required. She glanced out the window, and he silently urged, *Tell me. For God's sake share with me something for which you yearn.*

"The Cotswolds, I think." Her voice was soft, as though she feared if she spoke too loudly, she would burst the bubble of her dream. "A small cottage where I shall sleep late every morning as though it was Christmas and putter about in a garden in the afternoon."

"With whom will you reside?"

Her smile wistful, her gaze landed on him like a gentle caress that did nothing to diminish these urges suddenly bombarding him. "Sir Purrcival."

Her cat? "It sounds remarkably lonely."

"I am perfectly content to be in my own company, Your Grace. Besides, I want to be responsible to no one else. To do as I please with no worries I've let anyone down."

Had she disappointed someone in the past? She'd certainly never done so with him. "You do work for a tyrant, don't you, Pettypeace?"

Her smile brightened. "Perhaps I am the tyrant, making you feel you must keep me busy."

He kept himself occupied so he could avoid thinking about matters—his past, present, and future—that he'd rather not. A risk he'd taken when he was nineteen that still haunted him and often threatened his peace of mind. "Perhaps you are at that."

SHE ALMOST TOLD him about her idea for a business of helping ladies invest. She'd like to have his opinion on the viability of it but didn't want him to know she'd begun thinking of severing their relationship, giving up her post. It would only serve to make things decidedly awkward. Or perhaps she feared learning he was prepared to easily carry on without her.

The coach came to a stop. He held out his hand. "Give me your notes. I'll see them delivered to Beckwith."

"I can do it when I'm finished here."

"I have nothing else on my schedule."

While she'd known he had no other meetings on his calendar, she'd assumed he had some personal matters to see to. However, she appreciated his willingness to visit Beckwith. She was delaying her search for an assistant until after the ball. Simply too much on her plate at the moment, and nothing she was willing to hand off to anyone else. She reached into her pocket and removed her notebook. "The ribbon marks where today's meeting began."

"Of course it does."

"Are you mocking me?"

His smile was almost tender. "No. I would expect nothing less from my efficient Pettypeace."

My efficient Pettypeace. He didn't really see her as his, not in the same manner he would his wife, his duchess . . . his children. "Thank you for seeing to the task."

Shoving open the door, he stepped out and handed her down. "I'll return for you when I'm finished with Beckwith."

"I can hire a cab."

"No need when we'll be passing back this way on our return to the residence."

"I shan't tarry."

"No harm comes from having a man wait for you, Pettypeace."

He was wrong there. A great deal of harm had come from a man waiting on her—and she'd sworn to be forever punctual afterward. But she couldn't tell him that, wouldn't tell him that. Instead, she merely nodded and made her way into the dressmaker's, very much aware of his following her movements.

CHAPTER 10

$\mathcal{W}$EDNESDAY EVENING, STARING into the cheval glass, Penelope couldn't help but think that the dark rose gown with a neckline that dipped to reveal the barest hint of her bosom was the most elegant creation she'd ever owned. Her white gloves extended just above her wrists, leaving her arms bared. Lucy had pinned up her hair on the sides and left tight curls cascading at the back.

"Caw, Penn, you don't half look like a proper lady."

She rather felt like one, but there was danger in that. She couldn't forget her place. Slipping her hand inside the pocket she had insisted upon, cleverly hidden with an angled sash, she squeezed her familiar leather notebook. Having it near served to remind her of the reason behind attending tonight's festivities. "The ball is simply another job, Lucy."

"What if you catch the fancy of some lord?"

"That is unlikely to happen, but if it should, I will lose his regard as soon as he realizes I am in fact no lady but rather a secretary." Turning, she faced her friend. "I believe we discussed all this or something similar on another occasion."

"A girl can dream. I just read a story about a cinder girl who married a prince. It can happen."

"With your love for fairy tales, I do hope you don't go about kissing frogs."

"I kissed Harry the footman."

Taking delight in her friend's mischievous expression, she asked, "When?"

Lucy smiled brightly. "The other night when you were sick. I finished caring for you and was on my way back to my room and there he was in the kitchen, making a spot of tea. Invited me to join him but I started weeping, all worried about you like I was. The next thing I knew he was telling me not to cry and then he was kissing me. Gentle-like."

"Do you love him?"

"I don't know. Besides, servants don't marry, do they?"

Not if they wanted to remain servants. Oh, she supposed on the rare occasion an employer might accommodate a couple who had fallen in love, but they often faced challenges. "No, we don't."

"You're not a servant, Penn."

"I'm staff."

"Staff don't go to balls. And you doing so is not sitting well with some of them belowstairs."

She'd been so worried about what the nobility would think of her going with Kingsland that she'd failed to give any thought to how the servants would take things. "They already believe the worst of me. I can't be bothered with idle gossip. Besides, they'll appreciate my efforts on their behalf when I have all the information needed to select a duchess they will be proud to serve."

"I'd not thought of that. You're doing this for them." Lucy straightened her shoulders and set her mouth into a mutinous line. "I'm going to start pointing that out to the ungrateful lot."

Penelope didn't know if she'd ever had a more loyal friend. She'd had hardly any friends at all after her world had been turned upside down when she was a young girl. "Well, the proof of the pudding and all that."

Glancing at the clock on the mantel, she released a tiny squeal. They were to leave at half eight and it was already four minutes past their departure time. "I'm late."

She started to dash out and then stopped. No point in rushing now. As a matter of fact, a sedate and elegant entrance might serve her better. Going as his secretary didn't mean she couldn't exhibit all the grace of a lady.

Lucy followed her out, giving her a quick hug before heading for the servants' stairs. Penelope went in the opposite direction toward the grand sweeping staircase. Ascending and descending it still felt somewhat odd. Daring to look over the banister, she nearly stumbled when she caught sight of him in the foyer waiting for her. Blast her impertinent heart. Why did it always have to leap with joy whenever her gaze fell on him? Why did it have to yearn for what it could never possess?

He glanced up, his regard so penetrating he might as well have been touching her for all the power of it. She tried not to imagine the joy she'd experience at having him anticipating her presence—as a woman, not a secretary—at his side.

He was so devilishly handsome in his black evening attire. It fit him like a glove, outlining his broad shoulders, the jacket stopping short at his waist to reveal his narrow hips, the swallowtails draping along the back.

As she neared the bottom of the steps, a corner of his beautiful mouth hitched up. "When I said you should cause a man to wait for you, Pettypeace, I didn't mean it should be me."

"Apologies, Your Grace. This gown was more troublesome to get on than I'd anticipated." Along with all the undergarments it required in order for everything to fall properly and enticingly.

"I'm teasing, Pettypeace. It is fashionable to arrive tardy."

"That makes no sense whatsoever. What is the purpose of putting a time on the invitation if that is not when you want people to arrive?"

"I suspect you'll question the purpose of a good many things this evening." Reaching out, he took his hat and walking stick from Keating.

"If I may be so bold, you look remarkably lovely, Miss Pettypeace," the butler said.

She couldn't have been more surprised if he'd gone down on a knee and proposed, and she wondered if he was striving to signal his support of her, to ensure she understood he believed the gossip to be poppycock. "Thank you, Mr. Keating."

She preceded Kingsland out the door and down the steps to the gleaming black coach. She'd never had so much fabric to gather up as the footman assisted her inside. The vehicle rocked as the duke joined her, placing himself opposite her. His bergamot fragrance filled her senses, intoxicated her. As the horses took off at a trot, she knotted her hands in her lap to stop herself from reaching across to brush back his wayward forelock.

"Keating has a gift for understatement," he said quietly. "You're quite beautiful."

And nearly speechless at his compliment. It took her a moment to regather her wits about her. "Thank you, Your Grace."

"It wouldn't have done for me to say so with witnesses about."

"Of course not." He really shouldn't have said it now.

"The rose suits you."

"Apparently in her letter to the seamstress, your mother insisted on this shade." She'd have gone with green but couldn't deny the rose seemed to bring out the glow of her fair skin, soften her features.

"She can be quite formidable, my mother."

"I very much appreciate all the effort she went to on my behalf. The seamstress did a remarkable job. I love everything about the gown. It makes me feel elegant."

"You have no jewelry."

She touched gloved fingers to her throat. "That is an expense I can't justify for one night."

He reached inside his jacket, removed a long,

slim velvet box, and held it out to her. Staring at it with trepidation as though he'd withdrawn a vial of poison and presented it to her, she shook her head. "I can't."

"You don't even know what it is."

True. She nearly laughed hysterically. What a silly cabbagehead she was. He would never give her jewelry. Perhaps it was one of the pens that held ink inside the barrel. She could use it tonight instead of her pencil. Of course that was it. Something practical and useful. Something one gave his secretary.

Only it wasn't.

When she opened the box, it was to see an emerald teardrop on a gold chain. She jerked her gaze up to his. "I can't accept this, Your Grace."

"Pettypeace, you've been with me for eight years. Seeing all the little knickknacks spread out over your desk, recognizing most were from me, made me realize I have been remiss in showing my appreciation for all your hard work. This is but a small token—"

"It is not small."

"Large token, then. Most secretaries would have resigned if asked to select a wife for their employer. But you have poured yourself into the endeavor as you do every task that I ask of you. Please accept it."

She wanted to. It was gorgeous in its simplicity. Exactly what she would have chosen for herself if she ever indulged her *wants*. "It is so very pretty."

"No one need know it came from me," he said quietly as he crossed over to perch on the edge of the seat beside her, managing to avoid crushing her skirts while lifting the necklace from the velvet on which it rested.

She could barely breathe as his warm, bare fingers—he'd removed his gloves in preparation of the task, and she'd not noticed until that moment—skimmed ever so lightly across her flesh as he draped the chain around her neck, the emerald teardrop dangling just below the dip in her collarbone. Then he was gone, back to his side, proficiently tugging on his gloves as though he hadn't managed to turn her insides into a quivering mass of fluttering butterflies.

"Who are the ladies on your list?" he asked calmly, completely unaffected by the intimacy of the moment they'd shared.

List, what list? She seemed to have lost her wits, her ability to reason. Ah, the list of potential duchesses. They were returning to the business at hand, the reason she was now traveling in the coach with him, hoping her melted knees might regain their solidity before they reached their destination. "I've narrowed the number to ten. You should probably dance with each of them, since you might immediately find one unsuitable or perfectly suitable. I shall copy down their names for you."

She reached into her pocket and withdrew her notebook, in which she'd written her list.

"You brought your notebook?"

Glancing up at his amused expression, she felt her cheeks warm. "I wanted to make certain not to forget anyone and thought it best to have the ability to record my impressions. Otherwise, they might all begin to blend together."

"You are without equal, Pettypeace."

"I am attending the ball with a purpose, not to engage in frivolity."

He grew somber, serious. "I should think it would be quite interesting to see you engaged in frivolity."

She wasn't certain she even remembered how. "I shall reveal my frivolous streak when you do."

"Is that a challenge?"

While she was accustomed to speaking her mind with him, had never refrained from giving her honest opinion on matters, she couldn't help but reflect that she'd never been quite so bold and might be traversing along shaky ground. "I've never known you to be anything other than solemn. Even when you smile or chuckle, there is an undercurrent of gravity to it."

His jaw tightened, his eyes turned flinty, and he gazed out the window.

"I'm not being insulting," she rushed to assure him. "It makes us a fine pair, and is one of the reasons we work so well together."

"What would make you laugh, Pettypeace?"

"I laugh."

He swung his attention back to her. "Not that I've ever heard."

He sounded hurt, as though she'd disappointed him. She had an urge to laugh uproariously, but he was correct. It was not in her nature to do so. Fear. Fear kept any joy she experienced buried inside her, because happiness expressed tempted the fates to bring on sorrow. "I might say the same of you."

"Perhaps we both carry too heavy a burden for such lightness."

Not wanting to travel this path any further, not wanting to arrive at the ball with them both melancholy and despondent, she held up her notebook. "Possibly one of these ladies will make you laugh. I shall keep that in mind as I observe and speak with them."

His mouth twitched. "Maybe so."

He sounded unconvinced, but then, so was she. It would take a very special woman not to be intimidated by his sternness, in awe of his position, wary of the potency and power he projected. It would take a bold, daring woman to stand up to him, to brave delving beneath the surface of him to uncover all his truths, to learn her way around him well enough she would know how to make him laugh. It would take a woman in love with him to see all the goodness and kindness he fought so hard to keep hidden, that he saw as weakness while she saw it as strength. He'd given her an impossible task and yet she refused to fail at it.

She scrawled the names of eight ladies and two misses, gently tugged the page free of the notebook, and held it out to him. Their fingers touched, both gloved, and yet still a spark arced between them as though flesh had touched flesh. She held her breath as he glanced over the list, waiting for him to immediately dismiss some of the names. Instead, he merely folded the scrap of paper and tucked it inside his jacket, where her necklace had nestled close to his heart.

"It should prove an interesting night, Pettypeace."

"Indeed." And no doubt one of the most horrible of her life as she watched him take those women on a turn about the dance floor.

Pettypeace. Pettypeace. Pettypeace. He was calling her by name more than usual because if he didn't, he was going to begin to think of her as Penelope or Penny—no, she would never be a Penny. It was too innocent, and while he didn't know all the details of her, he was certain little innocence was to be found in her.

When he'd placed the necklace on her, when his fingers had grazed the soft skin at her throat, it had taken everything within him not to trail his lips along the path his fingers had forged. Not to taste her, not to want her.

When she'd pulled out her notebook, he'd nearly barked out his laughter, but he'd held it in check, fearing he would hurt her feelings. Only Pettypeace would hold true to her purpose in coming to a ball to ferret out the desirability of each of the ladies she'd identified as the possible future Duchess of Kingsland. Any other woman would have decided to make the most of the evening's entertainments by enjoying herself. And damned if he didn't want her to do so. In his arms.

After a slow journey along the circular drive filled with carriages, his coach finally came to a stop in front of the massive residence. A footman immediately leapt forward to open the door. King stepped out and reached back for Pettypeace, the teardrop at her throat catching his attention. It was an inappropriate gift, and yet he'd never experienced as much gratification in giving anything to anyone else. The manner in which her eyes had widened when she'd first seen it, the way her lips had parted as though inviting a kiss. The pleasure she'd fought not to reveal, had probably battled not to feel at all. He liked surprising her. Imagined the satisfaction to be found in a lifetime of doing so.

As she landed gracefully on the drive, he extended his arm and saw her hesitate at the intimate gesture, one he'd never offered to her before, but tonight seemed to call for it. Finally, her fingers came to rest on the sleeve of his jacket, and he had a spark of possessiveness, the likes of which he'd never felt before. But it was what he should have felt while courting Lady Kathryn, what he should experience whenever he was with his duchess. *She is mine and no one else shall ever have her.*

Only Pettypeace wasn't his. Not in so personal a manner.

Others disembarked from carriages and hastened up the steps. Ladies furrowed their brows or gave her a pointed glare; gentlemen tipped their hats. A few even acknowledged her. "Kingsland, Miss Pettypeace."

Any lord with whom he'd discussed investments, with whom he'd drawn up bills to bring before Parliament, or any gentleman who had dropped by his residence to ask something of him, knew Pettypeace because she was always on hand with her leather notebook to jot down all that was said. He hardly ever held a meeting without her.

As they stepped over the threshold, her eyes widened slightly at the grandeur of the foyer, and he realized that while she lived in a residence equally as spectacular, she wasn't one to take things for granted. He had a desire to show her majestic mountains and the vastness of the oceans and the small hummingbird he'd once seen on a trip he'd taken to America. With her sharp and inquisitive mind, she would take delight in every new thing encountered. She overlooked nothing, and he suspected she would be able to draw from memory every inch of the hallway they traversed, stairs they climbed, and rooms they glided through on their way to the ballroom.

"It's truly magnificent, isn't it?" she whispered reverently as they came to stand at the end of the receiving line.

"Indeed." Only he wasn't referring to their surroundings, but to her. The pride he felt having her at his side exceeded anything he'd ever experienced with any other woman. She exuded confidence, had weathered storms. Even if she'd never shared the tempests she'd survived, he had little doubt she'd been tossed around in them.

After they were announced—"His Grace, the Duke of Kingsland, and Miss Penelope Pettypeace"—he could sense a few stares as they descended into the ballroom. People judging, wondering, and curious. It was the reason he seldom attended these affairs. He didn't much care for the speculation or having mothers throwing their unmarried daughters at his feet. Or daughters looking up at him with hope-filled eyes. It was one of the things he liked about Pettypeace: she never misconstrued his intentions, and he never had to worry he would disappoint her and be forced to wipe her tears.

When they reached their hosts, the Duke and Duchess of Thornley, he gave a bow. "Your Graces, allow me the honor of introducing my secretary, Miss Pettypeace."

He was not surprised by the elegance of her curtsy, but rather suspected she'd spent hours practicing it. "Miss Pettypeace oversaw the ball I hosted last year and is managing this year's as well. I believe my mother wrote you explaining that as you are known for your hospitality, she thought Miss Pettypeace might benefit by observing the graciousness of your affair."

The duchess, who owned a tavern and was known for her skill at making people feel welcome, blushed at the compliment. "She did indeed. It's a pleasure to have you join us this evening, Miss Pettypeace. If you should have any questions at all, please don't hesitate to ask."

"I appreciate your offer, Your Grace, but rest assured I would never impose. I shall blend into the woodwork and you shan't even know I'm here."

She did have a habit of being inconspicuous, but tonight, wearing that gown, King didn't see how she wouldn't be noticed. The green had brought out the shade of her eyes, but the rose suited every inch of her. His mother always had possessed a knack for bringing out the best of her own features. It seemed she was able to do so with others. After exchanging a few more innocuous words, he cupped Pettypeace's elbow and led her away. Once they were beyond earshot, she asked under her breath, "Did your mother find fault with last year's ball? Did you?"

Was that a bit of hurt in her voice? "Nothing was amiss with your endeavors last Season, Pettypeace. Nothing ever is. But Mother couldn't very well tell them your true reason for accompanying me, could she? Nor could I. What if the couple behind us overheard and said something to someone else, and the ladies you wish to observe soon knew and sought to impress you?"

"I suppose there is some sense in that." She sounded slightly mollified.

"I assure you, there is a great deal of sense in it. Now we shall part here. I wish you success with the espionage."

"Thank you, Your Grace."

Her elbow slid away from his palm, and his empty hand felt hollow, less, as though a part of it had suddenly gone missing. He closed it into a fist, which only served to make him more aware of what it lacked. He didn't understand these strange reactions of late. It was almost as if Pettypeace was becoming part of him.

As he was snatching a flute of champagne from a passing footman, he caught sight of Knight and languidly began making his way over to the earl, acknowledging those he knew and even going to the bother to scrawl his name across a couple of dance cards. By the time he reached Knight, a trio of young lords had cornered his friend. While waiting, King tossed back what was left of his champagne and helped himself to another before stepping into the circle, acknowledging the gents with a firm scowl that sent them scurrying away.

"Do you have to be so curmudgeonly," Knight asked, "and chase everyone off? I was enjoying their company."

"As you are well aware, I have little patience for the young and inexperienced." He'd found they understood little about the ways of the world. Unfortunately, his duchess would no doubt fall into that category. He would have to think of her as unmolded clay to be shaped into what he required.

With an indulgent smile, Knight shook his head and took a sip of his champagne. "I see you brought Pettypeace."

Unlike with his hosts, he could be honest with Knight. "Yes, apparently she doesn't trust that all the ladies were completely honest in their letters when describing the qualities that would make them an accomplished duchess. She wishes to observe them and interview them in a clandestine manner in order to get a better sense of them and their suitability."

"I don't understand why she doesn't simply toss all the letters into a hat and draw one out."

"Pettypeace would never take so little care with any task I gave her."

"Still, finding a woman who is willing to put up with your exacting standards is no easy undertaking—especially as I have a hard time envisioning you being happy with anyone she selects."

"Why would you think that?" The woman Pettypeace chose would meet all his requirements. He was certain of it. No reason he'd find fault with her. He might not be ecstatic but would be content.

Knight gave a negligent shrug. "I have my suspicions."

"Suspicions about what?"

Another shake of his head, shrug, sip of the bubbly, and a glance around as though in want of more interesting company. Then a narrowing of his eyes. "So tell me, old boy, if Pettypeace is here to do your bidding by focusing on those who have an interest in marrying you, why is she dancing with Grenville?"

"The devil you say." He swung around to gaze out over the ballroom. In spite of the crowd moving in rhythm to the music, it took less time than needed for a blink in order to find her. Her diminutive size was no hindrance. She shone like a star whose brightness not even the glow of the moon could eclipse. Her smile was luminescent, her eyes twinkling as she gazed up at the deuced man. "Perhaps he has a sister on the list." He needed to look more closely at the names she'd written out for him.

"He has no sister."

"Then her actions are a ploy to throw the ladies off the scent regarding her reason for being here."

"May I be so fortunate as to find a woman here tonight who looks upon me with such unbridled interest."

King glared at the man he'd once considered a friend. "I don't know why I've never realized before that you're an irritating arse."

With a boisterous laugh, Knight clapped him on his shoulder. "As I said, I have my suspicions."

Then he strode away. King had no idea what he was on about, but when he turned his attention once more to the couples gliding about in rhythm to the music, he was keenly aware of one thing: he didn't like Pettypeace dancing with another man.

As it turned out, Mr. George Grenville was the fourth son of a viscount. Hence, the reason he qualified for membership in the Fair and Spare. It was highly unlikely he'd ever inherit his father's title. She'd been surprised to see him here, even more astonished when he asked her for the honor of a dance, but she saw no harm in it and decided people would find it odd if she never danced.

"When I first met you," she said as they circled the floor, "I thought I detected a bit of the street in your speech."

"I was in the army for a while. Knocked some of the polish off, I think. There's a bit of street in you as well, Miss Pettypeace."

"As is expected from one in my station."

"I'm not certain anything about you is expected."

She released a light laugh. "Do men prefer the unexpected in their ladies?"

"Some do."

Kingsland wouldn't. She was rather certain of that. It would irritate him to be surprised. He liked for things to be predictable. It was something she needed to keep in mind as she continued her search for his duchess.

"You've not returned to the Fair and Spare," Mr. Grenville said.

She couldn't help but be a bit pleased that he'd noticed, might have searched for her. "I've been rather busy handling the duke's affairs."

"How many mistresses has he?"

She laughed. "Not those sorts of affairs."

He was smiling brightly. "You have a lovely laugh, Miss Pettypeace."

She did hope he wasn't going to compliment the blush she was fairly certain was responsible for the warming of her cheeks. "You're too kind."

"Hardly. I am rather surprised he brought you. It's raised a few eyebrows, I can tell you."

"His mother thought I could benefit from attending and seeing how it's properly done."

"So there's nothing between the two of you? You and the duke?"

"Absolutely not."

"I have to say I'm relieved. I've thought of you quite often since we met."

After their dance ended, Mr. Grenville escorted her to a collection of chairs, lifted her gloved hand to his lips, and placed a brief kiss against her knuckles. "I hope to cross paths with you again at the club."

"I shan't have much time for socializing until after the duke's ball."

"I shall wait with bated breath until after the Kingsland ball then."

Watching him walk away, she had to admit she was flattered by his attentions and did rather like him, enjoyed his company. Where was the harm in a woman of her age taking on a lover or a series of them? Especially when the one she longed for was beyond reach. As she had no plans to marry, she wouldn't have a husband who on their wedding night anticipated having a barrier to breach, whose pride required no man had gone before him. Sex could no doubt be handled in a transactional manner. An equal pleasuring and then a parting of the ways. She might have to consider it. It would be nice not to have to see to her own needs and urges for once.

But all of that was for later contemplation. At the moment, she had work to do. Removing her notebook from her pocket, she studied the names. Lady Alice, youngest sister to the Earl of Camberley, was first on the list. She might as well begin there. Like the duke, she preferred order in her universe.

It took only a few inquiries to locate the lady on the upper level that circled the ballroom and allowed viewing from the railing. Lady Alice sat on a bench near an open doorway leading out onto a large balcony. Penelope recognized her immediately because she'd been wise enough to include a photograph of herself with her letter. "Lady Alice?"

The young woman, who had only recently turned eighteen, lowered the book she'd been reading and smiled softly. "Yes?"

"I'm Miss Penelope Pettypeace. I wondered if I might have a word."

"You may have as many as you wish."

Liking her immediately, Penelope returned her smile and indicated the bench. "May I?"

"Please." She scooted over and brought the skirts of her gown closer to her thigh, making adequate room for Penelope to join her.

"What are you reading?"

"*A Pair of Blue Eyes* by Thomas Hardy. Have you read it?"

"I've not, but it must be incredibly compelling to command your attention and force you to secret yourself away to spend time with it rather than the fascinating gentlemen below." She'd never imagined anyone would read at a ball.

"May I be honest, Miss Pettypeace?"

"Without question." She truly wanted to understand the girl's motivation.

"I find all the happenings in a ballroom not much to my taste. My dearest friends are to be found in books. But you said you needed a word. About what precisely?"

She rather wished she didn't favor this girl so much, had been hoping to find everyone on her list unsuitable. She'd intended to be a bit more circumspect, a bit more clever, when it came to obtaining what she needed, but deception—at least regarding this matter—didn't sit well with her. Therefore, she dispensed with the facade she'd not yet fully put into place and told the truth. "I'm secretary to the Duke of Kingsland."

"Ah. He has no doubt sent you to ferret me out in order to determine if I would be suitable as his duchess."

"Yes, he has."

"I wasn't expecting that. I assumed he'd find me frightfully boring based on my letter alone and pass me over without a second thought."

"Your letter was the most well-written and . . ." How could she describe it with any accuracy? The girl's honesty had fairly robbed her of breath. "And poetic, I suppose is the best way to describe it. Your words flowed so beautifully one into the other. He was quite taken with them." Or he would have been had he read them. But she had read them for him.

"I cannot tell you how touched I am. I've always enjoyed writing, have amassed an incredible number of journals because I can't seem to limit myself to only a few words about my day but describe it in some length. I've recently begun penning a novel."

"Jolly good for you. I look forward to reading it." The lady's laughter was soft and pleasant, like the last remnants of rain dripping from the leaves onto the soil. "I appreciate your faith, but I must finish it and find a publisher first."

"You will accomplish both. I have no doubt."

"You are kind to say so, Miss Pettypeace. I've always preferred time spent with books to time spent with people. Now that I've begun writing, I can go hours—no, days—without seeing anyone at all."

Lady Alice didn't realize it, but she was making her case for being the next Duchess of Kingsland. Lost in her world of stories, she would provide the quiet Kingsland sought. "You would not require his constant attention then."

"I doubt I'd require his attention at all, might

even be upset if he disturbed me when the words were flowing."

"Why did you write to him?"

She sighed. "My brother wishes me to marry. My eldest sister encouraged me because she is so deuced happy in her marriage." She'd married Aiden Trewlove, brother to the Duchess of Thornley. Penelope suspected they were about here somewhere. "I suppose I enjoyed the challenge of it as well, wondering if I could put words to paper in such a way that he might take interest. And he is devilishly handsome. Don't you think?"

Of course he was handsome, but he was so much more. "Is that how you judge a man? By his features?"

"I don't know that I judge them at all . . . unless they are in a book." Lady Alice studied her for a minute before leaning back slightly. "I have crossed paths with the duke. On occasion, he would visit the Duke of Lushing, my sister's first husband. Before she married, I remember Kingsland being particularly kind when my parents passed. I was quite young, in the garden, weeping. He gave me a cinnamon-flavored sweet and use of his handkerchief to dry my tears. I found him to be rather kind, although it might have been the circumstances and my youth responsible for that impression. What is he truly like, Miss Pettypeace?"

Where to begin? "He's brilliant. He gathers information, analyzes it, and makes his decisions based on facts. He identifies a problem and can determine how best to fix it. He appreciates a task done well, is not stingy with praise. He admires someone who can prove him wrong."

"Have you . . . have you ever proven him wrong?"

She smiled. "Oh, yes. On several occasions." And he had looked at her as though she'd conquered the world. "Although you mustn't tell anyone that. I shouldn't have told you . . . He has his pride, of course, and it wouldn't do— "

"I won't tell a soul."

"Thank you." She rose before getting too personal, before confessing he made her feel as though she could indeed conquer worlds. "I should let you get back to your book."

"Although I shan't be disappointed if he doesn't choose me, Miss Pettypeace, I would be quite honored if he did and would do all in my power to be a good wife."

"I don't think he could ask for more than that, Lady Alice. I shall speak very highly of you to him. I have enjoyed our chat."

As she made her way down the stairs, she couldn't help but believe Lady Alice would be a nice addition to the Kingsland household and was the sort of woman the duke could come to love.

She had only just entered the ballroom when a lady with striking red hair and bright blue eyes approached her. "Miss Pettypeace, may I have a moment of your time?"

"Yes, by all means."

The young woman, who had no doubt only this Season curtsied before the Queen, directed her to a small alcove. "I am Miss Angelique Seaton. Rumor has it that you are secretary to the Duke of Kingsland. I wondered if you know if he is considering me."

The lady was indeed on her list, but for some reason, unlike with Lady Alice, Penelope didn't feel comfortable divulging the information. "He is considering many."

"Pray tell me he is not contemplating marriage to Lady Elizabeth Whitelaw."

"It is not my place to reveal who is under consideration."

"She is my cousin and will lord it over me if she is chosen." Her lips formed a little moue, which Penelope had little doubt had been practiced countless times before a mirror in order to perfect and was used none too sparingly on gentlemen.

"Would you not do the same?"

"Absolutely not. Other than requiring she curtsy before me and address me as 'Your Grace.' I would be a duchess, after all."

At that moment, Penelope suspected she would not, in fact, become a duchess. Or at least, not the Duchess of Kingsland.

"I find the duke to be the most handsome of men. Perhaps you might be kind enough to inform him of my regard."

"He is more than his features, Miss Seaton."

"I would not argue differently. He is a duke, to be sure. With power and prestige, and I would gain all that."

"What would you do with it?"

With her nose tilted up, she glanced around. "I

would host the grandest balls and dinners London has ever seen, dress in the finest gowns, and visit the very best shops." She looked back at Penelope. "I would make him proud, Miss Pettypeace."

But what of good works? Helping the poor or disadvantaged? Kingsland's efforts in Parliament often served to better the working conditions of laborers or the fate of children. He believed in fighting to improve the lives of others. "If he were not a duke?"

The young lady blinked. "Well, we would not be having this conversation, would we?"

"No, Miss Seaton, I do not think we would." And that alone was reason enough to scratch her from Penelope's list.

CHAPTER 11

KING WAS NOT jealous. Had never been jealous of anyone or anything in his life. Jealousy served no purpose.

However, it was infuriating to watch Pettypeace waltzing about with one man after another. Perhaps he wasn't being quite honest with himself regarding the number of men. After Grenville, there had been three others. One was Knight, the traitor. He'd smiled at her. She'd smiled at him. And they'd laughed. King had been unable to hear the sound, but the joy wreathing her face— he'd wanted to smash his fist into something, his preference being Knight's nose. Not because he didn't want her happy, but because he wanted to be the one who brought a sparkle to her eyes and made her glow as though she'd swallowed moonbeams.

Where had that ridiculous thought come from?

It wasn't like him to think in preposterous abstracts. Besides, one couldn't actually swallow moonbeams. Oh, but she certainly had looked as if she had.

In between dances, she would speak with one lady or another. He lost sight of her for a while and a near-panic almost set in, which was ludicrous as he was not one to panic, but what if someone was attempting to steal her away? *His* Pettypeace. *His*. She wasn't an object or a possession, but she was his secretary, his right hand, his start to the day. His closest ally. Dare he admit, his dearest friend? He couldn't imagine a world in which she was not at his side.

Relief washed through him when he finally caught sight of her sitting among the wallflowers, matrons, and chaperones. Head bent, scribbling in her notebook. He smiled at the image. His Pettypeace would always be his Pettypeace. Duty before pleasure.

In long, measured strides, attempting not to appear to be rushing to her, he crossed the expanse that separated them until he stood before her. "You don't have to take your position so seriously as to jot down notes here, Pettypeace."

She looked up at him, a warmth to her features that made her appear almost ethereal. He would not even consider that the glow was a remnant from her time with Knight. "I wanted to record my thoughts while they were still vibrant."

He doubted the woman was capable of forgetting anything. Before he could think better of it or reflect on the ramifications of causing tongues to wag, he held out his hand. "Dance with me."

PENELOPE STARED AT that large gloved hand as though it was something discovered on an archaeological dig that had yet to be properly identified. The words that had accompanied the extension of it were not a request or an invitation but an order, a demand. Almost a command.

Dutiful soldier that she was, she wouldn't disobey, but it was more than duty that had her awkwardly stuffing the notebook back into her pocket, placing her palm against his, and relishing the feel of his fingers closing securely over hers as she rose to her feet. She'd dreamed of Kingsland doing exactly this: escorting her onto the dance floor. She'd been surprised when others had asked but was familiar enough with etiquette to know a lady did not refuse unless she had already promised the dance to another. Of course she hadn't. While she had a dance card tied to her wrist with ribbon, its purpose was to serve as a memento, not to actually keep track of any dance partners.

When the duke took her into his arms and glided her over the parquet, she felt as though she had ascended into heaven and was waltzing through clouds. None of her other partners were as graceful or accomplished as he.

"You may remove Lady Adele from your list. I danced with her. She talks incessantly about herself."

She smiled. "I noticed the same when I had a few minutes alone with her."

His gaze was so focused on her that she wondered how it was he avoided ramming into any of the other dancing couples.

"Unlike you, who reveals hardly anything at all about yourself," he said quietly, somberly.

"I'm really quite boring."

"Then bore me."

Her heart fairly skidded to a stop, or so it felt within the confines of her chest. Of late, it seemed he was delving more into her past, and along that route lay danger. Although surely she misread what he was seeking. She licked her lips. "Well, before you interrupted me, I'd made a notation about Lady Bernadette. She dresses garishly, but that can be addressed easily enough, especially as she finds you quite charming. Lady Louise Harcourt gossips snidely about the most inconsequential—"

"I don't care about them. Tell me something about you."

"You should care a great deal about them. You might marry one."

"Why are you so secretive, Pettypeace? What are you hiding?"

His eyes were fairly boring into her, mining deeply into her soul. Except he would soon hit bedrock that would allow him to go no further, but where was the harm in revealing a little of her past, the gale that had only hinted at the tempest that was to follow? "You asked about my father recently. He was a bookkeeper."

"He would have had a penchant for details, then. Did he teach you to be meticulous?"

She nodded, searching for the more pleasant memories of him. "He would sit me upon his lap and explain how figures worked. When I mastered penmanship, he would even let me make the marks."

"Why not tell the truth of him to begin with?"

After all these years, fourteen to be exact, still the shame and mortification struck her hard, and she wondered if a time would ever come when she could keep those particular emotions buried. "Because he wasn't a very good bookkeeper. At least not with his personal finances. When his debt became too great, we moved to London, where he had secured a position with a small export company. But eventually, he again got behind in paying what was owed. As a result, he packed us up and carted us to another area of London. A new adventure, he called it. A chance to see the world. But ultimately his less than frugal lifestyle caught up with him, and he was sent to debtor's prison." He'd made plans for them to run again, to another city, and begin anew. But she hadn't wanted to leave her friends. Even knowing she was expected at home, that all was packed, she had stayed away to play. The constables had arrived at their small residence before she did. "He took ill and died there."

Because she'd been tardy, because she'd been selfish.

"You said he packed *us* up."

"My mother and younger sister. But not long after he passed, they died as well."

The music stopped, and so did they, but he didn't release his hold on her. "I'm sorry for prodding you just now, for dredging up the memories. Dance with me once more, and I shall not utter a word."

She'd read enough books on etiquette to know it was a scandalous thing to do, to remain in his arms and have a second dance. People would talk. But she had suffered through the agony of having her mother turn her back on her. How could the backs of strangers even begin to compare with that? "Do you not think less of me?"

"You are not your father."

But oh, if he ever discovered all the truth of her. She should run now, should do as her father had taught her: when things got unpleasant, the only way to escape the past was to run, change her name, and begin anew. But matters were not yet so unpleasant that she couldn't face them down. And she'd not provided him with enough information that he could learn the rest.

Therefore, she stayed within the circle of his arms until the music began once more and became immersed in the fluid motions they created while they waltzed. She almost demanded he tell her a story in return, but after discovering how his father had punished Lord Lawrence in order to control his heir, she suspected other dark tales in Kingsland's life existed, and she didn't want to bring them into this grand salon where chandeliers glistened and happiness should reside.

Something different, a compassion, an understanding, was in his eyes now as they took turn after turn around the room. She shouldn't have been surprised he could relate to her misfortune. Had she not recently learned that his father hadn't the gift of managing money either and had left his estates in dire straits? A pauper and a noble facing similar circumstances, but Kingsland's position in Society meant he hadn't needed to take the unthinkable steps to survive that she had. She'd been too young to fully understand the scandal of it or how it would haunt her from the shadows, threatening ruination. Even now, as year after year passed and she moved further away from the moments that brought her shame, she couldn't be fully confident she'd escaped them completely.

"Where did you learn to waltz?" he asked.

So much for his not saying a word, but they were back in safe territory. "Last year, during your ball, I observed."

"No one danced with you?"

"No." She'd been too busy and had kept to the fringes.

"The same can't be said of tonight, can it."

Not a question, but a statement. The light from the chandeliers glistened over his dark hair, was occasionally captured in his obsidian eyes. "It seemed rude to tell them no. I assure you the lapses of focus are not interfering with my duties."

"I find no fault with you taking some time to enjoy the evening. We should have anticipated that gentlemen would approach you. Most like nothing better than to have a lovely lady on their arm. Were you keen on any of them?"

"No. The dances were merely a respite from my duties."

"I would regret losing you, Pettypeace."

"You won't lose me." *Not until you marry.* But even then, after he'd exchanged vows with another, after she'd left to pursue a life that no longer included him, he would have her heart. His name might as well be carved into it. It belonged to him and always would. "Were you keen on any of the ladies with whom you danced?"

"Not until this moment."

His gaze was intense as though he was conveying something else entirely, something larger, more grand than the two of them. Had the sun suddenly burst forth into the room, she couldn't have grown any warmer. Surely, he wasn't implying he fancied her, saw her as anything other than his secretary.

"You are anything but boring, Pettypeace. You don't talk incessantly. You don't boast about yourself. You don't giggle after every sentence I speak. Which reminds me. You may also remove Miss Susan Longfield. She titters like a squirrel fearful you're about to snatch away its acorns."

She couldn't help herself. She laughed softly at his disgruntled expression.

"You find it funny? She snickered after every sentence I uttered. My poor pride was taking a ferocious beating."

She laughed again, harder. "I cannot imagine you being undone by a woman's chortling."

His disgruntlement was gone, and he was staring at her with wonder, as though he'd just unearthed a treasure that had been buried for centuries. "I've never heard you laugh before."

"I apologize—"

"No, don't." His grip on her hand tightened, and his other palm pressed more firmly against her waist. "I like it. It's mesmerizing."

She swallowed hard. "I don't laugh very often."

"Not nearly enough. We need to do something about that, don't we?"

Drawing in breath became a challenge as she shook her head. "It's not your responsibility."

For the span of time during which a candle flame flickered, he appeared wounded. But then he was once again the Duke of Kingsland she knew, revealing nothing at all regarding what he felt. He was not a man to give his emotions free rein. Sometimes she longed for him to reveal everything about himself. But then he might ask the same of her, and if she did that, she'd lose him completely. He'd let her go in a heartbeat. From his employ, from his residence, from his life.

Very shortly he'd be releasing her from this dance, and already she couldn't help but regret that for the remainder of the night she would be seeing to her duties and he'd be seeing to the ladies. But for now, she had his attention, and unlike that of the other gentlemen with whom she'd danced, his focus didn't wander from her, not for a single second. He always had a way of studying things with a singular purpose, and he was presently scrutinizing her as though she was a puzzle box, and he was determined to ferret out how to plumb the hidden depths.

"What else have you learned from observing and not had an opportunity to practice?" he asked quietly.

As the image of some stray dogs rutting in the mews flashed through her mind, she almost laughed maniacally, but certainly he couldn't be referring to something of that nature. Not when he watched her with such seriousness, such interest. Her answer seemed important, and yet she was struggling to come up with anything remotely appropriate. Perhaps it was the way he held her or the closeness of him, but she seemed capable only of conjuring up all the various intimate actions she would like to participate in with him before he married. "I once saw my parents kissing rather enthusiastically."

His eyes widened slightly. It wasn't often that she surprised him, but she rather liked doing so. "You've kissed a gent, surely."

"When I was eight, a lad pressed his mouth to mine and bit my bottom lip. Does that count?"

His eyes darkened as his gaze dropped to her mouth. "In no manner whatsoever does that count. Is that how you acquired that small scar at the edge of your lower lip?"

She was taken aback that he'd noticed the thin quarter-of-an-inch-long line. "It's hardly visible."

"I don't miss much, Pettypeace." She knew that, of course. The man observed and cataloged everything. "At least what can be seen. I am beginning to question what I might have missed when it comes to you."

"Nothing at all. As I've said, I'm quite dull."

"Do you remember when we attended that scientific lecture on exotic species and we saw a chameleon from Africa? We observed it camouflaging itself as it was moved from one enclosure to another, from sand to ferns. I'm beginning to realize that's you. You have the ability to blend in, whether it's dinner with the Chessmen, facing some footpads, or attending a ball. Anyone here not familiar with you wouldn't realize you're not nobility. You adapt to your environment. Where did you learn such skill?"

"As I told you, my family moved around a good deal when I was younger. I quickly deduced it was to my benefit not to appear to be the new, naive person unfamiliar with the ways of the area. People will take advantage."

"If anyone here takes advantage, you have but to let me know and I shall put him in his place."

"Do you not think everyone here is civilized?"

"Unfortunately, no. On some matters, me least of all."

APPARENTLY, HE WASN'T at all civilized when it came to the matter of Pettypeace. He'd been both grateful when the music drifted into silence because things between them had been becoming too familiar, too intimate, and regretful the tune had ended because he'd had no choice except to escort her back to the sitting area. He'd barely taken two steps away before an earl approached her and asked for the honor of a waltz.

As King had no more dances lined up for the

evening, he'd come out onto the terrace and sought the darkest corner where he could . . . well, it felt rather like he was sulking. He wanted her to enjoy the evening, liked seeing her smile. But he'd been caught unawares by her laugh. The beauty of it, the depth of it, the wonder of it. The way it had invited him to join in. He'd been so tempted, but if his laughter had mingled with hers, he might have taken her into his arms and carried her out of the ballroom to someplace more private, where they could explore other sounds.

She had told him he wasn't responsible for creating her laughter. But what if he wanted to be? God help him, he wanted to make her laugh and sigh and scream with pleasure. He'd always viewed her as Pettypeace, his secretary. But of late, especially tonight, he viewed her as so much more, as a woman. An incredibly intriguing, fascinating, mysterious woman.

He should be dancing with the others on her list, taking one or two of the more compatible ones for a stroll through the garden, fetching refreshments, speaking with them if nothing else, and yet they held no appeal. Couples—a man and a woman, two ladies chatting away because they had no suitors—wandered onto the terrace, down the steps, and into the gardens. He'd always found these affairs tedious, had avoided them for the most part. Yet tonight he wanted another waltz with Pettypeace. He'd never been so enthralled with any woman he'd held in his arms, not even Margaret during the height of passion.

While he suspected speculation and gossip were

running rampant after he'd had her on the floor for two tunes, he'd not see her ruined. Not because it would make it more difficult for her to carry out her duties, but because he loathed the thought of anyone whispering anything unkind about her. She deserved only the highest of regard and admiration.

He was staring at distant shadows in the gardens when he became aware of Pettypeace. Glancing over his shoulder, he saw her standing on the terrace at the steps, the way one might hover at the edge of a cliff, contemplating whether to throw oneself into the tempestuous waves below. Then she began descending them. She was not going to take a turn about the garden alone, surely. It simply wasn't done. Except neither could he envision her headed for an assignation. Although before tonight, never had he imagined her dancing with gentlemen, smiling at them, or laughing with them. Proof of a lack of imagination on his part. What did he think she'd done with swells at the Fair and Spare? She wasn't a debutante, fresh out of the classroom. She was eight-and-twenty with experience behind her. She wasn't timid about offering her opinion or arguing her stance. Hell, she wasn't even afraid to stare down ruffians in his library.

Before she disappeared completely among the shrubbery, trees, and flowers, he glanced around quickly, saw no one else alone to join her, and followed. Gaslights lined the path, but she didn't stay on it. She detoured into the gloom. Perhaps she wanted a few minutes of solitude. He hesitated. It wasn't as though they were in the rookeries and she would be attacked, and yet he was reluctant to leave her with no protector, even if one wasn't needed. She was fully capable of taking care of herself but was too precious to risk. Therefore, he ducked off the path and into the foliage, wending his way through it until he reached the trees that lined the brick wall enclosing the Thornley manor.

The glow from distant lamps and lights illuminated her gazing up where the sliver of the moon hung in the sky and a few stars were visible. "Making a wish, Pettypeace?"

Her smile soft, she glanced over at him. "Simply striving to reorient myself, reclaim my balance. Since you waltzed with me, I've danced with three other gents. I'm here to work and still have ladies to interview or observe. I thought to give myself a moment's respite and the gentlemen some time to forget about me."

He doubted any of them would ever forget her. After approaching, getting near enough to see her more clearly, he leaned a shoulder against a tree and crossed his arms over his chest. "Do you not like the attention?"

"I put no stock in it. The gents are only asking because I'm a curiosity, an unknown."

"You might catch someone's fancy. Do you never think of marriage?" Was it the reason she'd gone to the Fair and Spare, because she had no other avenue for socializing, for finding a husband?

"I will never marry."

The conviction in her tone surprised him. What woman didn't long for a husband? "Never?"

"Never. A woman loses too much freedom when she says, 'I do.' Afterward, a husband is likely to say, 'You won't.' My mother never wanted to move elsewhere, always wept as she packed up our belongings. When I got old enough to not want to move either, I asked her why we couldn't stay. 'Because your father says we must go and so we must.' No discussion, no compromise. What if the man I marry doesn't want me working? Do I obey him? I don't know that I have it within me to do so, to be like my mother, when it's not what I want."

The relief that coursed through him was un-nerving. He wasn't going to lose her to some dandy who circled her about the floor. "Has there never been a man in your life for whom you thought you would give up everything?"

She hesitated, studied him, then looked away as though the answer resided in the foliage that was barely visible. When she swung her attention back to him, he caught a glimpse of sadness before she shuttered all thought. "Has there ever been a woman in yours?"

He'd never wanted a woman who would mean that much to him. It was part of the reason that he'd taken such an impersonal approach to find-ing a wife. Emotions weren't for him. They caused reactions that created havoc. He'd seen that often enough with his father. Yet he couldn't deny that of all the women he knew, Pettypeace was the most important, had the largest role in his life. The one who made waking up in the morning bearable, be-cause she would be waiting for him at the break-fast table. Rather than answer her, he decided to take the discussion in a different direction. "Was someone going to meet you out here?"

She jerked her head back as though slapped. "Why would someone do that?"

In spite of her age, she possessed an innocence regarding men and women that he was only just beginning to recognize. At a club such as the Fair and Spare that made no secret of its purpose—to provide companionship and intimate encounters with no commitment—she would be a lamb easily led to slaughter. "Sometimes at affairs such as these, trysts are arranged . . . especially for clandestine meetings in the gardens away from prying eyes."

"Is that the reason you followed me? Because you thought I was up to no good?"

"I followed to ensure no one took advantage of you wandering about alone."

"I'm fully capable of taking care of myself."

Her words brimmed over with confidence. How long had that been true? How old was she when no one else was about to watch over her? "How do you spend your evenings?"

"Working, usually. Finishing up matters I don't have time for during the day."

"No suitor to call upon you?"

"It would be a waste of his time and mine. As I said, I have no wish to marry, and therefore have avoided any entanglements."

Yet she'd gone to the Fair and Spare, so she was obviously open to receiving a gentleman's attentions. It appeared she simply didn't want anything permanent. While he knew it was none of his business, he couldn't help but be curious regarding her experience with men, especially as she'd cited earlier her parents kissing as something she'd only observed, but never done. Was she implying that as an adult she'd never been kissed or at least not enthusiastically? He found it inconceivable she had so little experience at it. "Has no gentleman ever kissed you?"

Glancing away, she shifted her stance slightly, and he was beginning to realize she did that when she was striving to determine exactly how much to reveal. So maybe there had once been a man for whom she'd considered giving up everything.

"When I was sixteen," she began before meeting his gaze, "a lad kissed me. I recall it being quite awkward. We bumped noses, then chins. Eventually, his lips landed on mine and lingered for a bit. To be honest, I didn't understand what all the fuss was about."

"A boy and a young, callow lad. Would you like to know what it is to be kissed by a man?"

CHAPTER 12

*H*AD SHE FALLEN asleep in the too-warm ballroom where she'd grown dizzy as one gent after another took her for a turn over the parquet? She'd come out here for a bit of solace, striving to determine a reason for all the sudden interest in her. And why she didn't enjoy the company of anyone else as much as she enjoyed his. She never felt she had to carry on a conversation with him. If she had something to say, she uttered it. He listened, he considered, he replied. And so they went with no pressure to be witty or interesting or clever.

However, those other gentlemen, not Knight or Mr. Grenville, but the last three in particular—the earl and the viscount and the earl after him—had all looked at her with expectation, as if waiting for something to be delivered. A promise of an action or an item. She'd always thought herself a woman of the world; certainly, she'd lost her naivety after her father had died, but tonight she felt like a gosling that had yet to learn to swim. And so she'd escaped the residence because that was the lesson her father had taught her: when matters became too complicated or frightening—run!

But she'd never in her life felt as scared as she did at that very minute. Terrified that he was teasing or mocking her. More fearful he meant what he'd asked, and afraid to believe him, she'd give the wrong answer and miss the opportunity to experience what she dreamed of every time she closed her eyes and drifted into slumber. Kingsland, tall, broad, and so incredibly perfect. Who studied her in the same manner he did his ledgers: with cool and controlled interest.

A couple of times tonight, however, she'd seen the heat in his eyes when he looked at her, had felt it down to the tips of her toes, had nearly lowered all her defenses so the love she felt for him would shine through, knock him back on his heels with the depth and breadth of it. But that way lay heartache because he could never be hers wholly and completely. His life didn't lend itself to running, and she never knew when the day would arrive that she would have to.

Yet the opportunity to know his kiss was too great a temptation to let pass.

"Yes, I rather think I would. Are you offering?"

While his slow sensual smile spread, he uncrossed his arms and pushed himself away from the tree. "Have you had another offer?"

When he began tugging off his gloves, her voice deserted her, and she could only shake her head as he tucked the gray cloth accessories into the waistband of his trousers. Then the warm, naked fingers of one hand were resting against the edge of her jaw. "Then, yes, I rather think I am."

Licking her lips, she ordered herself to relax, but every nerve ending felt like kindling just set alight, ready to ignite the whole of her. He began lowering his head. "Close your eyes," he whispered, and the low rasp shimmered through her.

She did as he bade. He touched his mouth to the corner of hers, so feathery light, and she imagined a petal felt the same softness when a butterfly landed on it. If a petal felt at all. It was an absurd thought. Then his mouth settled more firmly against hers, leaving no room for absurdity.

She was in no danger of having a scar added to her lower lip but feared she might very well end up with a damaged heart. It was dangerous to have this, to have him so near, filling her senses with his fragrance. His tongue traced the seam between her lips, and then the tiniest of pressures began to build as he encouraged her to part them. When she did, he dove in with a growl and a hunger that should have frightened her. His other arm came around her, drawing her up close. Of their own accord, her arms wound around his neck, and he responded with a groan and a deepening of the kiss.

The kiss of a man, especially this one, was wonderful, sublime, glorious. Just as she'd always imagined it would be. Leisurely but thoroughly, he explored the confines of her mouth just as she surveyed the interior of his. Hot, moist, and flavorful with a hint of champagne on his tongue. And dark—there was a darkness that made this moment much more sensual. She did wish she'd gone to the trouble of removing her gloves in order to determine if his hair was as soft as it looked. But even with the gloves, her fingers glided through it over and over, then down across his strong shoulders and back up to his scalp to hold him in place. She didn't want him to ever leave her and fought against thinking about the moment when he would.

While the fingers of one hand cradled her chin, his thumb continually stroked her cheek, adding to the sensations he was stirring with his mouth. It had been a mistake not to run when he'd made his offer, because how on God's green earth could she ever look at his lush, full lips and not remember what it was like to have hers cushioned against them?

With his muscled arm providing support, he leaned her back slightly and began nibbling along her neck, over her collarbone, down to her breasts plumped up by her corset, breasts straining for his touch. Her nipples had hardened and become so sensitive to the linen brushing against them that she was close to screaming. His ministrations coated her skin in dampness, caused dew to gather in her secret, intimate place that ached for release, for his touch, for her own.

His moan, low and tortured, vibrated against her flesh before his mouth returned to hers, and she greedily welcomed him with a mewling that resulted in him pressing her nearer as though he intended to absorb every aspect of her. She wanted it, him melded against her, buried inside her. She yearned for the impossible, for what she could never ask for, never possess. They shouldn't have done this, shouldn't have blurred the lines between employer and employee, between noble and commoner, between an upstanding peer and a woman who had betrayed her pride in order to survive.

Breathing heavily and harshly, he pulled back, his gaze boring into hers. "And that," he rasped, "is what all the fuss is about."

Her legs felt so weak she was amazed she didn't collapse at his feet. She might once he relinquished his hold, but he had yet to release her. Only now did she realize she was clutching his lapels. Stiffly, one by one, she unfurled her fingers and then smoothed out the cloth. "I hope you don't expect me to say anything," she murmured softly, "as you robbed me of coherent thought."

He chuckled low, and it took everything within her not to place her fingers against his throat to relish the vibrations she'd find there. Lightly he stroked his thumb over her lips, still tingling and swollen. "You should make your way inside now."

"Without you?"

"It wouldn't do for us to be seen exiting the gardens together. Besides, I need a bit of time to recover."

She wasn't so innocent as to not know what he meant, but refrained from looking down, not that she could have seen much anyway with the darkness surrounding them. "I'm not certain of the proper etiquette. Should I thank you?"

"God, please don't," he ground out.

After giving a small nod, she took one tiny step

to ensure her knees could support her. His hands fell away. And she was free, yet did not wish to go. But forced herself to walk away from the wall, from the trees . . . from him.

When she was beyond his sight, she began running, knowing she could never outpace herself or her desires.

ACHING WITH NEED, he turned and pressed his forehead to the tree and pounded a balled fist against the bark. Never before, with such a fervent passion, had he wanted a woman as much as he did her. He'd come so close to pushing her up against that blasted wall and taking her there, like a barbarian, a savage, a man without honor or scruples. Madness. It was total madness how desperate he'd become to know her in every way that a man could know a woman.

It was as though there had been something unknown bubbling beneath the surface that had erupted into an uncontrollable volcano the moment his mouth had met hers. The innocence and tentativeness of her initial welcoming had blossomed into a heated sensuality that had rocked him down to his heels.

Prim, proper, ever-efficient Pettypeace was a cauldron of molten desires. He'd wanted to make her burn with a fiery passion, watch her eyes smolder with want and yearning, hear his name echoing through her cries of pleasure.

Thank God, years of practicing not to be like his father, never to lose control, had allowed him to retain a flicker of sanity, enough to remember she was his secretary, and he couldn't risk taking advantage of a moment of weakness in her or himself.

Heaving several deep breaths, he stepped away from the tree. Fortunately, his cock had finally recognized it would go untended and was no longer plaguing him with need. He could return to the ballroom without embarrassment.

As he began striding back toward the lit path, he chided himself. Whatever had he been thinking to even offer to provide a lesson in kissing? But after knowing she'd gone to that new scandalous club and then learning about her two experiences with the males of the human species—it just seemed wrong that she should have nothing notable or worthy to compare with any future encounters. Ah, hell, who was he striving to fool?

That spark of jealousy that had first hit him when he'd seen her dancing had carried him through the gardens to her, had made him wonder what kissing her would be like, had taunted him to discover the reality of it.

"Ah, there you are."

He'd neared the stairs to the terrace, and glancing up, saw Knight standing a little off to the side, smoking a cheroot. After taking the steps two at a time, he joined his friend and shook his head when he offered him a cigar.

"Out for a little tryst?" Knight asked.

"Just a bit of fresh air."

"Then you're not the reason Pettypeace dashed out of the gardens?"

His heart slammed against his ribs. "She was running?"

"Only until she realized she might be seen. Then she slowed. I asked her if I needed to call anyone out. She told me not to be ridiculous then flounced inside."

Pettypeace did not flounce . . . ever. Although he took some comfort in her not confessing that he did indeed need to face a dueling pistol at dawn. "If anyone is going to call anyone out, it'll be me."

"Going to shoot yourself, are you?"

"You're deuced irritating this evening, you know that?"

Knight drew on his cheroot and blew out a series of smoke circles. "You might want to comb down your hair before going inside. You look as though you've been ravaged."

He felt as though he had been, inside and out, from the moment he'd stepped closer to her and she'd looked up at him with something akin to longing. Pressing his hands to his head, he flattened the strands that were sticking up and fought not to remember how wonderful it had felt to have her fingers going through them. "What were you laughing about while you were dancing with her?"

"I don't recall. Something to do with you, probably."

King wished there was a boxing ring nearby. He'd like nothing better than to knock Knight on his arse. "I didn't realize I was a source of humor."

"You're not usually." Knight had the audacity to smile at him. "There's nothing wrong in liking her."

If only it was liking, but it was something more,

something deeper, something he'd never experienced before, didn't quite understand. "She works for me."

"Then establish rules and make certain she understands them."

He made it sound so simple, but King wasn't certain anything with Pettypeace would ever be simple.

"TO BE HONEST, I only wrote the letter because I wanted to make someone else jealous," Lady Sarah Montague confessed.

After returning to the ballroom, Penelope had made inquiries until she'd been able to identify and locate Lady Sarah at the back corner of an arrangement of chairs, where she had been busily inputting cross-stitches through fabric to create a brown dog on her sampler. Penelope had almost immediately drawn a line through her name in order to move on to the next on the list because what sort of woman brought embroidery to a ball? But recalling how some of the servants judged her without knowing the truth of things, she decided to give the girl a chance to explain her odd behavior. She could have a perfectly logical reason for hauling her needlework around with her.

Extremely tiny, her feet hovering an inch or so above the floor, the blonde, blue-eyed debutante had a delicate elfin quality about her, and Penelope feared Kingsland might shatter the lady if he latched his mouth onto hers with as much enthusiasm as he'd exhibited in the garden. While giving him freedom to kiss her had been a mistake, it had made her realize he required a sturdy wife who could survive his breath-stealing passionate nature.

"I didn't truly believe he'd seriously consider me," Lady Sarah continued.

Sitting beside her at an angle, Penelope was able to keep an eye on the doorway opening onto the terrace. Kingsland had yet to return, and she was beginning to worry he might be struggling to recover from their encounter, that perhaps it had weakened him as much as it had her. Her limbs still felt languid, as though she'd just emerged from a strikingly hot bath. "But you wrote so glowingly about yourself."

"Well, I suppose I did hope he might mention to a gent or two how difficult it was to pass me over, and the one who has captured my heart might soon hear of it and become intrigued." She wrinkled her delicate brow. "I'm beginning to realize I didn't think my strategy through completely."

"Sitting near the fronds might not be the best way to catch anyone's attention."

"Miss Pettypeace, have you ever longed for anyone with every fiber of your being, only to have him never notice you, to act as though you don't even exist, to never have even asked you to dance?"

As though he'd been summoned, the one for whom Penelope yearned chose that precise moment to walk into the ballroom and glance around. His gaze landed on her with an almost audible thud. He gave an abrupt nod of acknowledgment and moved on. Apparently, he'd recovered quite nicely. While she had yearned, she certainly couldn't claim he hadn't ever noticed her or asked her to dance, so she fudged the truth a bit to spare the girl's feelings. "No, I can't say as I have."

"It's the most awful thing in the entire world. He gives more attention to his hound than to me."

She nodded down at the sampler. "Is that to represent his hound?"

Lady Sarah smiled, a tiny dimple forming on either side of her mouth. "I thought to slip it into the pocket of his jacket or into his hat at some affair where he left one or both in a cloakroom. To be secretive about it, to make him wonder who his admirer might be."

"Perhaps, then, you shouldn't risk him seeing you working on it at a ball."

"Drat," she said, the one word filled with a universe of disappointment. "I'm not very good at this subterfuge thing, am I?"

"Have you ever considered asking him to dance?"

The blue eyes widened. "That's simply not done."

"Sometimes doing what is simply not done is the only way to gain what you want. When the duke placed his advert for a secretary, he specifically stated he was in need of a gentleman with certain skills, which he then listed. A gentleman, Lady Sarah. And yet in I walked."

"That was dashed bold of you, Miss Pettypeace."

"I must confess, I thought he would toss me out on my ear, and my knees trembled during the entire interview. But I got the position. Nothing ventured, nothing gained, Lady Sarah."

"I will certainly give it some thought and try to find my courage."

"Shall I remove you from consideration for the position of Duchess of Kingsland?"

"I think it would be best. The duke actually terrifies me. So large and bold, and he has this determination about him that is overwhelming and unnerving."

It was one of the things Penelope admired most about him. Funny how people could perceive attributes differently. What one person favored, another rejected.

Those thoughts continued to rumble around in her mind after she bade Lady Sarah goodbye and while she made notes regarding her impressions of the ladies with whom she'd spoken or observed. She was still applying pencil to paper when Kingsland approached and told her it was time to take their leave.

He didn't offer his arm as he guided her out of the ballroom and followed her up the stairs. He didn't touch her at all until they reached his carriage and he handed her up. It was a shame he was again wearing his gloves, although they did little to stop the heat from his skin seeping into hers. As she settled onto the squabs, he took his place across from her. Unlike the night they'd had dinner with the Chessmen, at least he wasn't leaving her alone in order to go off in search of other entertainments.

However, it might have been far less stressful if he had. She didn't know whether to make a comment regarding the kiss or to pretend it had never happened. Although it made it difficult to read his expression, she was grateful he'd not brought a lantern inside. Traveling in darkness brought some comfort with it.

"Did you accomplish everything you'd hoped?" he asked, his low voice shattering whatever calm she'd almost achieved. "Regarding your list, I mean."

Did he believe clarification was needed? Did he think she'd gone there with the intention of kissing him, of learning the joy to be found in having his lips pressed to hers? "Two of the ladies didn't appear to be in attendance. I'll see about calling upon them. I don't want them to be at a disadvantage."

He issued a grunt before looking out the window. Perhaps she should say something about the kiss. *It doesn't change anything between us.* When in fact, it had changed everything.

"Pettypeace, I've been giving some thought to our situation."

Even as his words took her by surprise, his voice was a deep, slow caress in the darkness. She'd mucked things up royally. He was going to let her go. A secretary who engaged in such scandalous behavior was not to be tolerated. "It shan't happen again. The kiss, it was"—*wonderful, incredible*—"I"—*wasn't myself, wasn't thinking clearly, still aren't, seem unable to form any sort of coherent explanation*—"You need not dismiss me. I shall most certainly behave in the future." There. She was claiming the fault as hers, taking full responsibility for what had transpired in the garden.

"Dismiss you?"

"Is that not what you're considering, regarding our situation?"

"Not really, no. Did you not enjoy it? The kiss?"

She would surrender her small fortune for another. "That is beside the point, is it not?"

"It could very well be the point. Was it to your liking?"

He was studying her, his gaze homed in on her as though he could detect every facet and reaction from her, in spite of the darkness. "It was very much to my liking."

"To mine as well. Men have needs, Pettypeace. As do women. Although most men would deny that the gentler sex does indeed harbor needs."

Her heart began hammering. She didn't think he was referring to the need for food, housing, or clothing. "Needs?"

She was pleased her voice didn't squeak like a frightened dormouse.

"For a touch, a caress . . . camaraderie . . . companionship . . . or even carnal urges that must be met. Do you not ever *yearn* for what a man can provide? Do you never seek it?"

Such confidence in his tone. Oh God, he already knew the answer, somehow knew she'd gone to the Fair and Spare. "Lord Lawrence told you."

He seemed taken aback for a minute, and then his grin flashed in the darkness. "That you went to the Fair and Spare? Yes. It slipped out. Unintentionally. He didn't mean to betray a confidence. Did you meet anyone there whom you fancied?"

Even though she couldn't see him clearly, she looked out the window because it seemed a safer place. "No, but I only went the once. It wasn't tawdry, but I'm not quite certain it suited me. My flirtation skills are abysmal. However, it was just before I got ill, so perhaps I wasn't at my best."

She heard the rustle of his clothing, and when she turned back, it was to see the shadow of him leaning toward her. "Do you plan to return?"

Clutching her hands in her lap, she squeezed her eyes shut, then opened them because this was Kingsland, a man she'd known for eight years. "Probably not before the ball. So much remains to be done."

"We are both incredibly busy people. We work long hours, attend investment meetings, explore options, read journals and newspapers, and strive to stay ahead of an ever-changing world. Why should we not take some time for ourselves, you and I, at the end of the day, when we are within easy reach of each other, to see that those urges are satisfied? You have no desire to marry, and I presently have no wife. Who would we harm by getting up to a bit of mischief, as long as we both acknowledged and understood going in that there would never be a commitment? We would enjoy a temporary liaison. As long as we owed no allegiance to another. Although here is the rub, as I see it. I am your employer. It would not do for me to seek you out. But if you should ever have a *need* that I could fulfill, you are welcome to come to me."

He settled back against the squabs as though the matter was settled, as though at that very second, she didn't yearn to cross over to him and have him press a hand, a thigh, or a cock against the pulsing spot between her thighs. "I would not wish to get with babe." But even as she said it, she knew it for a lie. She would very much like to have his child.

"I know how to ensure that you don't."

Of course he did. She was the virgin, not he. "I would remain your secretary?"

"Absolutely. Nothing between us would change in that regard. It is only the nights that would differ, become more interesting, more satisfying."

She nodded, although uncertain as to whether he could see the motion. His proposal was certainly worth considering. She'd gone to the Fair and Spare because she'd wanted a male companion. But it required time to become comfortable enough with a man to even consider engaging in the sort of intimacy she craved. Yet here was a man to whom she'd already given her heart. Sharing her body with him seemed reasonable, especially when she'd already experienced the power of his kiss. To enjoy more involved encounters with him, even for a short time, was preferable to never having anything else of him.

CHAPTER 13

THE ARGUMENTS PENELOPE had made to herself as they'd continued their journey back to the residence in silence had all seemed rational and clear. But now, sitting on the edge of her bed in her nightdress, she recognized they were dangerous and rife with pitfalls. She could fall more deeply in love with him. In spite of his reasoning that only their nights would change, she suspected it was a rare occurrence indeed when an encounter between the sheets did not affect those that took place beyond them. Yet her yearning for him was so great, she was willing to risk that a tryst might shorten their time together, that she might have to turn in her notice before he married.

But at least she would have this night with which to console herself.

If she could only find the courage to put her feet on the floor. She understood why the decision had to be hers. She had the most to lose but also the most to gain. Although he didn't know the last part.

For him, it would be only lust and a physical release.

For her, it would be a clandestine delivering of her heart. But it was already his. To take this step would simply be acknowledging it as such. Lifting her legs, she wrapped her arms around them and squeezed them to her chest. Lowering them, she slid off the bed until her bare feet rested against the floor and glanced over at her cat curled on the pillow. "I shan't be too long, Sir Purrcival. Don't get into any mischief while I'm gone."

Quietly crossing the room, she didn't bother with slippers. After they'd arrived at the residence, she'd immediately retired to her room, while he'd headed down the hallway, no doubt going to the library for a bit of scotch. It had been only twenty minutes or so since she'd heard the door to his chamber close. He might already be asleep. Although if the ensuing silence was any indication, he'd not yet rung for his valet. But then, he was a grown man, fully capable of undressing himself.

Opening her door, she glanced up and down the corridor. No one was about, not even his valet. Inhaling deeply, before her courage could desert her, she padded over the thick carpeting to his chamber and rapped softly on his door. She was taken aback by how quickly he opened it, as though he'd been hovering on the other side, simply waiting for her arrival. The buttons on his shirt had all been given their freedom, the material parted to reveal an enticing V of naked chest with a light sprinkling of dark hair. His feet were bare, large and perfect, and the sight of them seemed far more scandalous than his chest.

After swallowing hard, she confessed, "I've never done this before."

His features shifted to reveal a wealth of tenderness that chased away any of her lingering doubts. He held out a large, powerful hand. "I'll be gentle."

She slid her palm over his, relishing the strength in his long, thick fingers as they closed around hers and he drew her into his bedchamber. He closed the door, locked it, and led her farther into the room twice the size of the one in which she slept.

"Would you like some brandy?" he asked.

She shook her head. "I've already had two glasses. You might want to get to it before my courage deserts me."

Affectionately he cradled her face. "If at any time you want me to stop or you change your mind, you have only to tell me."

"I appreciate that, Your Grace."

He touched his thumb to her mouth. "It is only the two of us in this room, two people with needs. No duke, no secretary. No peer, no commoner. Call me Hugh, Penelope." He'd never addressed her by her given name before. She'd always liked how he referred to her as Pettypeace, but at that moment her heart blossomed into the most beautiful bloom that had ever existed.

She smiled softly. "Hugh."

Then, as though all the preliminaries had been

settled and were out of the way, his mouth blanketed hers with unbridled purpose and passion, stealing what little breath remained to her after hearing her name on his tongue. This time when her fingers tangled in his hair, she was without gloves and able to appreciate the sable-soft curls. His moan bordered on a rough growl that made her want to laugh, dance around the room, and then leap back into his arms. He was kissing her as though she meant something to him, as though he was unable to get enough of her, would never have enough of her.

Even so, she worried that she was simply opening herself up to more heartache. After having had him, how could she survive when the time came that she couldn't have him again? She didn't want to think about that now. She wanted only to savor the moment, to savor every sensation he sparked within her. She wanted to return the favor, to know more than his mouth on hers, her fingers in his hair. Trailing her fingers along the corded tendons of his neck, she relished his feral groan, only then becoming aware of her own sighs. How could a man of such power and strength have such silken skin? Grateful the buttons were no hindrance, she slipped her hands inside his shirt and glided her palms over his firm, broad chest.

Breaking from the kiss, he lifted his arms, grabbed the back of his shirt, dragged it over his head, and tossed it aside, giving her a view of his splendid chest to admire. A flat stomach . . . and scars, peering out from along his side. A large area of discoloration and puckered skin. Her fingers went toward the marred flesh, but his hand covered hers before she reached her destination and drew it away. "Those are burn marks. How did you get them?"

He pressed the tips of her fingers to his mouth. "An accident." Unfurling her fingers, he kissed her palm. "It's of no consequence now." He flattened her hand against his chest. "Ignore them."

Then his mouth was back on hers, distracting her from seeking answers to his past, encouraging her to become lost in the vortex of the present where nothing mattered except passion and pleasure.

HE'D FORGOTTEN ABOUT the damned scars. After all these years, they were simply a part of him. He should have expected the mottled flesh would draw her attention and thus should have kept his shirt on. But when she'd begun exploring what his loosened buttons had exposed, he'd wanted her to have the freedom to explore all of him. When she was ready, he'd be shucking his trousers. He'd promised to be gentle and that meant going slow, but bloody hell if he wasn't already aching to be buried deep inside her.

She made the sweetest, most sensual little mewling sounds he'd ever heard. And she seemed to appreciate having the luxury of touching him. He'd known women content to receive pleasure, thinking little of giving it to their partner, but as in all things, Penelope was an equal. She wouldn't take without giving, and he had a feeling when they were done, he was going to feel as Knight had described him earlier: ravaged. Inside and out.

He hadn't realized how badly he wanted her, needed her, until he'd begun preparing for bed, stripped down to his shirtsleeves and trousers, and then started prowling through his chamber, not wanting to be completely nude if she should come. With each passing minute, the tension had ratcheted up until he'd convinced himself to go to her, simply to wish her pleasant dreams and give her a kiss to take into slumber with her. He'd been reaching for his door latch when she'd knocked, and the relief that had swamped him very nearly had unmanned him.

Now there she was in her modest nightdress that left everything to the imagination, and yet it might be the most alluring garment he'd ever laid eyes on simply because she was in it, running her hands over his chest, shoulders, and arms as though she couldn't get enough of touching him, while he'd contented himself with cradling her face or skimming his fingers over her linen-covered back.

Without taking his mouth from hers, he brought his hands around and began to push the buttons lining the front of the nightdress through the holes until none remained tethered. The gentleman inside him wanted to take a bow for his patience while the savage within growled with need. Tender, slow, he reminded himself, not wanting to frighten her, to give her any cause for regret.

Leaning back, holding her heated gaze, he fought not to look at the skin revealed, waiting for her to grant permission for him to go further, to signal she was comfortable enough to shed the armor. When the signal came, it nearly felled him.

Provocatively, she rolled her shoulders, causing the nightdress to slither and slide down the length of her, revealing her perfect petite form with its enticing dips and curves. He intended to take a journey over each one, but first he latched his mouth back onto hers, lifted her into his arms, and strode to the bed.

THE APPRECIATION IN his dark gaze created a dizzying array of sensations traversing along her nerve endings. She knew the look of lust, but that wasn't what he was displaying. Certainly, want, need, and desire were there, but they were tempered by a hunger that ran deeper than mere lust. An ache that she recognized in herself, a craving to know every aspect of him, to savor and relish. She was remarkably glad she'd taken the initiative to slip out of her nightdress, signaling she wasn't timid or missish about what was to come. At an early age, she'd dispensed with modesty, as it served no useful purpose.

He kept his word to be gentle. She was barely aware of the bed greeting her back as he slowly set her down on the sheets, the duvet folded at the foot of the bed. Stretching out beside her, he reclaimed her mouth as one hand cradled her breast, practically swallowing it, and tenderly kneaded, his thumb and forefinger toying with the nipple straining for attention. How was she to have known it would feel so different to have someone else's fingers taunting the sensitive flesh? She could hardly wait to have his fingers elsewhere, to discover the sensations his touch would bring forth.

Flattening her palm against his chest, she dragged her hand down to his trousers and pulled back from his questing mouth. "These need to go."

"For a virgin, you certainly are bold."

"I said I hadn't done it before. I didn't say I hadn't thought about it."

Chuckling, he pressed a kiss to her throat, and she felt the vibrations of his happiness travel along her nerves. "Are you certain?"

"I've seen statues as well as paintings in museums." Although she did wish he could undress without leaving her.

He rolled off the bed, unfastened his trousers, and soon stood before her in all his naked splendor.

"When I fantasized about being with a man"—*with you*—"my imagination fell . . . far *short* of the reality."

His smile was the most beautiful he'd ever bestowed on her, and his laughter echoing around them filled the well of her longing to overflowing. "Glad to have surpassed expectations."

Then her laughter mingled with his as he rejoined her. She'd not expected the joy, the happiness, the absolute delight of being with him. It was as he'd said. Only the two of them. No burdens, no worries, no fears.

Reaching down, she wrapped her hand around the hot, velvety length of him. His chest rumbled with his growl as he peppered her throat and shoulders with kisses, while she stroked and explored what she had vastly misjudged. "You would tell me if I was hurting you."

Rising up, he held her gaze. "A touch has never felt better."

"I like touching you."

"Good, because I like touching you, too." He glided his hand along her side, over her hip. "But I also want to taste you."

He cupped her mound and waited, seeking permission for what he wanted, what she yearned to experience at his hands.

"You can do anything you want," she whispered.

"Ah, Christ." Burying his face in the curve of her neck, he suckled at the tender skin. Then he began licking and kissing, moving down her torso until she finally had to release her hold on his shaft, but she touched whatever she could reach: his back, his shoulders, his neck, his hair.

So many varying textures. She hoarded every sensation, what it felt like to caress him, to have him caressing her. He was skilled at combining his mouth, his hands, his fingers, his growls and groans, to make her ache and throb in spots she hadn't known she could. These memories of his hunger for her would sustain her through the years.

He dipped his tongue into her navel before dragging his jaw across her sensitive skin to the hollow of her hip, and she realized she felt no whiskers. To be that smooth, he had to have taken a razor to his face after they returned from the ball. Why would he do that unless he was hoping, anticipating, she'd come to him? She thought her love for him had reached its peak, but she was wrong. It swelled within her with his thoughtfulness.

After kissing the inside of her thigh, he slid his hands beneath her hips and tipped her up slightly. Using his thumbs, he parted her, exposing to his gaze the small, throbbing button that ached for him. "So perfect, so pink. Do you ever touch yourself here?"

"Yes."

His gaze, heated and dark, came up to slam into hers. "You're not modest."

"No." Doing the things she'd done to survive had chased any sort of potential embarrassment regarding her body out of her. It was all only a shell. The inside was what counted. Although at the moment she was incredibly grateful for everything he was doing to that shell.

"I didn't think you would be. You're too confident."

"As you said earlier, women have urges as well. It's silly to deny them."

"But you've never been with a man."

Pushing herself up, resting on her elbows, she shook her head. "Not like this."

He grinned, a devilish, boyish grin, and she envisioned him as a much younger man, before he was duke and had responsibilities. "How fortunate for me, to be the first."

The only. She couldn't imagine anyone would come after him.

He lowered his head, and his velvet tongue traveled over her, circled, licked. Her entire body turned into molten candle wax. "Oh, well, that's certainly something I've never been able to do for myself."

His deep chuckle rumbled against her. "And I've only just begun."

She'd always admired his single-mindedness, the way he devoted himself to a project or an endeavor, and he was certainly ardently dedicating himself to his current task. She was unable to hold back the whimpers and sighs. Soon they evolved into moans and cries as sensations coursed through her. With smoldering eyes, he watched her the entire time, peering over her mound, daring her to look at him as he feasted.

His fervent stare was enough to cause pleasure to ripple through her, but combined with the attention to detail provided by his talented mouth and clever fingers, she was beginning to doubt her ability to survive the onslaught of sensations that began gathering, promising more, more—

Until she could no longer contain them. Her body curled forward, flung back, as the deluge of pleasure ripped through her, tore his name from her lips in a joyous sob, a grateful benediction. She wrapped her legs tightly around his shoulders, held him close while the spasms undulated through her. He slid through the shackle she'd created until he was able to claim her mouth, and she tasted herself mingled with him.

Oh, the pure intimacy of it. It had been a mistake to come to him, to know this and to know she couldn't have it forever.

He rubbed his cock against her. "You're so hot, so wet. You're still throbbing."

"My release has never been that strong or powerful."

"Normally I would wear a sheath, but this time, only this time, I want to feel you, Penelope. I'll leave before I spill my seed."

"I want you inside me with nothing separating us."

He bracketed his hands on either side of her head. "Just so you know, sweetheart, this will be a first for me, not using a sheath."

She smiled. "How fortunate for me, to be the first."

Another low chuckle from him that settled in to reside within her heart. After adjusting their positions, he nudged against her opening. "Stop me if it hurts."

She nodded, but the movement was a lie. She wasn't going to stop him, wanted too much to be joined with him.

He'd prepared her well. She barely noticed the discomfort, too enamored of the wondrous notion that he was pushing into her, spreading her, filling her. She'd dreamed of this and was discovering the reality was so much better. When he was seated to the hilt, he stilled. "Are you all right?"

"More than all right. I like the way it feels."

"And we haven't even gotten to the good part yet." Then he was slowly moving against her, easing in and out, never taking his gaze from hers. He lifted himself up, bracing his arms on either side of her. "Wrap your legs around my hips."

She did as he bade. He withdrew almost completely, then thrust hard.

"Oh." That little button he'd licked earlier suddenly woke up.

"That's what I was looking for. Now, hold on." He pistoned into her, and her lethargic body came fully awake as the promise of pleasure took hold.

She scraped her fingers up his back, loved the feel of his muscles bunching with his movements. His groans mingled with her sighs. His errant forelock flapped against his brow. His eyes darkened, his jaw tightened.

Her nerve endings sparked as her muscles contracted and ecstasy whipped through her. But she couldn't stop watching him, the sight of him only adding to her gratification. His breathing grew harsh and heavy. The tendons at his neck tautened.

With a resounding curse, he left her. As his seed pulsed onto her belly, she wrapped her hands around him and milked all she could from him. He dropped his head back. "Ah, Christ."

He pressed his forehead against hers. "Give me a minute and then I'll clean you."

He kissed her, just a quick claiming of her mouth, but it was as powerful as any of the other kisses they'd shared. Lifting her head off the pillow, she pressed her lips to the center of his chest. She'd never known such contentment.

AFTER WIPING HER stomach, he'd tenderly and gently cleaned between her legs, grimacing at the small bit of blood that appeared on the cloth.

"Did it hurt terribly?" he'd asked.

"No," she'd lied.

Now resting on his back, he held her against his side, with one arm wrapped around her, the fingers of his other hand playing over her hip as lightly as a musician testing the strings of an instrument. With her head nestled in the crook of his shoulder, she skimmed a palm over his chest, taking delight in the hairs tickling her skin.

"Is Penelope really your name?" he asked quietly.

"Yes." It was easier that way, to keep part of the old so she didn't have an abundance of new to remember.

"And Pettypeace?"

"No. My father always changed the family name when he moved us around. He used to say, 'When you have nothing, you never have to prove who you are in order to obtain it.' It was a habit I continued after he died, and I found myself moving from place to place."

"That explains why my spies could find nothing on you."

"I find that remarkably reassuring." It proved she'd done an excellent job of leaving no crumbs to be followed, when she became someone who hadn't existed before.

"What is your real name?"

"It's of no consequence. I've been Pettypeace longer than I've been anyone else." Lifting up on an elbow, she gazed down into his eyes. "Now you have to share something. How did you get the burns?"

"I'd rather share my cock."

When he started to roll her over, she stayed him with a hand flattened to his chest. "How did the *accident* happen?" Because the truth was, she couldn't envision it wasn't something deliberately done.

With a sigh, he dropped his head back onto the pillow. "I was twelve. It was night, late. I was already abed. I don't know what Mother had done. Penned a letter he didn't like, written something unbecoming about him in her journal." Another sigh, this one longer, harsher, filled with frustration. "I can't imagine it was anything truly untoward. But I was awoken by her protests and apologies and promises to never do it again echoing down the hallway as he dragged her along it. I ran out of my chamber and rushed after them. To the kitchens. The servants had retired. Keating emerged to see what the commotion was about. My father ordered him to put on a pot of water to boil and then to make himself scarce. My mother went to her knees, begging for forgiveness, for understanding. I stood in that doorway, terrified. Too frightened to try to stop him, too horrified to leave."

He went quiet, but she could see in his eyes, as he stared at the ceiling, that the horror was still there, visiting him. She wished she hadn't asked but knew it would do neither of them well to leave it there, to have the memories lingering in his mind without conclusion. "What happened?"

He flattened his mouth, shook his head, and released a shuddering breath. "He jerked her to her feet and commanded she put her hand in the pot. The water was boiling by that time. I could hear the bubbles rumbling, see the steam rising. When she refused, he tried to force her hand inside, but she fought. My God, how she fought. He released his hold, picked up the pot to toss the water on her—and I shoved her out of the way."

Covering her mouth, she fought not to retch, to be ill.

Gently, with his thumbs, he gathered the tears rolling down her face, pooling at the corners of her mouth. "Don't cry. It was a long time ago. My nightshirt provided little protection and my screams seemed to bring him out of that dark place into which he'd gone. He had a physician sent for, but the damage had been done."

"He was a cruel man, your father."

"More often than not, especially when his temper was pricked."

She considered the past eight years. "I've never known you to get angry."

"I work very hard to remain in control of myself and to keep the world around me on an even keel. Do you know, others have asked, but you are the only one I've ever told? What does that mean, I wonder?"

"That you know all your secrets are safe with me."

"What of your secrets?"

"They are safe with you." He studied her, and she sensed it was with an expectancy that she would reveal more. "I've shared them all." She hated bringing the lie into the chamber, into this bed.

He touched the scar near her bottom lip. "You've had your own share of misfortunes."

Misfortunes was an understatement for both of them, but this time when he began to roll her over onto her back, she didn't stop him. She was weary of talking and wanted him to do all those wickedly wonderful things with her that made her forget, for a short time, that the past never left completely and could always make an unexpected appearance.

CHAPTER 14

Four weeks until the Kingsland ball

THE NIGHT BEFORE had seemed a wonderful, glorious, magnificent dream. Waltzing with him, kissing him in the garden, going to his bedchamber, joining him in his bed. But with the light of morning, she soundly cursed every minute that had passed since their arrival at the ball. How could she have been so reckless, so careless, as to think that any intimacy between them would not linger and interfere with her day?

As she drew on her no-nonsense dark blue frock, she wished for the rose ball gown that would leave some of her skin bare so he could deliver a light touch or a press of his lips. As she yanked her hair back into its tight knot, she longed to have it loose so his fingers could become entangled in it, so he could spread the tresses out over his pillow. As she headed down the stairs to breakfast, she yearned for the sustenance he could provide in his bedchamber.

When she walked into the dining room, she staggered to a stop, arrested by the sight of him sitting at the table, reading his newspaper. Carefully he folded it, set it aside, and came to his feet.

"Good morning, Pettypeace."

Well then, apparently, he was completely unaffected by their encounter, and she rather resented it should be so. "Your Grace."

Briskly, she marched over to the sideboard and began scooping the offerings onto her plate, giving them little attention, realizing too late she didn't favor half of the items. Turning about, she made her way to the table, surprised when he waved off the footman and saw to pulling out the chair for her himself.

When they were settled, he lifted his cup of coffee—he seldom favored tea when he'd had a grueling night—and studied her over its rim as he drank, and she fought not to be jealous of a bit of china because it was fortunate enough to have his lips resting against it. Moving the cup away, he asked, "How did you sleep last night?"

"Very well, thank you." Nestled up against his side until just before the servants began stirring. Then she'd scurried back to her bedchamber for another couple of hours. "You?"

"I didn't sleep. The light spilling in through the window across my bed made it appear particularly lovely, and I didn't want to miss the opportunity to savor the splendor of it."

It had also been spilling across her. She rather hoped the butler and two footmen standing at attention in the dining room didn't notice she was blushing up to the roots of her hair. Down to her toes as well, she imagined. "You must be tired then."

"Strangely, I'm not. I'm quite revitalized, actually." Another sip. A small, secretive smile, which she dared to return with her eyes if not her mouth.

It wasn't fair that he should be so handsome, even after a rousing night of little sleep. Or that he should be making innuendoes regarding what had transpired between them. He had promised only their nights would be different, although it wasn't his fault she couldn't stop thinking about what had passed between them, continued to experience the wondrous sensations coursing through her as though they were once again engaged in the forbidden.

"What is on today's agenda?" he asked.

A kiss in your library, a caress in my office. Perhaps a taking of me on your desk or my taking of you against a bookcase. But his voice was serious with no hint of wickedness reflected in it. She cleared her throat. "I thought you might wish to see how your brother is doing, ensure he has no questions or problems with the manufacture of the clocks."

"Splendid idea, although I don't expect him to be available at my beck and call. Why don't you send a missive to invite him here for dinner tomorrow evening? If that doesn't suit him, ask him when a better time would be. What other matters do we need to address?"

"I thought to call on the two ladies who were not at last night's ball."

"Do you not agree with my mother's assessment that a natural habitat would serve you better?"

"They are not creatures in a zoo."

"Still, I've met them before, would recognize them on sight. I propose we take a turn about Hyde Park during the fashionable hour."

"You usually ride your gelding, and I'm not an accomplished horsewoman."

"We'll take the open carriage. I assume you have a bonnet or parasol for such an outing."

"Do I strike you as the parasol sort?"

A corner of his mouth lifted and his eyes warmed. "No, you don't, to be honest. I suspect you forbid the sun to shine on you and give you freckles."

She liked when his eyes sparkled with teasing. "Would that I could. I do have a bonnet."

"Splendid. See that the carriage is readied for us at the appropriate time."

"Yes, Your Grace."

"And see if there is another affair we should attend, for research purposes, of course."

"I shall look over the invitations recently received."

"Very good." He picked up his newspaper.

She lifted and unfolded hers, although making sense of any of the words seemed a challenge this morning, because even though her gaze was traveling over the print, her attention and focus were on him. While she'd always been aware of him sitting beside her, as his fingers closed around the china cup, she now knew how they felt closing over her breast. When his lips touched the rim of the cup, she recalled their warmth and softness as he'd touched her intimately. The coffee would travel over his tongue just as her juices had when he had lapped at her. She knew precisely what he looked like beneath the jacket, waistcoat, and shirtsleeves.

When he slid his heated gaze over to her, she suspected he was remembering what she looked like beneath the dark blue. Shame on her, because she wanted to refresh his memory by standing up and attacking buttons, shredding the serviceable cloth until it was no more, until he was able to once again feast upon the sight of her.

She'd always known she possessed a wanton side that had allowed her to do things she ought not, but she'd tamed it, subdued it, shackled it— until last night, until him, until it was roaring with triumph at its freedom, and she was battling mightily to force it back into submission since they were not alone. It would not do for the servants to suspect a change had occurred in her relationship with the duke. She picked up her napkin and daintily tapped it against her lips, striving to give the appearance of being civilized when at the moment her desires bordered on the barbaric. "I should get started with my day."

"You haven't eaten much. Perhaps you have an appetite for other things." His smoldering gaze told her he knew exactly what her appetite craved. "If you prefer something else, we could send word to Cook and have her prepare it."

Oh, the wicked man, as though a poached egg rather than buttered ones would squelch the embers that were threatening to fully ignite. Did he want her to admit, here in front of staff, that the duke was what she wished to nibble on? She had decided last night would be it for them. Just the once. To know what it was like to be in his arms. Now she knew herself for the liar she was. The night couldn't arrive soon enough.

"I think I drank too much champagne at the ball last night. My digestion is a bit out of sorts."

He sobered immediately and leaned toward her. "Should I send for my physician?"

At his alarm, his caring, she smiled softly. "I'm certain the distraction of working in my office shall be sufficient to set me back to rights." *To remind me of my true purpose in this household.*

"I'll escort you to your office. Keating, have fresh tea made and delivered to Miss Pettypeace."

"Yes, Your Grace."

Kingsland was out of his chair and assisting her before she'd had a chance to even shove back her chair. He didn't offer his arm—that might have clued the staff in to a change in their relationship—but clamped his hands behind his back as he walked with her from the room.

"Rest easy. I'm not ill," she told him once they were traversing the corridor.

"I suspect what ails you does me as well."

She glanced up to find him studiously watching her. "What would that be?"

"Discovering the urges I thought would be assuaged by one night have not quieted in the least. I find I want all the more."

"Is that not always the case?"

"No, Penelope, it is not." His brow furrowed. "Such a large name for so small a creature. Yet Penny seems too frivolous for you."

"Some friends call me *Penn*."

"Would you consider me a friend?"

She considered him a lover. And he was correct. One night was not enough. "Perhaps during late hours, when only the wicked are awake."

His smile was one of triumph and knowledge. "Quite right."

They entered the hallway housing his library and her newly appointed office. The footman opened the library door and then crossed over to do the same with the entrance leading into her office.

"I have too many damned servants," Kingsland muttered.

"You're a duke. You're supposed to have too many servants."

"But they keep me on my best behavior, when I'd rather they didn't." They stopped outside the room where they'd shared brandy, and she couldn't help but believe that one night had served as the impetus for matters changing between them. "I'll see you at luncheon. We can discuss your progress."

Usually, she had a tray brought to her office and worked while she ate, but she wasn't willing to turn away an invitation—more of a command—to be in his company. "I look forward to it."

Feeling his eyes boring into her back as she walked away, she—who had never swung her hips when walking—was terribly tempted to do just that in a rather undignified manner to signal she was aware of his watching. Heat was suffusing her face by the time she was settled at her desk. Perhaps she was imagining everything: the innuendoes, the heated glances, the interest, the desire.

But he had admitted to the urges. She would definitely be crossing over to his bedchamber tonight.

Reaching for the large rosewood tray where a footman placed the morning's post as well as any invitations delivered by hand to the residence, Penelope decided she would start by finding an event she could attend with the duke. A dinner, perhaps, or a recital.

She took the vellum envelope resting on the top of the stack. Odd that it wasn't addressed, but then, it had no doubt been delivered by someone's footman. Still, the name of the person for whom it was intended was usually scrawled across. Using her gold letter knife, she efficiently slit the envelope and withdrew the folded paper.

Opening it, she stared at the oddest thing she'd ever seen. Someone had cut words from newsprint and apparently glued them to the parchment. Then the message struck her, sending a chill skittering along her spine.

I know what you did.
My silence will come at a cost.
Prepare to pay.

KING BEGAN EACH morning studying his investments, determining which were a waste and needed to be gotten rid of, which were worth keeping and warranted further investing, and what new ones had come to his attention that might be worth taking a risk on. But at the moment, sitting at his desk, he seemed incapable of nudging his mind away from memories of last night, of Penelope Pettypeace in his bed, beneath his body, moving enthusiastically in tandem with him.

It wasn't that memories of encounters with other women didn't often linger, but with her it was more of a savoring, like the tasting of a fine wine that required some time to cherish before indulging in another sip. He definitely wanted another sip of Penelope Pettypeace. And based on the manner in which he'd caught her looking at him with yearning during breakfast, she wanted to be sipped. Leisurely. Methodically. Enticingly.

Oh, his ever-efficient secretary had certainly been there, striving to appear unaffected by what had transpired between them, but she'd never blushed at the breakfast table. However, this morning she'd been all blushes. More than once he'd cursed the dark blue that hid her shoulders and chest, along with the upper swells of her breasts, from him. He'd have liked to see the pink traveling over that skin.

What a fool he'd been to think she wouldn't pour all of herself into lovemaking, just as she did every task he gave her. All these women she was considering as his duchess—he doubted a one would be more suited to him than she was.

It wasn't unheard of for a duke to marry a commoner. Thornley had married a tavern owner with no pedigree whatsoever. But King cared too much for Pettypeace to inflict upon her what was to come: a cold husband who could not risk his passions taking hold or jealousy rearing its ugly head.

That was the reason he'd placed an advert, the

reason he'd taken such an impersonal approach to securing a duchess: he needed a woman who would be content with the title if not the man. Someone who would never come to love him because he'd never give her any reason to.

Marry a woman and gain his heir and his spare. Then grant her freedom from him. No emotional attachments. No fear of having his temper unleashed, no worries of her ever discovering the unconscionable actions he'd taken.

The door to the library opened and closed. Pettypeace was marching toward him, concern mirrored in her features. How was it that he knew her so well, knew the meaning of every nuanced expression? He came to his feet. "What's the trouble?"

She staggered to a stop before his desk. "I was in the process of going through the post and invitations when I ran across this. It is the strangest missive and has me worried."

He took the paper she extended and read the words that had been clipped and arranged in an ominous message. His neck tightened as though a noose had been placed around it. It took everything within him not to ball it up, build a fire in the hearth, and burn it to ashes. "The envelope?"

She pulled it from her pocket. "Completely blank. It had to have been delivered. A servant must have placed it in my correspondence box."

He gave a nod. "I'll see to the matter." Although he didn't know where to begin, with so few clues. He couldn't risk hiring his usual sleuths and having them discover what he'd done. It would make him too vulnerable by placing those he'd trusted in the position of having to betray him or they might be lured into following the path of this blighter and extorting him.

"What does it mean?"

"It's not important."

"It's so unimportant as to cause all the blood to drain from your face? This person believes you have a secret worthy of blackmail. Hugh, what have you done?"

He did wish she hadn't used his name, because it indicated she was viewing him as more of a man than a title. It was much easier to deal with the entire matter, with the consequences, from the perspective of his title rather than himself.

"Let it go." He did ball up the offending parchment then, tossed it into the rubbish bin, and strode over to the window. He was aware of the hushed footsteps on the thick carpeting as she joined him, inhaled her comforting jasmine fragrance, and felt her steady—damn it, trusting—gaze on him.

"You're being threatened, and based on your reaction, this threat carries some merit," she said softly.

He clenched his back teeth until they ached. He'd said all he intended on the matter. If he held his silence, she would leave.

"Let me help you."

"It doesn't concern you." He felt a tiny shimmy in the air as though the words had struck her like a physical blow. There. He could be as cruel as his father when he needed to be. With tears streaming down her face, she'd run now, out of his office, out of his residence, possibly out of his life.

Only she didn't. She placed her hand on his shoulder. How could he forget this was Pettypeace? She ran from nothing, had stared down ruffians in this very room. He wanted to turn into her and have her wrap her arms around him.

"Did you really think what passed between us last night was not going to change things between us?" she asked quietly. "Whatever your secrets, whatever you've done, it can't be worse than what I'm imagining. Yet here I remain and will continue to do so, ever your loyal servant . . . your devoted . . . friend."

Slamming his eyes closed, he bowed his head. "It is so much worse than whatever you are imagining. Please, Penelope, leave me to it."

"I have stood by your side for eight years. Why would I abandon you when I can see how badly you need someone to be here for you? Who else is there, Hugh?"

Only you echoed through his mind, through his heart, through his soul. Was there a greater fool than he in all of Britain? She admired him, respected him. That would all change. Taking a shuddering breath of surrender, he opened his eyes and dared to meet her gaze. "I stole the titles from my father."

Her delicate brow pleated; her green eyes reflected confusion. "How can you steal what was yours by right at birth?"

Another ragged breath before forcing out the words. "They become mine only after he draws his last breath, and he has yet to do that."

CHAPTER 15

$\mathcal{P}$ETTYPEACE STARED WITH confusion at him. "He's not dead?"

"No."

"Then where is he?"

"I had him locked away and declared him dead."

She rubbed her arms as though to warm herself, as though a frigid wind had whipped through and chilled her to the bone. "I see."

He very much doubted that.

"I need a drink." She strode over to the marble sideboard and splashed scotch into two glasses. Returning, she handed him one. "Sit down and tell me everything."

After all this time, he shouldn't be surprised she always faced matters squarely. No accusations, no voiced judgments. But she wanted answers, and after what had transpired between them last night, she deserved them. Hell, she deserved them because of her loyalty all these years. He chose

two chairs by the window so the morning sunlight could warm them. He hardly knew where to
begin.

"I told you how he punished Lawrence, how I
came to have my scars, what he intended for my
mother. He was a cruel man, Penelope. I was always left with the impression he enjoyed being
cruel. When I was nineteen, I'd had enough. I convinced him I wanted to go on a hunting trip to
Scotland with him. Just the two of us. I'd planned
to kill him there, claim it as a shooting accident,
but in the end, I didn't have it in me."

With gentle fingers, she brushed off his brow
the wayward locks he'd never been able to tame.
"Of course you didn't."

Her faith in him made him feel that something
inside his chest was shattering. Perhaps it was the
ice surrounding his heart. It hurt, and yet at the
same time it was as refreshing as spring arriving,
filled with promise. "Instead, I dragged him to a
small and extremely private asylum."

"That doesn't sound like something you could
have done in a very clandestine manner. There
must have been witnesses aplenty."

"You'd be surprised what a desperate man can
accomplish when he sets his mind to it. Although
I must confess, I was terrified the entire time that I
would be caught." He took a sip of the scotch. "We
have a small hunting lodge in Scotland. Minimal
staff. We went there. He liked to do his stalking
in the early hours, just as daylight crept over the
hills. He'd sighted the stag he wanted and was so
focused on lining up his shot that he didn't hear

me approach. I jabbed the barrel of my rifle against his skull and felled him. I was afraid I'd hit him so hard that I had managed to kill him. I decided then and there to confess and go to the gallows without a fuss, knowing Mother and Lawrence would be forever safe."

Threading her fingers through his, she squeezed. "And you claim to have no heart."

He gave her a wry grin. "Perhaps when I was younger I did. But as fate would have it, I'd only served to knock him out cold."

"How did you get him to the asylum?"

"You know me, Penelope. I do nothing without planning. Aware I might have second thoughts about killing him, I'd researched an asylum located a little over an hour away from our lodge. I'd brought a sleeping tonic with me and poured it down his throat, bound him up with rope I'd packed in a satchel I carried with me when hunting, and covered him with brush. Then I hiked to the nearby village to let a wagon and horses. People knew me, of course. But no one questions why the son of a duke does what he does. I returned to where my father was, hauled him into the wagon, and drove him to the asylum."

"So perhaps after all this time someone there decided to take advantage of you."

He shook his head. "They don't know who he is. I gave him and myself false names, told those in charge that he believed himself to be the Duke of Kingsland. Assured them he was not. I go there every year and pay them, in currency, not a bank draft."

"Does your mother or Lord Lawrence know?"

Gazing into her eyes was a balm to his guilty conscience that had ravaged him for years. "No. I claimed the hunting accident I'd originally intended as an explanation for his demise. On the way back from the asylum, I passed a village I'd never before visited and purchased a casket. I filled it with brambles and branches and rocks I found along the way to give it weight. Nailed it shut. I told them he'd tripped, which had caused the rifle to fire accidentally, and the angle of the shot had decimated his face, head. The casket was never opened. I thought the family physician or some official might require a look in order to claim him dead . . . but no one doubted my word. Until a few minutes ago no one knew except me." Strange how the burden of it somehow seemed lighter. "For fifteen years, I thought I'd completely gotten away with it. I need to speak with the staff, determine who brought the envelope."

"I should do it; otherwise, they'll view the whole affair as being more important than they should."

"I don't want to bring you into this, Pettypeace."

"Too late. I became involved as soon as the letter arrived on my desk."

She spoke with her usual aplomb. Nothing ever unsettled her. He thought of the young ladies on her list. How many would swoon? How many would weep? How many would be horrified? "This afternoon, I may need to leave for Scotland, rather than going to Hyde Park."

He wanted to ensure his father was where he'd been left, that it wasn't the eighth duke intent on creating havoc who was responsible for the letter. It was inconceivable that it would be him, but neither could King envision it being anyone else. He'd been damned careful over the years.

"Completely understandable."

"Come with me." The words were out before he'd given them much thought. Any journey into Scotland always took him to a dark place, but if she was with him, he'd be carrying sunlight into the black corners of his soul.

Her face softened, and he wondered if she understood the magnitude of what he was asking. "I would be honored to accompany you on this journey."

The relief swamping him should have served as a warning that where she was concerned, he was in trouble.

"MR. KEATING, PLEASE have the staff gather in their dining hall as I need to have a word."

The advantage to being the duke's secretary was that when Penelope placed a request, it was treated like an order. Within five minutes, she was counting heads in the room where the servants took their meals. Since she was the one who saw them paid each week, she knew exactly how many were employed and was satisfied when the tally matched.

She did have to stand on a fruit crate that Harry always provided when she needed to address the crowd, but she'd become quite skilled at throwing out her voice with authority, so her diminutive size didn't undermine her. "Thank you all for gathering promptly. This morning as I was going through the duke's correspondence, I ran across a letter that was not addressed, nor did it have any markings to indicate where it might have been posted, leaving me to believe it was delivered by hand." She held up the envelope. Although it was plain, nothing special about it, she hoped someone recalled it. "If you received it, please step forward."

No one did. She saw merely blinks and blank stares. "You're not in trouble. You've done nothing you shouldn't. You won't be let go. It's simply that the sender neglected to sign the letter, and I'm therefore at a bit of a loss as to where to deliver the duke's response. I was hoping someone might recall the livery worn or some other tidbit of information regarding the person who brought the missive."

Nothing. "It could have been delivered yesterday evening." After they'd left for the ball, but she might as well have been addressing a room full of statues. "I see. It's rather odd, is it not? All right then, if you should recall receiving it, please do let me know." She stepped off her box.

"Come on, lads and lasses," Mr. Keating suddenly blurted. "One of you had to have taken it at the door. It couldn't have flown in. If you were given a coin, even though the duke doesn't approve of that sort of thing, you can keep it. No harm done. But help Miss Pettypeace out here."

A few shuffles occurred, but she suspected everyone was anxious to get back to their chores. No reason existed not to come forward. Mr. Keating looked rather defeated. "I'm sorry, Miss Pettypeace. It's a mystery to be sure."

"I'm certain it'll sort itself out. When the sender doesn't get a reply, he—or she—is bound to send another. Perhaps the next time more information will be provided."

But he was correct. It was a mystery. And would no doubt not provide the satisfying ending that she'd enjoyed when reading Benedict Trewlove's *Murder at Ten Bells*.

"You worked for the previous duke, did you not, Mr. Keating?"

He studied her thoroughly before saying, "I did indeed."

"What was he like?"

"I do not believe in speaking ill of the dead, Miss Pettypeace, but I did not mourn his passing. Why do you ask?"

"I was simply curious. He'd already passed before I began working here. No one ever mentions him."

"For good reason. He was not worth remembering. I assure you the same will not be said of the present duke."

He had the right of it there. She would remember the present duke as long as she drew breath.

CHAPTER 16

"*W*HAT IS IT you hope to discover in Scotland?" Penelope asked as the coach fairly raced along the road that had taken them out of London. It was not yet noon. She'd been disappointed to report to Kingsland that she'd had no luck determining how the letter had come to be on her desk. The tension in him was palpable as he sat across from her, his attention focused on the passing scenery—or at least it looked that way. In truth, she suspected he was battling his conscience and his worries.

"I want to make certain he's still there."

"Would he not stride into his own residence if he weren't?"

"I don't know what he might do, Pettypeace." Exasperation threaded through each word.

She was firmly back to serving as his secretary. Even as she knew it was for the best, that she needed the reminder of her position in his life, she couldn't forget that for far too long she'd struggled with thinking of him as only her employer, and she dearly wanted to be seen as more than staff, even if only for a short time.

"My apologies, Penelope. I probably shouldn't have brought you with me."

Oh, how she did wish her impractical heart didn't flutter madly every time he addressed her using her given name. But he had the ability to make it sound like he was issuing an endearment. His voice always dropped lower, went softer. While he might consider the name too long, she treasured each syllable he uttered. Striving not to let on how easily he could turn her thoughts to mush, she forced a reassuring smile. "I've seen you worse."

"But things between us were different then."

She almost told him that his coach needed a sideboard of spirits in it, because she was in the mood to toss something back, something to loosen her tongue and his, so they could discuss exactly how different things between them were now. She glanced out the window. "Looks to be day to me. Only the nights are to be different."

He stretched out his long legs, a shiny boot landing on either side of her skirt. "I misjudged, which, as you are well aware, is a rare occurrence for me."

The man could come across as humble and arrogant at the same time. "What exactly did you misjudge?"

"How much you would touch me."

She was rather surprised she didn't combust, considering the heat engulfing her as images raced through her mind of not only how much or how often, but precisely all the various portions of him—nearly every inch—she'd touched. Confusion quickly followed the embarrassment. "Do ladies not generally touch you often when you are fornicating?"

He chuckled softly. "I'm not talking about the physical touch, but something deeper. I haven't the words to explain it. I have always valued you, Pettypeace, but there is this strange undercurrent now. Suddenly you are more precious, Penelope, more important, more a fabric of my life. I have made this journey alone countless times, and yet this morning, I couldn't envision making it without you." He balled his gloved hands on his thighs and looked back out the window.

Reaching across, she cupped her hand over his, felt the tension radiating from that fist to every endpoint, making him brittle, easily shattered if struck with the proper force or the wrong words. "I couldn't envision you going without me."

Turning his hand over, he wrapped his fingers around her wrist, so their palms touched. "We may have mucked things up between us," he said.

"Well, if we were going to do it, I can't think of a more pleasant way to have gone about it."

HE WANTED TO give a slight tug on that hand that fit so perfectly inside his, pull her onto his lap, and take possession of the mouth that so easily uttered words capable of destroying a man. But having tasted all of her last night, if he took so much as a nibble, he was going to want to feast, and the glorious sounds she made would be heard by the coachman and footman. He didn't have it in him to cover her mouth in order to strangle the noise. He enjoyed too much her moans and cries of pleasure.

In spite of his promise, his *belief*, nothing would change between them, everything had. Profoundly and irrevocably, and he was in danger of losing the very best secretary in all of Britain, probably all of the world, because he'd been unable to resist her allure.

But they needed to keep matters between them unemotional and detached. He wasn't capable of giving more than the physical. While she'd gone into this arrangement knowing the limitations, he had little doubt eventually she would want more. All women did. He couldn't give her hope of having it. So he slid his hand out from beneath hers, watched with a sense of loss as she settled back against the squabs.

"Do you think one of the servants might be responsible for the message?" No hint of hurt marred her voice, for which he was grateful. Ever practical, she was bound to understand the necessity of restricting any sort of closeness to the moonlit hours.

"I don't see how."

"Perhaps the driver or footman who accompanies you to Scotland thought to take advantage."

"Once we arrive at the family hunting lodge, I travel alone by horse to my destination. A good bit of the journey through the countryside provides nowhere for anyone to lurk about. I would see anyone following. Knowing the stakes, I've been extremely cautious."

"The staff at the lodge?"

"Unlikely. It's very small. Butler, housekeeper, maid, footman, cook. A man who tends the cattle, one who sees to the hounds and grounds."

"Right then." Reaching into her pocket, she withdrew the familiar leather notebook and a pencil.

He couldn't help but smile. "Do you go anywhere without those?"

She gave him a heated, sensual look that made him feel as though the sun had suddenly risen inside the coach. "To your bedchamber."

Slamming his eyes closed, he ground out a curse. "You're going to be the death of me, Pettypeace."

"You wanted to kiss me a few minutes ago."

"Yes." He opened his eyes to find her watching him with satisfaction and understanding. "And more."

"We are both so terribly disciplined."

"Would you have had it in you to stop me, then?"

She looked down where her finger was stroking the leather, and he thought of her stroking other things. "I'm glad you didn't test me." She lifted her gaze. "He or she—I don't think we should discount the possibility that this person could be a woman—must have thought you might recognize the handwriting. Otherwise why go through all the bother of cutting out words and gluing them to paper? Therefore, we should make a list of everyone whose handwriting would be familiar to you."

Her conclusion made sense, but he didn't like it. Was it someone he knew intimately? How many people could he identify by their handwriting? A ghastly few. "Or they might have feared you'd associate the handwriting with them. You read more of my correspondence than I do."

In spite of the rocking of the coach, she went still, remarkably still. "Yes . . . I suppose I do."

Her gaze drifted to the window and beyond. If he wasn't mistaken, she was taking a journey somewhere that he couldn't follow. It was unlike her not to remain focused. "Penelope?"

She snapped her attention back to him. "Yes, you're correct, of course. We need a thorough, comprehensive list of anyone either of us could identify by their handwriting. Although it's also possible that whoever it was simply wanted to be unnerving."

"That's probably more likely. I can't imagine anyone I know well would threaten me with a missive rather than directly to my face. But let's see who we can come up with. It will at least allow the time to pass more quickly."

WHAT IF SHE had the wrong of it? What if the missive had not been for him but for her?

The thought haunted Penelope as she wrote down each name mentioned—and soon scratched through after they concurred it was ludicrous to even contemplate the person would be responsible for so ominous a message and the method of delivering it. And then it became too dark to write anything at all, which left her with nothing but her tangled imagination spinning one scenario after another like an industrious spider not content with only one web.

They stopped twice to change horses and have a meal at a tavern. Kingsland intended for them to travel through the night so they would arrive at his lodge late tomorrow evening. Now she was beginning to dread they were on a fool's errand, which she'd sent them on because she had not considered all possibilities.

She'd left her past behind, changed her name, moved to a section of London never frequented by those with whom she'd associated when younger. She never received correspondence because no one knew where she was, so it had never occurred to her that the envelope had been meant for her. But what if someone had somehow discovered where she resided, what she was doing? What if she'd been found?

She'd had countless encounters with Kingsland's business associates: solicitors, traders on the London Stock Exchange, business owners, tradesmen, merchants. As well as those with whom she'd personally invested. She was always at risk of someone recognizing her. Recently an abundance of new people had entered her life: those she'd met at the Fair and Spare, those to whom she'd been introduced at the ball. Mr. Bingham at Taylor and Taylor, with whom she'd not felt comfortable. Even new servants within the Kingsland household were suspect. The footman Gerard in particular. The night she'd gone to dinner with the Chessmen, had he stood with Harry and studied her a bit too closely? He certainly had access to her desk, to placing something on it. But then, all the servants did.

She'd become too complacent, thinking herself safe, when the truth was that she was never safe from discovery. She could go entire swaths of time without contemplating what she'd done and how it had caused her mother to disown her. Her mother had preferred to face death to the shame her daughter had brought her. Penelope would run before enduring Kingsland's disappointment in her.

But it was too soon to panic. The letter could have been for Kingsland. He certainly seemed to believe it to be.

"You've been subdued since our last stop," the duke said quietly. "Is something amiss?"

"I can't seem to cease running that letter and the strangeness of it through my mind."

"I believe we've given it enough hours of consideration."

The lanterns hanging outside the coach along with the bit of moon and multitude of stars provided enough light for her to see his massive silhouette crossing the short expanse separating them. "What are you doing?"

"It's night, Penelope, when we are at liberty to allow things to be different between us." His arm came around her and he drew her up against his side, positioning her head so it rested in the nook of his shoulder. "Here, let me provide you with a pillow."

"Do you truly believe I'll be able to sleep?"

"I think you should try. It's amazing how much

sitting in a coach can drain you, and we have another day of it."

As she burrowed her head more cozily against him, she was grateful to be employed as Society didn't require a working woman to have a chaperone. Although she'd never had one because it wasn't expected of the middle class. Another reason it had been foolish to fall in love with him. It would not do at all for a peer to marry a woman who had not been guarded during her youth. On the other hand, she was glad not to have experienced the suffocation of being under someone's watchful gaze.

"Tell me about this club you visited."

She couldn't stop herself from smiling. "People aren't supposed to talk about it."

"People aren't supposed to speak about the people who frequent it. That's not the same as not talking about what transpires within those walls."

"You seem to know an awful lot about it."

"I should. The woman I selected to court last year married the man who owns it." She'd known that, of course. "I stopped by one night but wasn't allowed to see much beyond the foyer. Is it as scandalous as rumored, with orgies and such?"

"Not that I saw. It was all very tame. Dancing, imbibing, darts." Although she may have discovered something very different if she'd gone to the top floor with Mr. Grenville. "Tell me about the woman you went to see after we had dinner with the Chessmen."

Snuggled against him, she was aware of his stiffening, relaxing, and she wondered if he intended to lie.

"Her name is Margaret. We see each other from time to time . . . when the mood strikes. But nothing happened that night. Nothing has happened between us in a good long while."

The woman was his lover . . . or had been. She wished she hadn't asked, that she didn't now know the truth of where he'd gone. "She is not as convenient as I."

"Nor does she hold my interest as you do." He eased away from her slightly until she could feel his gaze on her, and his warm hand was cradling her face. "Urges, Penelope. When I had them, she satisfied them. When she had them, I did the same for her. That night, I didn't realize they had a specificity to them. I didn't want any woman. I wanted you."

His kiss was perhaps the gentlest touch, caress, encounter she'd ever known. He was encouraging her to long for the nights, to long for those moments when she wasn't Pettypeace. When she wasn't his secretary, but something more. Something he craved. No, not something. Someone. *I didn't want any woman. I wanted you.*

Now she had another task set before her, another condition the woman she selected for him would have to meet: she would have to make him no longer want Penelope. With each passing day, passing hour, the chore of selecting his wife became more unbearable.

But that was for consideration at another time, after this journey reached its end and they were back in London. For now, all she wanted was to get lost in his kiss, lost in him. She breathed him in, a long, deep inhale, as their tongues engaged in an ancient ritual, for surely even the druids had discovered the magic of two mouths fused in passion.

His arms slid under her, around her, and with very little effort, he shifted her until her legs were on the bench and she was partially reclining on her side, pressed up against the squabs, creating enough room so he could sit at the edge of the seat without tumbling to the floor. Facing him, resting up on an elbow, she welcomed the deepening of the kiss. His groan of satisfaction was probably heard by the coachman, and she did not care. Not one whit, one iota.

He trailed his mouth along her cheek to her ear and nipped at her lobe. "I thought the darkness would never come." His voice rasped with his need, with his hunger, and her body responded in kind with a sluicing of heat that threatened to turn her clothing into ash.

She thought of the months to come when the darkness would arrive earlier in the evening, fade away later in the morning, when she'd have more hours with him. More minutes, more seconds.

He slipped his hand beneath her skirt and closed his fingers around her calf. His gloves were gone, and she relished the intimacy of his touch. "The things I want to do to you."

She hoped he could see her smile. "The things I want you to do to me."

"Most ladies I know would be scandalized at the thought of my taking liberties in a moving conveyance."

"Firstly, I'm not a lady. Secondly, I find the notion of you taking liberties anywhere rather tantalizing."

"You couldn't scream."

"I can hold in the cries. I've done it before when traveling through London."

His fingers flexed against her calf while the rest of him went completely still. "Jesus, Penelope, have you seen to your . . . urges in a carriage?"

"In this very one." She could hear his breath sawing in and out of his chest, could feel his eyes boring into her. "Are you shocked?"

"When?" Demanding, insistent.

"The night you abandoned me in order to call on Margaret."

"Because of Bishop, because of that damned wink he gave you?"

Was that a fissure of jealousy in his tone? "No, you daft man, because of you. Because of the way it felt to have you touch my hand. The manner in which you looked at me like you wondered if you'd find a taste of me as satisfying as that of your wine."

Although it was low, drowned out by the horses' hooves pounding the road, his howl was that of a beast calling to its mate. His mouth came down on hers, hard and with purpose, as his hand glided up her leg until it reached the apex between her thighs. His fingers made short work of slipping through the slit in her drawers to nestle within her curls. She wanted his coat gone and his waistcoat and his shirt. But there was hardly room for disrobing, and how would he explain his absence of clothing if a wheel suddenly broke or a horse went lame?

So she settled for cupping his jaw, for circling

her palms over his prickly, thick stubble, realizing she was correct about the night before. He had taken a razor to his face before she knocked on his door.

His fingers parted her curls, parted another set of lips, and began stroking her, drawing forth the sensations that hovered on the surface, all the while keeping his mouth plastered to hers. When she proved herself wrong, when her release came and she couldn't hold back her scream, he held fast, absorbing her cry as her body bucked and shuddered.

Drawing back, he studied her, and she wished for a lantern in order to see him more clearly. "You're so quick to respond."

Because she'd lived on fantasies for a couple of years and now was discovering the reality was far better than she'd foreseen. "I'm a wanton."

His grin flashed in the darkness. "I wasn't complaining, nor was I finding fault with you for knowing what you want, what you deserve."

"You deserve as well. We should see to your pleasure."

He drew her up into the nook of his body and held her close. "I found incredible pleasure in your reaction. It's all I require at the moment."

She burrowed against him. "You're quite the comfortable bed."

"Sleep well, Penelope."

How could she not when she was nestled in the arms of the man she loved?

CHAPTER 17

"WE SHOULD ATTEND the theater together," Kingsland said. "You're bound to see some of the ladies you're considering there. It'll provide you with a chance to observe them in a different atmosphere, give you a clearer picture of their suitability."

Penelope nearly pointed out that he should be the one doing the *considering*, every aspect of it. But the task had the benefit of being with him in differing atmospheres, and she wasn't silly enough to give that up.

Shortly after she'd awoken that morning, gathered up in his arms, they'd stopped at an inn for an hour. He'd secured them rooms so they could wash off the dust of travel and tidy themselves. But they'd somehow ended up in the same room, then the same bath, then the same bed. When they'd entered the dining room to break their fast, she'd feared that everyone could tell she'd been well and truly ravished. When the sun was out, barely above the horizon, but still visible. She fought not to read too much into the encounter. She suspected it had been a temporary escape from all the worry that weighed on him.

When they returned to the coach with its fresh set of horses, he'd taken his position on the squabs opposite her, effectively declaring she was again Pettypeace. It was the most comfortable form of herself. She understood her duties, was adept at navigating her way through her responsibilities and their business arrangement. She kept her heart caged, but at night it was like an imprisoned canary, testing its wings and wanting to bend the bars enough to slip through so it could take flight.

"It might prove helpful if you told me more of what you wanted in a wife. Other than being quiet."

Narrowing his eyes against the sunlight, he looked out on the passing greenery. "I'd rather she not be in love with another."

"But you don't want her to love you."

With a sigh, he shifted over the leather. "Have you ever been in love, Pettypeace?"

"I have, yes."

His jaw tightened. "Did he toss you over?"

He seemed truly offended on her account. "He never knew. I never told him. No good would have come of confessing my feelings."

"Unrequited love. The worst kind."

"I think it would have been worse to have never felt it, to have never known . . ." With a shake of her head, she let her voice trail off. How could she tell him that it was so much better to have loved him than not, especially when he was unaware of how deeply her feelings for him ran?

He crossed his arms over his chest. "What did you experience? How did you know you loved him?"

"Have you never loved?"

"I've told you before that I have no heart. I do believe having one is a requirement. What made you love him? His handsomeness, his physique, the color of his eyes?"

"He could have been an ogre and that wouldn't have mattered. I liked the way he treated me, valued my opinion, and viewed me as an equal, even when Society didn't. I loved him because he didn't measure my worth based on my features, my curves, or the shade of my eyes."

She might have said all that with a bit more vehemence than was expected—nay, allowed—when a secretary spoke to a duke. He didn't respond except to study her as though she'd suddenly become a puzzle he couldn't decipher. A flexing of his gloved hand followed, then a tugging on the leather. "You didn't marry him."

"No, he married another." Or would before long. He would marry the woman she chose for him.

"Someone you fancied before you came into my employ." Statement, not question.

"I don't know why we're discussing this."

"I've kept you too busy for any sort of social life, so it would have had to have been. So, you were, what? Sixteen, seventeen, eighteen, when you thought you were in love?"

"I didn't *think* it. I knew it." Let him believe she'd been a child instead of a woman. She certainly didn't want him to guess he was the love of her life, didn't want to see regret in his eyes because he couldn't love her back. "Besides, those girls on my list . . . how many years do you think they have? Some are barely out of the classroom."

"Don't select one of them. I want a wife with some worldliness to her."

The man was so deuced irritating. "Do you think you might give me a complete list of your requirements instead of doling them out like a miser his pennies?"

He grinned. He actually grinned. "I like the fire you exhibit when you're cross."

"I'm not cross." Although grinding out the words probably disproved her claim. "I'm merely frustrated. I'm striving to find the perfect woman—"

"There is no perfect woman, Pettypeace."

"I want you to be happy with her. I don't want her to make a fool of you like the last one. I want her to be what you need. And, yes, I want you to come to love her. A life without love is . . . even if it doesn't last, even if it's only for a short while . . . to find joy in the giving of yourself, to look forward to the day because that person will be part of it. To share your thoughts and not have them judged. To be able to disagree and know the person will listen to your argument and not think less of you for making it. To feel you're better than you were before that person came into your life. And to weep when they no longer are."

"Did you weep over your lost love?"

She would, she would indeed. She smiled sadly. "Buckets."

"It sounds devastating, and yet you wish it upon me."

"I haven't the words to explain it adequately. While I had him, while he was in my life, what I felt was like sustenance to my soul. The sun, the moon, and the stars were all inside me." She sighed and rolled her eyes with embarrassment. "And now I sound like a blithering idiot. It's so very complicated and impossible to describe. Poets try, but they can only capture portions of it. It's too big, too grand, to be reduced to what we mere mortals can clarify." She removed her notebook from her pocket. "Let's start from the beginning, shall we? You want a worldly woman who does not speak. What else do you require?"

LOVE. UNTIL THAT moment he'd thought he'd be content without it, but to hear her wax on so passionately about it made him yearn to experience that depth of caring. He felt rather sorry for the chap she'd loved because the poor bugger had never known. What an incredible thing it would be to have her regard.

But how did one know if he was in love? That's what he'd been asking her, the answer he'd been seeking. Ever since he'd tucked those stray strands behind her ear that long-ago morning when they met with Lancaster, his feelings toward her had become perplexing. In spite of the

Society matrons' raised eyebrows, it had seemed right to waltz with her. Having her in his bed-chamber had felt as though she was where she belonged. Making love to her—when had he ever made love to a woman? He had sex. Good, rous-ing sex, and yet he couldn't deny that with her, it had been more than fornicating. Then to make matters even more bewildering, he hadn't wanted to take this journey without her.

What else do you require? You hovered on the tip of his tongue, but he couldn't give voice to it when he didn't understand what had prompted it.

Odd that he'd given more thought to what he re-quired in a secretary than what he did in a wife. He tried to envision his future duchess sitting across from him now as he'd once imagined she might be: prim, proper, hands folded on her lap, gaze turned toward the passing countryside, and quiet. Not ut-tering a word. Not disturbing his concentration as he pondered business dealings.

Certainly not giving him a pointed and chal-lenging glower, her green eyes practically shoot-ing daggers at him, demanding he provide what she asked. He knew men who mumbled in his presence, shuffled their feet about, all the while refusing to meet his gaze. But he had never intimi-dated her.

Over the years, especially of late, their relation-ship had shifted into something more, something he was only just recognizing, couldn't quite place. Friendship, perhaps. Yes, that was it. Although it differed slightly from what he experienced with the Chessmen. Of course it did. She was a woman, after all. He certainly never yearned to plant his mouth on Bishop's and turn a glare into smoldering embers. "I would want in a wife what you want in a husband."

"As I have no plans to ever take a husband and have given it no thought, that is hardly helpful."

"What about this fellow you loved?"

"We were never going to marry. I knew that from the beginning, so I didn't bother to consider him in the role. Besides, as I've already explained, I don't want a husband."

"And I don't want a wife."

"Then why the hunt? Why now?"

"I need an heir. And I'm not getting any younger. I'm certain you're a better judge of women than I, Pettypeace. Trust your instincts."

She tapped her pencil against the notebook. "We have miles to travel yet. Ruminate on what you want. I stand ready to write down your requirements."

Perhaps he didn't require a quiet wife, but rather one who would speak her mind, would challenge him.

She began scrawling—probably all the reasons she was miffed at him. Although perhaps she was noting all the requirements that she thought he should request. No, she would have done that before she ever began opening the missives the ladies of London had sent. She would, of course, select someone she could accept as mistress of his household. Someone amiable. Someone who wouldn't mind that his secretary didn't sleep in the servants' quarters.

Except any duchess would mind. Once he married, Penelope certainly couldn't traipse across the hallway to his chamber. Their intimate association would come to a halt. Although they hadn't addressed the issue specifically, he knew she was not the sort to dally with a married man. Nor was he one to be unfaithful to his wife.

He would have his duchess and Penelope would have . . . someone else. That she didn't already was a testament to her devotion to her work. But she possessed too much passion and fire, was too intelligent, too competent, too bold for some man not to pursue. He was surprised a gentleman hadn't already claimed her. Certainly, several had noticed her at the ball, had been intrigued enough to risk censure by dancing with a duke's secretary. And if none of them called on her, she would go to that damned club and make further acquaintances there. The strength of the jealousy that tore through him took him aback. It was far stronger than what he'd experienced at the ball, and he could no longer deny what it was. He could not bear the thought of her with another, and yet it was selfish of him not to want her to find a man who could appreciate her as she deserved. She might not wish to marry, but that did not mean she had to spend her life alone. She could take a lover and still maintain her independence.

Just as things had changed between them two nights ago, they would change when he signed the registry at the church. She would return to the servants' quarters. They would return to all business. Until some gent swept her off her feet, and he became her focus, became more important to her than the work that presently brought her satisfaction.

He regretted posting the damned advert so quickly after Lady Kathryn had rejected his proposal. But he hadn't wanted to be viewed as the to-be-pitied, cast-aside duke. He cursed his bloody pride. He wanted another year without courtship, without a wife. Another year with Penelope.

But he knew with a conviction that shattered his peace, more than the strange letter had, that the night of his ball would be the last he had with her. Afterward, she would be only his secretary and no longer his lover. He intended to make the most of their time together.

CHAPTER 18

$\mathcal{I}$T WAS LATE into the night, full dark, by the time they reached the hunting lodge. She'd visited his other estates, properties, and residences, but not this one, and a chill swept through her as she stood in the foyer while the doddering butler, awoken from slumber, began lighting candles and lamps. Although Kingsland had told her that he didn't suspect these servants of being responsible for the missive, she had remained doubtful, but based on the slight trembling in the older man's fingers, she didn't see how he could cut out words in the newspaper and glue them into place without making a mess of the task.

"My apologies for the disarray, Your Grace, but we weren't expecting you until November. I'll wake Mrs. Badmore and have her prepare you a meal."

"Not necessary, Spittals. We dined before arriving. A bath would be welcome, however."

"I'll set Johnny to it straightaway."

A faint light appeared at the top of the stairs, and she assumed the maid had made her way there using the back staircase and was readying the rooms. The footman, Harry, who'd traveled with them and had been standing just inside the doorway holding their bags, started up.

When she thought of a lodge, she imagined something considerably smaller than a four-story stone dwelling that, if she had to guess, housed just fewer than fifty rooms. Holding an oil lamp, Kingsland approached and placed a hand on the small of her back.

"Shall we go up?"

She wanted to explore but was also incredibly weary from the worry and the travel, so she simply nodded, taking comfort in his steady hand guiding her up the stairs. The shadows wavered and dispersed in front of them, revealing paintings of hunts, men standing with shotguns aimed at birds in flight, men astride horses galloping while foxes scurried.

"Are those images of hunts held here?" she asked.

"No, just something found or commissioned to put on the wall."

"No family portraits?"

"Maybe one or two, but we seldom stayed for long. It's not particularly cozy, as you'll find."

They reached the landing, and a long hallway stretched before them. A dozen doors, only two open. He directed her through one and into a bedchamber that seemed chillier than it should. Perhaps it was the whistling of the wind or the fur on the bed or its matching counterpart on the floor. A fire was crackling on the hearth, but it failed to generate much heat. Moving away from him, nearer to the large stone fireplace, she rubbed her arms.

"We'll have the maid assist you in readying for bed."

With a smile, she glanced over at him. "I don't require assistance, have never had a lady's maid. My clothing is simple, designed for ease in putting on and removing."

He leaned against the post at the foot of the bed. "I suppose I could assist you."

"That might lead to a bit of naughtiness."

"Would you mind?"

No, absolutely not, never. But instead of voicing the words, she simply shook her head. He took a step toward her—

The London footman appeared in the doorway. He didn't make a sound, but Kingsland must have felt his presence, because he immediately stopped and glanced over his shoulder.

"We have the tub for Miss Pettypeace," Harry said.

He gave her a small nod. "I'll leave you to enjoy your bath." He strode past Harry and another footman, possibly Johnny, as they lugged in the copper tub.

After they set it before the fire, they left to begin hauling up the water. Penelope walked to the mullioned window and gazed out. She wondered if they might have some time to see the area. Probably not. They were here for a purpose and when that purpose was done, they needed to return to London.

THE FOLLOWING MORNING, King was already seated at the circular table in the small dining room when Pettypeace strolled in, wearing her dark blue frock and looking far more at ease than she had last night when she'd knocked on his door.

"The wind shrieking beyond the window is a bit unsettling," she'd said.

"My father always told me it was the ghosts of our ancestors seeking attention, even though he was the one who purchased the residence, so I've no idea how the spirits of our ancestors found their way here."

Then he'd pulled her into his chamber and done all in his power to ensure her cries of pleasure drowned out the screeching that had put his brave Penelope on edge. But then, something about this place had always seemed more fitting to the dead rather than the living.

Now he rose to his feet. "Good morning, Penelope."

Staggering to a stop, she looked past him to the windows, and he supposed she was confused by his brazenly not calling her Pettypeace, signaling her role as secretary, as he normally would when they were in London. "Is the sun not out?"

"It is, but—" How to explain that it wasn't his secretary he needed at the moment, but a friend, someone who was more than a friend?

As he was searching for the words, she wandered to the chair beside him and smiled softly. "I know. Who we are in London doesn't seem to fit here, at least not at this precise minute."

"I couldn't have said it better myself." He pulled out the chair for her. After they were seated, she poured herself some tea and added a splash to his cup to rewarm it. The footman left to retrieve her plate. "Things are run rather simply here," King said, "except for the few times when we had guests during stalking season."

"Do you enjoy hunting?"

"Not really, no. It's part of the reason I have so few staff to see after the place. Probably should sell it. Will eventually." When he had no reason to return to this part of Scotland with its morbid memories—although now he had memories of her here, and the others seemed to carry less weight.

The footman returned and placed a plate with buttered eggs, tomato, toast, and ham in front of her. She reached for her fork. "What time will we be going out today?"

She said it so quietly, so calmly, that it took him a minute to realize she was referring to the journey to the madhouse. "I'll be leaving as soon as I've finished eating."

"I'll be ready."

"I was planning to go alone."

"Then what is my purpose in being here?"

To be here. It was that simple, that complex, and that ludicrous. When had he ever needed to have someone with him for anything? But he had no plans to take her to the asylum, which would no doubt haunt her and give her nightmares. He always came away feeling as though he'd left a bit of his soul within those walls.

"I would think it would be helpful to have someone about to take notes," she continued. "I intend to accompany you."

"Then we'll take the curricle."

Her smile of triumph stole his breath. He needed to tell her to add to his list of requirements a woman whose smile made him feel as though he'd conquered the world.

"I'll ask the cook to prepare a small basket in case we decide to stop and picnic somewhere along the way," she said.

He wasn't surprised she was already comfortable enough to begin making requests of the servants. Would his wife appreciate her taking charge of things? Pettypeace was a natural at it, had been so from the beginning. She was right not to want to marry. Most men desired a demure mate, not a strong, independent one. An idiot might strive to tame her, to put her under his thumb. "Splendid notion."

It would also give the servants something to speculate over, to believe they were simply going for a ride and a picnic. Not that any of them would dare ask where they were going or the reason for their leaving, but doing something so natural as heading out in the curricle with a picnic basket in hand would make it appear that they weren't hiding anything other than possibly a personal relationship. In any case, the gossip wouldn't make it back to London, so no harm would come of the natter.

An hour later, reins in hand, he was urging a

pair of matching grays to travel at a fast clip along the narrow road.

"It's so beautiful here, with the heather in bloom," Penelope said.

More of it would coat the land in another month, not that he'd ever paid any attention to it, not that he'd taken the time to appreciate the lakes and rolling hills dotted with sheep in the distance. He'd hated coming here because with his arrival came the memories of how he'd placed his father in the grave before he was dead. At nineteen, he'd been terrified that what he'd done had been written on his face, that family, friends, and strangers would take one look at him and claim him a thief.

In response, he'd separated himself as much as possible from Society, had buried himself in shoring up the estates so the next in line would have no need for worry if King found himself stripped of his titles and standing on a scaffold.

But looking about him now, perhaps he had judged the area too harshly because of the memories. Pettypeace had always managed to make him view things differently. It was one of the reasons he valued her opinion. She brought a different perspective to matters. And she was correct that leaving her at the lodge would have served no purpose, whereas having her with him might reap rewards. She might notice things he hadn't: a dodgy-appearing staff member or someone with guilt written all over them. On some matters, she was much more observant and perceptive than he. He focused on the large items, while she concentrated on the small.

He turned down a narrow lane. At the end of it was a wrought-iron fence, the gate left open destroying the notion that the enclosure served any real purpose.

"They're not trying to keep them in, are they?" she mused.

"They lock it at night when they aren't watching the residents as closely."

Looming ahead was the dark brick monstrosity with spires poking the sky.

"It's rather ominous looking, is it not?" she asked.

"I wouldn't want to live here."

"How did you ever find it?"

"I overheard my father threatening to have my mother committed to Greythorne Manor. Afterward I made a few inquiries."

"Ironic as well as justifiable that he should be here."

"I thought so at the time."

She settled her hand comfortingly on his arm, and he wondered if an occasion would come when he wouldn't crave her touch. "You did what needed to be done to ensure life was more pleasant for others."

"I tell myself that every time I come here. But it always rings hollow. Yet there was no way to undo it without grave consequences once it was done." He drew the horses to a halt, leapt from the chaise, and secured them, before coming around to assist her in disembarking.

"You'd think they'd have someone seeing to arrivals, but I suppose they aren't expecting visitors."

"I have never seen anyone other than staff and

patients." The isolation of the place had appealed to him. Nothing and no one about for miles. It had seemed secure. Or at least he'd thought so fifteen years ago when emotions had driven him to be reckless. It was only later that he'd realized he had limited not only his father's chances for escape but his as well. He'd set his course without thinking everything through. Since that time, he'd never made any decision in haste, had learned to consider every angle.

She tucked her hand within the crook of his elbow as they ascended the steps to the large oaken door. It seemed the sort of place where hinges should creak, but they remained silent as he released the latch and shoved on the heavy wood.

A woman a little younger than his mother popped up from behind a desk in the massive foyer. "Mr. Wilson, sir, welcome to Greythorne. I'll fetch Dr. Anderson." She scurried off and disappeared around a corner.

If Penelope was bothered by the moans and cries echoing from unseen rooms, she gave no indication but merely glanced around at the two sets of sweeping stairs and the high windows. He wondered if the shrieks had brought true madness to his father.

"It's not the most welcoming of places," she said in a hushed tone that the atmosphere required.

"No, but I've seen the staff interacting kindly with the patients." Although his father's violent tendencies had sometimes required that they handle him less than gently, going so far as to subdue him with the use of a strait waistcoat.

A slender man of short stature came around the corner. The alienist's hair had been raven-black when King had first brought his father here, but now it and his beard were almost completely silver, with only a hint of the shade they'd once been. He didn't think the doctor, extending his hand, was even a dozen years older than himself. "Mr. Wilson, I'm grateful you've paid us a visit."

His grip was firm and strong as he shook King's hand.

"Dr. Anderson, allow me to introduce—"

"Mrs. Wilson," Penelope interrupted with ease and a demure bowing of her head. Although she wore leather gloves that would make it difficult to discern if she wore a wedding ring, she'd slipped her left hand inside her frock pocket, where it was no doubt caressing her beloved journal. He had the right of it. If he ever needed her to lie for him, she had the talent mastered. Pretending to be his wife and not even blushing while doing it.

"Mrs. Wilson, a pleasure." Then his crystal-blue eyes were back on King. "It seems we didn't gather adequate information from you. I had no idea where to write to let you know your father is no longer with us."

King felt as though he'd been dunked in a vat of icy water. "He escaped?"

"No, no. My apologies for not being clearer, but he passed. Not quite a month ago."

If Penelope's hand hadn't closed around his and squeezed reassuringly, he might have reeled back from the unexpected blow of realizing his father was dead. After all this time. He should have felt like rejoicing, but instead he was hit with an un-expected soul-crushing desolation, grief. "How? How did he die?"

His voice sounded far away, seemed to be echo-ing around him as though he stood within the depths of a dark cave.

"His heart. Simply gave out, I'm sorry to say. His erratic behavior and violent outbursts no doubt put a strain on it. He became more agitated, had to be restrained on occasion. His delusions were so ingrained, he was beyond help, to be honest. He claimed to be a duke until the very end."

Of course he had, because he had been.

"It was as I was looking for information on how to contact you that I realized we had none, so we did for him as best we could."

"What did that entail?"

"We laid him to rest in our cemetery at the rear of the garden. Proper services. We will need to col-lect on the casket, I'm afraid."

"Naturally."

"I know this must be a shock, but at least his suffering is over. He's in a far better world now."

King doubted very much that hell was better.

"Would you care to visit his resting place?"

PENELOPE WOULD HAVE let him mourn the previ-ous duke alone if Kingsland had released his hold on her hand. Instead, he tightened it, and so she walked with him and the alienist through a very lovely and peaceful garden until they passed be-neath a pergola covered in fragrant honeysuckle and into a garden of stone. Larger than she expected for a place such as this.

Dr. Anderson guided them to a lengthy mound of dirt. The grass surrounding it had yet to reclaim most of it. The spot was marked with a simple wooden cross, William Wilson carved deeply into it.

"If you wish to have a proper headstone made and sent to us . . . or I could provide you with the name and address of a fellow in a nearby village who would see to the task."

"Thank you," Kingsland said, his voice rougher than it had been a half hour earlier.

"I'll give you some privacy to mourn. When you're ready, come to my office and we'll settle your accounts."

The doctor walked away. Kingsland held still for a minute, two, his dark eyes never lifting, never glancing around, but focused on the place where his father now rested.

"I despised him," he finally grated out. "What he saw as strength, such as bullying people—my mother, my brother, his friends—I saw as weakness." While he didn't say it, she knew Kingsland had been bullied as well. "I told you how he punished Lawrence."

"Yes."

"When I was eighteen, I'd come home from Oxford for Christmas. I'd made an investment and it had paid off. I was so cocky and full of myself. He commanded me to do something—I can't even remember what it was, something trivial—and I told him I was at last a man and couldn't be ordered about. He was adamant that *he ruled* and I would kneel before him and pledge fealty as a demonstration that I understood his power over me. Like he was some medieval king. I refused, believing if I stood my ground, he would respect me as a man and stop with his childishness."

He never looked at her, never blinked, never stopped staring at the mound of dirt as though he could see through it and into the earth.

"But he called for Lawrence. I could see in my brother's eyes that he knew why he'd been summoned. He looked at me and then he stepped right in front of our father, who struck his spare with such force that he fairly flew backward. And I dropped to my knees. One blow and I crumbled."

She fought to hold the tears at bay, not wanting him to see how much his confession ravaged her heart. "One blow and you showed mercy."

"I should have shown it before Lawrence was ever asked to pay the price for my obstinance. But I swore I would never again go to my knees for anyone." He emitted a brittle scoff. "Do you know, when I asked Lady Kathryn to marry me, I did not kneel before her. She took offense and decided it was an indication we should not marry."

"I think it was her love for another that did that."

He shook his head. "Add to your list of my requirements for a duchess a woman who will not insist I go down on a knee for her, because I will not."

"Consider it done."

"You must think me vile and heartless not to shed a solitary tear for this man. The last few times I saw him, he was in a terrifying rage and didn't even seem to know who I was. I think he may have actually gone mad. I suppose I should feel some remorse for the horror of his last few years, but I don't."

"You spared your mother and brother further hurt at his hands. You mustn't forget that. And you took the burden of carrying this secret alone onto your shoulders, so I consider you neither vile nor heartless."

He brought the gloved hand he still held up to his mouth and pressed a kiss against her fingers. "I'm sorry you had to endure all this, but I'm incredibly grateful you're here."

She almost told him that she wouldn't want to be anywhere else except at his side, that wherever he needed her, she would be there. But it seemed too much to confess, too much to admit when on his part nothing deeper existed between them than the satisfaction of urges. "Would you like a few minutes alone?"

His smile was small, sad, regretful. "No, I just want to leave this hell behind."

AFTER HE SORTED things with Dr. Anderson, they went to the nearest village, and Kingsland paid a stonemason to create a simple headstone for William Wilson that, other than his name, showed only his birth and death dates. On the way back to the lodge, they stopped by a babbling stream and laid a quilt over heather. Beneath the boughs of one of the massive trees dotting the area, they ate the meal the cook had prepared for them. Well, mostly

Penelope ate while Kingsland drank a good bit of the wine that had been packed in the basket. "You know I've never driven a curricle," she said lightly.

Raised up on an elbow, his body stretched the length of the quilt, he tore his gaze from the rushing water. "Would you like to?"

"No, but I'm thinking if you get too deep in your cups, I won't have a choice."

"It'll take a good deal more than a bottle of wine to get me drunk." Reaching out, he poured some wine into the glass resting near her knee. "Although you can save me from myself by drinking your share."

She took a sip. If not for the melancholy brought on by their morning visit to Greythorne, it would be a lovely day, even if a few dark clouds threatened rain. This area was so pastoral and peaceful. Not a single person had passed them. No one was about. It became more clear that no soul had ever followed him while he made this journey. "I know today was a bit of a shock."

"In a way, but also expected. I feel a great sense of relief that I am now, legally, the Duke of Kingsland."

Sitting with her legs beneath her, she turned so she could face him more squarely. "I've been thinking about that, about the letter. *My silence will come at a cost. Prepare to pay.* I assume the person wanted to collect money. However, with your father gone, I don't see how he—or she— can prove anything. It would be his or her word against yours, and unless they're royalty, I find it difficult to believe anyone would take their word over yours, a duke. Assuming of course that it was this matter to which they were referring."

"I can't imagine how it could be anything else. Although I don't know how he—or she—would have proven the claim. Either help my father escape and parade him through London or bring someone up here who knew him well enough to identify him."

"Your mother perhaps?"

"It's unlikely she would have traipsed off with a stranger without alerting me—and then I would have put a stop to it. However, if she made the journey, leaving me unaware of it, she would have been stunned by the sight of him but would have quickly deduced a lie was in order. I think she would have claimed him a madman. I was taken aback when you introduced yourself as Mrs. Wilson."

"I thought it would lead to fewer complications if he assumed I was your wife."

"Clever girl. I may have to exercise my husbandly rights this evening."

Warmth suffused her cheeks. She certainly hoped he would. "The point I was coming to is that I think any further worry over that threat is unfounded."

"Unless he brings Dr. Anderson to London and introduces him to me. Then things might get complicated. Anderson will surely discern the truth if he learns my identity. So I don't know that I'm fully out of the woods yet."

"I was a bit surprised you purchased a headstone."

"I needed his place marked because I intend to leave instructions—sealed until my death—for my heir to move him to the family crypt. It's a finer resting place than he deserves, but, well, he was my father."

She felt a tightening in her chest, a knotting in her throat, as tears threatened. "He did not deserve you as a son."

He barked out a dark laugh. "I suspect he spent the past fifteen years thinking the same thing."

She lobbed a piece of bread at him. "I'm serious. You're a good man."

"Not so good that I don't have wicked thoughts." He grabbed her ankle and pulled her toward him. Losing her balance, she fell on her back but didn't try to get up as he was suddenly hovering over her. "How is it that the sight of all these buttons drives me mad with wanting to give each one its freedom, to reveal what is being covered?"

"I'd have thought you'd prefer a gown to my daily attire."

"I'd have thought so, too, but something about you being all tucked away makes you so much more tempting."

She threaded her fingers up into his hair. "Am I tempting?"

"Most certainly."

"No one is about to bother us."

His eyes darkened just before he lifted his gaze and glanced around. "We are quite alone." Lowering his head again, he nipped at the underside of her jaw. "How many shall I undo?"

"All of them."

His deep growl reverberated through him and into her. Then he was watching his fingers as they saw to the task. When the last button escaped its mooring, he spread the material of her bodice wide before dipping down to trail his tongue along the upper swell of her breast. She couldn't stop her sigh as pleasure curled in her belly. "You are so wicked."

"You make me so."

"I doubt that," she said. "You were wicked before me."

"Not outdoors. Not where the gods could watch from the heavens." Slipping a finger beneath her chemise and corset, he pulled the fabric until her breast escaped the restraint. He latched his mouth onto the nipple that was already hard and begging for the relief he could provide.

"I know we can't see anyone, but are we being watched, do you think?" she asked.

"Hmm. The birds, the sheep, and the hares." A splash sounded, and she felt his mouth form a smile against her breast. "Seems the fish are anxious for a look."

"Maybe we should head back to the lodge."

"Not until you scream my name."

She did scream, because the skies suddenly opened up and a deluge rained down. Since he was beside her and not over her, she managed to slip away and scramble to her feet. He grabbed the hem of her frock. "Where are you going?"

"It's raining."

"You're sweet, Penelope, but unlike sugar, you're not going to melt."

She hadn't considered herself *sweet* in years. "I'd have thought you considered me more tart."

He gave her skirts a little tug. "Come back here so I can have another taste in order to properly determine which applies."

Digging her fingers into the material, she jerked it free of his hold. "If you want a taste, you're going to have to catch me."

"Think you I can't?"

His smoldering gaze and the depth of the challenge in his eyes had her doubting she'd make it two steps before he had her back in his grasp. Oh, but she wanted to accept his dare, wanted him coming to her for a change. "I suspect you misjudge my swiftness."

And she'd misjudged his. Damn if he didn't practically vault into the air. With a shriek, she spun on her heel, lifted her skirts, and raced for the tree, barely managing to put it between them. The rain pelted her, and she could feel her hair listing to the side, the strands threatening to break free of the pins holding them in place.

"A little tree isn't going to stop me from getting to you," he yelled as thunder boomed.

A little tree? It was a mighty oak. She saw his shoulder coming around to her left. With his massive shoulders, she was at an advantage, would always know where his attack would come from. With a laugh, she rushed around to the other side of the tree, barely in time as his hand grazed over her elbow. He stopped. So did she. One side of his chest became visible, then disappeared. The other side made an appearance before vanishing. She should run, run for the carriage, not that it would provide any shelter as it wasn't covered. The boughs of the tree stopped some of the rain from reaching her, but still drops trailed down her face, soaked her hair, her clothing.

Seeing his shoulder, she darted in the other direction—

And crashed into his chest, his arms encasing her as his laughter, deep and rich, echoed around her. With a feint he'd fooled her, and she'd fallen for it.

He was grinning brightly with triumph as he pressed her back against the bark. She couldn't stop herself from reaching up and skimming her fingers over his lips. "I love your laugh." *And your smile. And your eyes. And the absolute happiness that is emanating from you at this moment.*

His breathing was as harsh as hers. His smile faded, his gaze becoming more intent. He plowed his hands into her hair, the last of the pins giving way so the wet tresses tumbled down just before his mouth blanketed hers with passion and promise. His low groan reverberated between them, sent pleasure spiraling through her, joy traipsing along closely behind it. He wanted her, needed her. Theirs wasn't a dispassionate coming together. It rivaled the intensity of the storm that pounded the earth and roared through the heavens. The leaves on the tree were abundant enough to protect them from the harshness of the rainfall. Not that it mattered. Her focus was all on him and the manner in which he was deliciously devouring her, exploring her mouth with an eagerness that served to ratchet up her own hunger for him.

She dragged her fingers up the corded muscles of his neck, slipped them beneath the collar of his coat and along his shoulders. Breaking away from her, he shrugged off his coat and tore off his waistcoat. She went to work on the hooks of her corset, loving the way he stilled and watched, as though mesmerized, as though he hadn't already seen what she was on the verge of unveiling. With the stiff material parted, she loosened the ribbons of her chemise and gave freedom to the buttons. Dipping his hands inside the cloth, he cradled her breasts, the heat of his skin chasing off the chill of the breeze fluttering over her that had caused her nipples to pucker all the harder.

Lowering his head, he took one into his mouth and suckled. She moaned low as sensations rippled through her. Perhaps it was the wickedness of doing this where they shouldn't, outside in the open, as though they were wood nymphs, that heightened her pleasure, but she felt mad with desire. Hastily, she managed to cast his neckcloth aside and un-button his shirt, so she had the luxury of waltzing her fingers over his bare flesh. So heated, so hot. He was fire, and she loved it. Loved him. Thought she would never get enough of touching him.

"Hang on to me tightly," he growled, before gath-ering up her skirts, cupping her bottom, and lifting her, until she could look directly into his eyes. She clamped her legs around his waist and clutched her arms around his shoulders. She became aware of movement, and then his cock was sliding into her, inch by glorious inch, stretching her, filling her.

His eyes burned just before he latched his mouth onto hers, kissing her deeply, thoroughly, hungrily. He rode her, she rode him. He pumping, she welcoming and meeting his thrusts, while the insistent rain found its way through the leaves and branches to fall over them.

She had no fear of tumbling, of losing her purchase. He held her securely, increasing the tempo. Breaking free of the kiss, she watched his features shift, grow with furiousness, nearly feral as the pleasure built. The depth of his power, his strength, his command only served to heighten her own enjoyment. Ecstasy cascaded through her, her cries of fulfillment echoing around them as his roar of completion sent the birds into flight. She'd never seen anything as beautiful as him at that moment, had never known such satisfaction. She had no words to describe what had transpired during the storm that had swept through them and around them. They clung to each other as their bodies cooled, their breaths slowed, and their tremors diminished.

. The rain had stopped. Now only an occasional drop landed on an eyelash, a nose, a cheek. She brushed his forelock back from his brow. "I've decided I like Scotland very much."

Laughing, he buried his face in the curve of her neck and pressed a kiss against her damp skin. "I must confess to just now developing a fondness for it myself."

She held him a little tighter. They might not have danced in the rain, but she considered what they had done to have been much more enjoyable.

WITH HIS FOREARM pressed to the mantel, King stared at the flames dancing on the hearth. The rain had returned, necessitating fires be lit to ward off the chill of the dampness. It had also prevented an immediate return to London. Not that he'd minded having another night here with Penelope. For so long, he'd carried the burden of what he'd done with his father, had always felt the imposter. Now he was truly the Duke of Kingsland. And he felt . . . free. Light. As though he was worthy of experiencing joy.

This afternoon, chasing Penelope, having her in the outdoors—

I love your laugh.

He couldn't remember the last time he'd done so with such abandon. Wasn't certain he ever had. Even in his youth, the specter of his father hung over him, and he'd been keenly aware he could easily ignite his father's temper if he was anything other than serious at all times.

He did recall the first time he heard his mother laugh. It was six months after he'd had his father committed. She and Lady Sybil were having tea in the garden, and his mother's laughter had floated into his office through the open terrace doors. Sitting there mesmerized, he had known a depth of hatred for his father that had shaken him to his core—that the man had created an environment that kept such glorious sounds of merriment imprisoned. King had done what he had as a means to protect his mother and Lawrence. But at that moment he'd seen the larger picture, had seen the greater potential for good that his actions had wrought. They were free.

And now at last, so was he.

Hearing the light rap on the doorjamb, he glanced back over his shoulder and smiled at Penelope hovering in the doorway.

"Your door was open."

"I was waiting for you. Come in and shut the door." He picked up the bottle on the table beside his chair, filled the snifter, and set it on the table beside the chair into which she settled, her toes peering out beneath the hem of her nightdress. He dropped into the wingback chair opposite her.

"You look . . . lighter," she said. "I noticed it during dinner."

It had been simple fare, shared by the two of them, in the dining room.

"Only adjusting to finally being whom I've pretended to be for so long."

"You weren't pretending. You embraced the role and made it your own."

"Still, I couldn't quite forget it wasn't yet mine. Now it is. I'm torn between waiting for another missive or hiring someone to discover who sent the first."

Looking to the fire, she took a sip of her brandy. "I think you should wait. Perhaps the person won't have the courage to send another. Or perhaps it was a jest all along."

"Hell of a jest. I don't fancy being threatened." He'd hire a trusted sleuth to get to the bottom of it as soon as they were back in London. He stretched out his legs until his bare feet touched hers. "I always thought I would sell the lodge when the time came, when I no longer had need of it, but now I have memories of you here. And they are so much stronger than what went before."

Her toes skimmed over his. The woman had such tiny feet.

"My father taught me that when you're running from the past, you have to sever all ties to it. I think if you keep the lodge, you run the risk of history haunting you or catching up with you."

"You left everything behind?"

"I thought so, but there is always something we can't control. Who is to say that Dr. Anderson won't someday discover the Duke of Kingsland has a hunting lodge within an hour's ride of his asylum? Perhaps curiosity will get the better of him and he'll pay a visit. In this matter, the greater the risk would not mean the greater the return."

"You're quite right." Rising, he held his hand out to her. "We'll be leaving in the morning. Let's make another memory before we go, shall we?"

As her fingers threaded through his, he wondered if a time would come when he wouldn't crave making one more memory with her.

CHAPTER 19

AFTER THEIR RETURN to London, each morning Penelope approached her desk as though a black adder poised to strike was hidden among the various bits of correspondence stacked and waiting for her attention.

On the third morning it struck.

The blank envelope balanced on top of the heap drew her eye before she'd reached her chair, before she'd pulled the pile forward to sort through it. Instinctively she knew nothing would be written on the other side either, that it had not gone through the post, but had been personally delivered. Or had originated within these walls, created by a staff member who possessed no loyalty.

She didn't bother to sit. Some things were better done standing. While it felt like her heart was quivering with fear inside her suddenly too-tight chest, her hands were steady as she picked up the

envelope and letter knife. The ripping of paper had
never sounded so ominous or loud, grating on her
nerves. She pulled out the parchment, unfolded it,
and stared at the letters cut from newsprint forming the words *Cremorne Gardens tonight. When wickedness reigns.*

She could no longer imagine that the first letter
had indeed been meant for Kingsland. What he had
done could not be considered wicked. Deceitful, but
not wicked. Whereas not a single soul in all of Great
Britain wouldn't condemn her for what she'd done.
There were laws against it, but more than that, it
was immoral. She would burn in hell for it. If the
truth were discovered, she would not be allowed in
polite society. Would not be allowed in any society
at all.

She was the target, the one to pay.

Thank goodness for all the money she'd hoarded.
Surely, it would be enough to pay for her sins.

Still, the note seemed rather short on information. No indication regarding where precisely
they should meet at the Gardens. No hint as to
what he might be wearing. Devil's horns perhaps?

She despised and loathed this person, whoever
he—or she—was. The method of drawing her out
seemed mean and abhorrent.

She walked to the window and sank into the
plush chair where she'd begun working when she
tired of her desk. It was quite possible this person
was planning to meet Kingsland, and yet from
the moment he'd suggested she was the one who
would be able to identify the handwriting, she'd

worried that he had the right of it and the missive had been created for her.

While he'd been so careful in covering his sins, she'd been equally so, and yet there were aspects to hers over which she had no control. Anyone of her acquaintance, even casual or just in passing, who favored wickedness and had a keen eye could uncover her secret. The fear had plagued her for years, but as time passed with no discovery, she'd begun to think herself safe. But the truth was, for her, everlasting safety was but an illusion, a dream.

She'd been found out when she worked as a shopgirl. That time it had been a customer who had threatened to tell her employer if she didn't bare herself to him. She'd promised to meet him at his residence that evening. Instead, she'd snuck away and disappeared in Whitechapel. When she'd hired on as a maid-of-all-work in a successful tradesman's home, it had been the tradesman himself who had gained the knowledge and thought to exploit her, insisting she lift her skirts for him. When she'd refused, he'd tried to force her, but she'd managed to escape his hold and had been quick enough to make her way to the street, where she'd taken refuge in a crowd of passersby.

Why shouldn't she be found out again? She'd become reckless, going to the Fair and Spare, attending a ball and being seen, rather than keeping to the shadows.

If she was correct, and she was the target, then her days as Kingsland's secretary and Hugh's lover were numbered. He'd become too important to her, and she'd not have her shame visited upon him.

SOMETHING WAS AMISS. King sensed it as they strolled through Hyde Park, finally carrying through on the suggestion he'd made before they'd left for Scotland. But Pettypeace was distracted, as though mentally scrawling notes in her mind if not in her notebook.

"That's Lady Rowena over there, surrounded by a bevy of gents," he said.

"Hmm." She looked up at him, confusion etched in her features, when he'd never known her to be confused. "I beg your pardon?"

"Lady Rowena. She is on your list, is she not?"

"Oh yes. Which one is she?"

"The one with the flaming red hair. Four gents vying for her attention."

She glanced past him and studied the woman twirling her bright pink parasol. "She's rather comely."

"I can hear her laughter all the way over here."

"She won't do then, will she?"

He was beginning to think no one would do, not when it meant giving up his nights with her. Would he look the fool if he declined to reveal his choice of duchess at the ball or canceled the affair altogether? He could announce in the *Times* that too many qualified candidates were in the running and he required more time to make such an important decision. Would anyone care? Probably the ladies who had written the blasted letters. "No, she won't."

"I suppose I should still speak with her, although it would be rude to interrupt when she is holding court."

"Was that a bit of waspishness on your part?"

"I don't understand why she sent a letter when she has so many admirers."

"Because not a one of them is a duke."

"You are more than your title. I daresay they should want to wed you even if you had no title."

He didn't know why it soothed him to have her defending him so. "Should you not be making notations?"

"I'll remember. That leaves only Lady Emma Weston. Do you see her about?"

"I do not." However, he did see trouble. Wearing a red riding habit, she rode up on a bay mare.

"Good afternoon, King."

"Margaret, how are you on this fine day?"

"Very well, thank you. Are you going to make introductions?"

He'd rather have a tooth pulled but didn't want either lady to feel he was ashamed of his association with her. "Pettypeace, allow me to introduce Miss Barrett."

"My pleasure, Miss Barrett."

He noted her tone was flatter than usual when greeting someone, her smile completely absent. She no doubt had correctly discerned which Margaret this Margaret was.

"Miss Pettypeace, it truly is a delight to meet you. You are often a topic of conversation whenever King spends time with me enjoying . . . tea. He has naught but praise for your capabilities. I daresay none could ever compete with you when it comes to keeping him happy."

"Margaret," he fairly growled in warning.

"What, darling? Is it not true?"

He touched Penelope on the small of her back. "I believe that is Lady Emma near the Serpentine. Why don't you go on and I'll catch up with you in a bit?"

"All right, yes." She bade her farewell to Margaret and began wandering toward the lake.

He stepped up to the rider and horse. "What are you doing, Margaret? I've never spoken to you about Pettypeace."

Dropping her head back, she released a throaty laugh. "Oh my God, King, she is practically the only thing about which you talk."

He furrowed his brow. That couldn't be true, could it?

"You poor man. You don't even realize you're doing it, do you?"

"What did I tell you?"

She sighed, clearly exasperated with him. "She's competent, clever, smart . . . I don't recall everything. I listened with only half an ear. It wasn't really conversation I wanted from you."

"I feel as though I owe you an apology."

"Nonsense. You allowed me to prattle on about Birdie. Don't let her get away."

"I have no plans to dismiss her."

"You think she'll remain after you marry?"

Until some gentleman comes along and changes her mind. "I would give her no reason to leave."

"Oh King, how can you know your way so well around a woman's body but be such a novice when it comes to a lady's heart?"

"I don't know what you're on about." Although he might. Had Pettypeace given him her heart?

Surely not. She was too practical for that. It was one of the reasons they were so compatible. They didn't let inconvenient emotions get in the way of their relationship.

Her smile was indulgent as she glanced over her shoulder. "She seems to be having difficulty locating Lady Emma."

Looking toward the Serpentine, he saw Pettypeace simply standing there, gazing in the distance. Something was definitely wrong. "I have to see to her."

"You're never going to come to my door again, are you?"

He shook his head. "No, but then, I think you knew that the last time I left."

"What one knows doesn't always coincide with what one hopes. Do be happy, King."

"You as well, Margaret."

As she urged her horse on, he strode with purpose toward his secretary who was now more than a secretary, and the feelings stirring within him were confusing, difficult to reconcile. He'd had such an easy, uncomplicated relationship with Margaret. When urges struck, they were satisfied by a visit to her bed. He'd expected the same when it came to Pettypeace. When urges clamored for attention, she in his bed would calm them. But it wasn't that simple with Pettypeace. The moments when she was his secretary—or his lover—were beginning to blur. He was losing sight of when she was Pettypeace and when she was Penelope.

It was Penelope appearing so forlorn that was a blow to his chest, a knife to his heart. "You need to tell me what's wrong," he said without preamble as soon as he reached her, "because it's obvious something is."

His strong Penelope looked as though she were on the verge of weeping as she shook her head. "It's embarrassing to admit."

"I promise not to blush."

"My monthly curse is upon me."

Christ, was she referring to her menses? He never spoke of that particular aspect of woman-hood with *anyone*. He feared he did actually blush.

"It has me out of sorts," she continued.

"You should have said something. We could have delayed our trip to the park."

"It is not to be spoken of. But I do hope you'll understand why I won't come to your bedchamber tonight."

"Without question. You never *have* to come, sweetheart. Nor should you ever feel obligated to provide a reason for your absence."

She looked as though he'd struck her, and he wondered if it was his use of an endearment. It had slipped out with no thought, and yet using it had seemed as natural as breathing.

"Things between us are becoming confusing . . . Hugh."

"Yes, I know."

"We probably should have drawn up rules and parameters to keep us in line. Signed a document with them all spelled out."

"I don't know if that would have helped." Knew it wouldn't have. "Considering your situation, shall we head back to the residence?"

"What of Lady Emma?"

She'd never been about to begin with, had been an excuse to move Penelope beyond Margaret's tart tongue, but he glanced around as though she had been within the vicinity. "We seem to have missed her." He offered his arm, grateful when she slipped her small hand into the crook of it.

As they strolled along, she said, "I believe I should go with my original plan of interviewing the remaining ladies in their homes. I am quickly running out of time."

"I prefer my idea of going to the theater."

"I should think one would need to be quiet so as not to disturb others' enjoyment or to interfere with hearing the performers."

"Precisely. Perfect place to judge a lady's ability to remain silent."

"Was Miss Barrett silent?"

"Not often enough." He peered down on her. "Not jealous, are you?"

"Why should I be? I have no claim to you."

"Neither did she."

"Your wife will be a different matter entirely."

"Yes."

"I will move back to the servants' quarters when you marry."

"It will be a while yet. I intend to court her first, confirm she suits."

"She will suit. I shall ensure it."

He wondered why the words sounded more like a threat than a promise.

CHAPTER 20

*W*HEN *WICKEDNESS REIGNS.*

Penelope had no idea regarding the exact hour she was expected but was familiar enough with the reputation of Cremorne Gardens to know it was becoming tarnished by unsavory activities that occurred after the more polite people left. It was no doubt reckless of her to be strolling about without any sort of protector, but she'd learned at an early age to look out for herself. She wasn't proud of all the ways she'd had to do that, but her experiences had taught her that she might be bowed but she'd not be broken.

Although that might change tonight if her fears were realized and she had to leave Kingsland. It had nearly killed her to lie to him that afternoon and claim the monthly curse was upon her when it wasn't. She'd lied to others with such ease. In the beginning, she'd even lied to him. But this afternoon it had felt like claws scraping through her soul and shredding it. However, she'd needed an explanation for why she wouldn't come to his bedchamber shortly after they'd retired. In the end, it hadn't been necessary because he'd gone to spend time in the company of the Chessmen. She hadn't even needed to sneak out of the residence. She'd simply left and walked for a while until she was able to hail a hansom cab.

And now here she was, where she truly didn't want to be, remaining steadfastly aware of her surroundings while striving to communicate that she wasn't here for any sort of cavorting. Having decided that keeping on the move was her best recourse for avoiding any unwanted advances, she assumed the message sender would approach her eventually.

Solitary women sauntering by gave her a curious look, probably because she was buttoned up to her chin while their breasts were in danger of spilling out of their low-cut frocks. Some tarts clung to gentlemen's arms. Some swells staggered and lurched. Others studied her with speculation until her frigid glare caused them to scamper away. She wasn't the innocent she'd been when forced to cast aside her pride. She was not so easily manipulated or taken advantage of now. She would see what this scapegrace wanted, and then—

"Miss Pettypeace?"

With a start, she swung around. "Mr. Grenville." What the deuce was he doing here?

He smiled warmly. "Fancy seeing you here, especially this time of night. You do realize it's not the fashionable hour."

Although she recalled he'd thought they'd met before, he seemed surprised by her presence. Surely, he wasn't the person who had sent the missive. She detected nothing threatening or sinister in his demeanor. "I'm afraid my curiosity was piqued by the recent spate of articles in the newspaper reporting on the questionable activities that occur when the good folk have gone home. I thought to simply have a quick peek."

"Are you quite alone?" he asked, a measure of concern reflected in his tone.

"I am, yes, but you need not worry. I won't be staying long." Trepidation building, she glanced around. Was his nearness going to make whomever she was supposed to meet hesitant to approach her?

"I'm rather surprised Kingsland would let you come by yourself."

"I am not his possession. I'm free to do as I please."

"Are you certain he's not lurking about somewhere?"

Distracted, searching the shadows for anyone she might see watching her, she said, "He had plans for the evening, enjoying time with friends."

"No one else came with you?"

She really needed him to go on his way. He was mucking things up for her. "I'm fully capable of taking care of myself, thank you."

"Are you?"

"Yes, quite."

"Splendid." He slipped his arm around hers. "Why don't we walk for a bit?"

When he took a step, she stood her ground and

wrenched her arm free. "Don't take liberties with me, please. It was good to see you, Mr. Grenville—"

"George. You must call me George, as we're going to become very good friends."

"Mr. Grenville, I really prefer to wander about on my own."

"Then how in the world will you pay me for my silence, Miss Pettypeace?"

The affable tone was gone, replaced by a hard, biting edge, and his eyes suddenly appeared cruel. Talons of ice danced down her spine. "I don't know to what you're referring."

"Oh, I think you do. I finally realized where I'd seen you before: in my collection of salacious photographs. But not to worry. I'll hold your secret, my dear, as long as you pay my price."

Oh God. He did know her secret. She'd only posed a dozen times for the photographer but had been too young and naive to know the images could be duplicated, printed on paper over and over. The practice had helped to spur an industry that thrived in the darkened corners of London. People had recently begun referring to the sexually explicit materials as pornography.

"Why all the earlier questions?"

"To ensure you were truly alone, and Kingsland wasn't skulking about somewhere. I didn't think you'd tell him but had to be certain. I suppose you didn't want him to know his sainted Pettypeace is such a wicked girl. Or was, anyway. How old were you?"

Too young. Her father had died, and she'd blamed

herself. If only she had returned home when she was expected, if only she hadn't been late, if he hadn't been waiting on her. Then they would have all escaped again and begun anew elsewhere. But she had been late. And he'd gone to debtor's prison. With no other means for survival, she, her mother, and her sister had lived there with him, as was a common practice. But after he'd fallen ill and died, they'd been cast out on the street, where their companions had become starvation and cold, where they often slept in alleyways.

Then one day a man had approached her with an offer. All she had to do was wear very little clothing, perhaps none at all. Stand still, sit still, lie still. And he would place coins in her palm.

Posing with all her secret places on display had been difficult at first, but eventually had become easier . . . until she'd actually begun to enjoy it. That realization had shamed her more than the posing.

"I do not know you well enough to recognize your handwriting, so why not simply pen me a letter?"

"I thought it might be a bit more ominous, make you think twice about ignoring my summons."

That aspect of his plan had certainly worked. "How much do you want?"

He laughed, harshly, bitterly. "You think I am so crass as to want money? No, my dear, no. I yearn to see the Fallen Angel as a mature woman, compare you with what you once were. That's what we call you, you know. Collectors such as myself.

The Fallen Angel. You had such a transcendent innocence about you, almost ethereal, that came through in the photograph."

She didn't care what they called her or how he perceived her image on paper. She was focused on his earlier comment regarding what he yearned for. Was he saying what she thought he was? Did he expect her to strip down for him? "You're mad."

"Oh, Miss Pettypeace, don't say that. I have several photographs of you. It would be à shame if one were to show up on Kingsland's desk. I suspect I'm not the only one in the upper circle who has a penchant for indulging in the erotic."

"You purchased it; you look at it." She didn't want to consider what else he might do with it. "Yet you fault me for posing for it?"

"If you didn't position yourself in such carnal ways, I would not have access to the sin of looking."

"That makes no sense whatsoever. You're a hypocrite."

"That may well be, but you are familiar enough with Society to know I would be given a slap on the wrist and you would be stoned. And unemployed. Do you honestly believe Kingsland would keep you on when he learned the truth of you?"

He wouldn't. He'd have no choice but to let her go. "How did you manage to get your letter on my desk without using the post?"

"I must keep some of my secrets."

"You paid a servant." Paid him well, apparently. Not only for the delivery but for his silence.

"We're rummaging around in details that have no bearing on the matter. Here is what I'm proposing. You come with me to my lodging house, where you will pose for me as you did when you were younger."

"That's all you require? That I simply pose for you?"

"Perhaps you might be good enough to fulfill my fantasy of knowing the Fallen Angel more intimately. I can't imagine you've not given yourself to others."

"Then you haven't much of an imagination." Which was no doubt the reason he relied on the photographs.

That didn't seem to sit well with him. "We're wasting time here. Let's be away, shall we?"

"No."

He was already reaching for her before he comprehended her answer. If she weren't so appalled by what he wanted, she might have laughed when his movements froze and his face revealed his shock. "I beg your pardon?"

"I'm not going with you. I have no intention of fulfilling your fantasies."

"I will see you ruined. Not only you but your precious duke." Her heart sped up and her chest tightened at the mention of Kingsland. "How do you think he will be perceived when people learn that within his residence lives a woman who exposed her cunny to the world? I have that photograph, Miss Pettypeace, and I will show it far and wide until not only you can't show your face, but neither can he."

"Actually, I don't think you will." The deep voice rumbled out of the darkness, a split second before a fist slammed into Mr. Grenville's jaw and sent him flying backward to land with a bone-crunching thud on the ground. Then a tall, broad specter was standing over him. "We're going to your residence now to retrieve those photographs. And if you ever threaten Miss Pettypeace again, I shall see you destroyed."

Reaching down, he grabbed Mr. Grenville by his lapels and heaved him to his feet. With a firm grip on the man's collar—Kingsland towered over him in size and bearing—he dragged the scapegrace toward her. There was not enough light to see the duke's features clearly, to look into his eyes, to discern what he was thinking—or more importantly, what he was feeling. "My carriage awaits."

Based on the heat slithering through his voice, he was not at all happy. Not that she blamed him. To learn about his secretary's—his lover's—scandalous past in such a manner. Then another thought occurred: what the devil was he doing here? Coincidence? Had he come with the Chessmen? Glancing around, she didn't see them anywhere.

"Pettypeace, we're leaving."

She jerked her attention to where he stood a few feet away, his grip on Grenville holding firm, even as the man fought to break free of his grasp. She hurried to catch up, taking a position on the side opposite where Grenville struggled. Kingsland gave him a hard shake. "Still yourself or my fist will do it for you."

"Do you know what she is? Do you know what she did?"

"Quiet. Your voice carries, you insolent sod. Behave yourself or your father will hear about your questionable pastime."

"What? You've never looked at any erotic images, never read any sensual books? It's all wildly popular at present, you know." In spite of laws against the selling of what was considered obscene. Penelope wondered if that was part of the appeal. Although it certainly hadn't seemed obscene at the time. The photographer had told her it was a new form of art, and she would be a pioneer, leading the way. "Now that you've taken her to a ball and such, how long before others recognize her as well? I doubt I'm the only acquaintance of yours with photographs of her."

Kingsland swung around and wrapped his hand around his throat, tilting Grenville's head back. "We are not acquaintances. But trust me on this, I do have acquaintances you do not want to meet. So hold your tongue and forget you know anything at all about Miss Pettypeace. Otherwise, you will meet one of them who is very skilled at making people quietly disappear. Are we clear on that matter?"

Grenville nodded, as much as he was able with Kingsland's hand serving as a tight collar.

"Good." He released his hold on the man completely. "Now, let's carry on with our plans, shall we?"

A much subdued Grenville walked to the waiting coach. It was Kingsland who handed her up, with no tenderness in his hold on her hand, no squeeze of reassurance. No warmth in his eyes, no smile. She rather suspected he very much resembled the mien of the man who had dragged his father to an asylum. He would be dismissing her tonight, and she doubted he would give her a reference.

She heard voices, couldn't make out the words, but assumed directions were being given to the driver.

Grenville appeared in the doorway and stumbled forward as Kingsland shoved him into the conveyance. He scrambled up and onto the bench while the duke settled himself, with all the poise and grace of a seasoned warrior, beside the cad. Reaching up, he rapped on the ceiling, and they were off.

She had so much to say to him, to explain, to make right, but didn't want to speak in front of Grenville. Perhaps Kingsland felt the same, because he sat there silent and stoic, unmoving, but oh, she could sense his gaze boring into her.

"The tart lied to me, told me you weren't about," Grenville whined.

"If you wish to arrive at your residence with all your teeth, you'll keep your lips pressed together for the remainder of the journey," Kingsland said, the threat evident in the hard edge of his tone.

Crossing his arms over his chest, Grenville tucked himself into the corner to sulk. Sulking when she was the one who was on the verge of losing everything while he would lose only a few photographs.

The tension was palpable. She could hardly stand it. Angry men, hurt men, wounded men. But she cared about only one, knowing he was no doubt feeling betrayed. He understood the ugliness of her past now. She'd done what any decent, respectable girl wouldn't. She should have found another way to earn a few coins, but at the time all she'd wanted was to eat. And to get some food for her mother and sister.

The coach slowed and came to a stop.

"Wait here," Kingsland ordered her just before shoving open the door and disembarking. He reached back, grabbed Grenville, and hauled him out.

She contemplated leaving, clambering from the carriage, and wandering away. Away from the life she'd built, away from London . . . away from Hugh. It would be the easiest and the hardest thing to do. But the same could be said if she stayed. He knew the truth of her now. She could barely stand the thought of the disgust she'd see in his eyes.

But if she left, she wouldn't get her hands on those photographs—for surely, he would give them to her—and she'd be unable to see them destroyed. It was imperative that she set them alight, watch them burn.

She knew a couple of shops on Holywell Street where salacious books and photographs were sold. Over the years, wearing widow's weeds and a hat with a thick black veil to disguise herself as much as possible, she'd visited, searched through the inventory, and found a few of the prints that now brought her shame. She'd purchased them, then burned them. She'd always been uncomfortable standing in a room in the back of the shop and glancing through the offerings, searching for images of her younger self. Now she knew she only had to ask if they had any photographs of the Fallen Angel on hand. The Fallen Angel. How appropriate. She wanted to weep for the young girl she'd been.

The door was yanked open with such force she was surprised it didn't come off its hinges as the carriage rocked. Kingsland slammed the door shut, sat opposite her, and banged on the ceiling. The vehicle lurched forward as though he'd startled the horses.

"Here," he said quietly.

The streetlamps they passed allowed her to see the small packet he held toward her. Her fingers were stiff and cold as she took it from him and pressed it against her stomach, covering it with both hands, not to shield it but to hide it. "Did you look at them?"

"No."

"But based upon what you overheard, you've deduced what they are."

He held silent, but the tension building within the confines was suffocating.

"Hugh—"

"You took off your clothes in front of a man and let him take photographs of you." It sounded as though he spoke through clenched teeth. She couldn't help but believe he was livid.

"Technically, yes."

"Technically?"

"You make it sound lurid, and it didn't seem so at the time."

He scoffed. "You were so uninhibited when you

came to me the first time, and I thought . . . Christ, you were accustomed to removing your clothes in front of men."

"No, it wasn't like that. There was only one. The photographer. No one else was about. Well, maybe another girl or so. But no other men."

"Did he touch you?"

"Sometimes, but only to show me how to place my arm or tilt my head. He never did anything untoward."

"He was taking photographs of your naked body. How in God's name is that not untoward?"

"If you shout a little louder, perhaps the coachman and footman will be able to explain to the rest of the staff what was going on tonight."

She heard him inhale deeply, exhale. When next he spoke, his voice was lower, quieter, more in control. "I can hardly stand the thought of what you did."

It would have hurt less if he'd shot an arrow straight into her heart. But it also caused the anger simmering within her to flare at the unfairness of it all. "Do you know I have gone to museums, art galleries, and exhibitions to study portraits of nude women and men? The *Sleeping Venus* by Giorgione comes to mind. What defines it as art? I posed similarly, and yet it is defined as obscene, to be sold in dark alleys and in secret rooms in bookshops." And it had made her mother look at her as though she'd developed leprosy.

"I don't know the answer to that," he said so quietly she almost didn't hear him, but there was also a note of resignation in his voice that made her want to weep. Perhaps in the deepest recesses of her heart, she had hoped he cared for her enough that her past wouldn't have made a difference in how he felt toward her. But it did. It always would. "So these photographs are available throughout London?"

"Probably beyond."

"Why didn't you come to me when you received the second letter?"

She had considered it for all of a heartbeat. But knew she'd never be able to bring herself to do it. Should she try to explain that to him? Would it ease the hurt she heard in his voice? Or would it only make matters worse? "How did you know about it?"

"The chambermaid, Lucy. She told me he paid her to place it on your desk. The first as well. Only she opened the one delivered this morning."

"But it was sealed."

"Apparently she has a skill for removing wax and putting it back into place without it looking disturbed. She told me what the letter asked of you. Therefore, I knew where you would be, although Cremorne is so large that finding you was a challenge."

"You lied about spending your evening with the Chessmen?"

He scoffed. "Is that annoyance in your voice?"

As irrational as it seemed, it rather was. "Why didn't you tell me that you knew, intended to be at Cremorne ferreting out this fellow?"

He looked toward the window, where beyond carriages rattled, horses trotted, and a few people strolled. "I suppose I wanted you to come to me.

I shared my secret when it might have seen me hanged." His attention came back to her. "But you didn't trust me with yours."

Did he not understand her shame and mortification? Why would she willingly confess to doing what laws forbade? "It wasn't a matter of trust."

"Then what was it?"

She heard the anger, the disappointment, the hurt. Perhaps he was justified in his feelings. In a way she'd betrayed him. All these years they'd shared breakfast and ideas and opinions. Only lately had they shared a dance, a kiss, a bed. With the last, matters between them had changed, but maybe not enough. Perhaps she'd clutched her secret close because working for him had helped her gain respect for herself, and she'd feared losing his respect for her, which would have meant losing him. But then, he'd never been hers. She was the scribbler of notes, the one who kept him organized. The satisfier of urges. But he didn't love her. He hadn't come for Penelope tonight. He'd come for Pettypeace. He'd come for his secretary, not his lover.

Suddenly she felt weary, melancholy, and tired beyond measure of being Pettypeace. She wanted to be Penelope. Pettypeace hadn't existed before that afternoon when she'd stepped over the threshold into his office. Pettypeace was who he knew. She was terrified of introducing him to Penelope.

Her fingers spasmed, shook. She flattened them against the parcel, crushed it against her belly, took a deep breath, clutched the packet hard enough for the paper holding everything together to crackle.

Slowly, painstakingly, as though she was climbing an impossibly high mountain with a peak that always seemed beyond reach no matter how many steps she took, she leaned forward and set the packet on his lap. "Open it, look at them, and then burn them. I trust you to burn them."

CHAPTER 21

$\mathcal{K}$INGSLAND DIDN'T SAY a word, didn't touch the packet. It just sat there balanced on his upper thighs as the carriage turned onto the drive. He didn't move when the conveyance came to a halt. Or when the footman opened the door. Or when the liveried gent handed her down.

Penelope walked up the path to the steps and ascended them. At the door, she glanced back. He had yet to emerge. Probably for the best. She fought to shore up her defenses, to gather up all the feelings pouring forth and shove them back into a box that resembled Pandora's, where items were held that should never be set free. But they had been, and locking them back up was hard.

After entering the residence, she made her way to the servants' rooms, passing only Keating and Harry on her way. It was late and most of the staff were finished with their chores, had retired in order to be up early to see to all the monotonous tasks that were repeated every day. Perhaps she would sleep in her old room tonight. Or lie in it. She doubted she'd be able to drift off.

When she reached the room she sought, she tapped lightly on the door, hating the idea of waking Lucy but needing to speak with her, to set things right between them.

The door opened and Lucy peered out. Her eyes widened. "Oh, Penn! You're all right. I've been so worried."

Most of the words were said directly into Penelope's ear because Lucy's arms had immediately come around her, hugging her tightly as her friend swayed. "I know you're cross with me," Lucy said.

"No, no." She leaned back. "But I would like to visit for a bit if you're not too tired."

"Yes, please come in." She grabbed Penelope's hand and pulled her into the room, shutting the door behind them.

Quickly they made their way to the bed and followed a routine that had become theirs after so many late-night chats. Lucy grabbed her pillow, tossed it to Penelope, and then plopped down near the head of the bed. Penelope settled in at its foot, tucking the pillow between her back and the brass. She must have tried a hundred times to convince Lucy she didn't need to give up her pillow, but her friend had insisted a person was always to ensure their guests were comfortable. Lucy treated her bedchamber as though it was the fanciest of parlors in the grandest of houses.

"Did everything get sorted?" Lucy asked anxiously.

Not everything. "Yes." She leaned forward. "Lucy, that morning when I called all the servants together, why didn't you tell me you put the envelope on my desk? You must have known I would have protected you, would have seen you didn't get into trouble."

Lucy knotted her fingers together. "You were so serious, and looked so worried, and said the duke had received the letter. I couldn't imagine what the bloke had written to make you think it was for the duke. Because the duke was involved, well, I knew I'd done wrong and worried I'd get the sack if I confessed. The first one, I only done it because I thought he was a chap you'd met at the ball who'd taken a fancy to you. His clothing was so fine, he looked like he could have been a lord."

"Close. His father is a viscount. Why did you decide to read the letter he gave you this morning?"

"Because of how concerned you were with the other one. I kept waiting for you to tell me what the first one said, tell me about him. But you never did. Then, when he showed up this morning and offered me a quid to put it on your desk, I told him I would. But then I got curious about it. After I read it, I got scared. *When wickedness reigns.* He sounded like a bloke up to no good, one I didn't want to cross, so I sealed it back up and delivered it like I promised, because maybe he just had a strange way of wooing and was someone you were keen on." Lucy shook her head. "But then I worried about it . . . all day. I saw you a couple of times, just staring out a window. I thought, 'Something's not right.' When I overheard the duke's valet telling Mr. Keating to have the coach brought round at half seven because His Grace was going out tonight, I panicked a bit and thought if something was wrong, he wouldn't be about to make it right, so I waited in the foyer and told him as he was leaving. He still left but assured me he'd sort it. I'm frightfully sorry, Penn. I should have told you. Probably shouldn't have told him."

"I'm glad you did. Things needed sorting, and he . . . well, he has the strength, power, and determination to make certain it gets done." Scooting to the middle of the bed, she took Lucy's hands and squeezed them. "Lucy, I want you to know you are the most wonderful and precious of friends. I shall always treasure my memories of you."

Lucy wrinkled her brow. "I love you, too, Penn. Are you sure everything's all right?"

"Right as rain." Or at least it would be fairly soon. "Now, tell me. Have you kissed Harry again?"

THE PACKET RESTED at the edge of his desk, mocking him, taunting him, daring him, while he stared at it from his place in the wingback chair near the fireplace. No flames flickered upon the hearth. The weather didn't call for them. Yet he felt chilled all the same, in spite of the abundance of scotch he'd downed.

After reaching for the bottle on the floor beside him, he refilled his glass and took another slow swallow. He'd not seen Pettypeace since she left the coach. It had been a while before he'd been able to clasp the remnants of her past that she'd left in his lap. He hadn't caught all of the conversation she'd had with Grenville, but he'd heard enough to know what those photographs represented. A woman with no morals. A woman who displayed herself so men she didn't know could feast upon the sight of her. Little wonder she'd changed her name and sought out a new life. Grenville had the right of it. He could indeed see her ruined, and in ruining her, he would ruin King.

But King was struggling with more than what was revealed on paper. He wanted to howl out his frustration and anger. She hadn't trusted him. Not with the truth of her past. Not with the second missive that had arrived. Not with tonight's rendezvous with a vile rodent. It had wounded him that she'd not trusted him enough to come to him when she'd needed him. Hadn't trusted him to handle the matter, to protect her.

Or perhaps he was struggling more with the fact that she hadn't needed him. Didn't need him. Not the way he needed her.

She had become such an integral part of his life. When he'd had to face his past, he'd found solace in having her at his side, offering support, providing comfort. For the first time in his life, he'd felt as though he wasn't truly alone.

Certainly, he had the Chessmen, and his brother, and his mother—but Pettypeace was somehow more. More substantial, more important. More . . . crucial.

He wanted to be more essential to her. More than a salary, a roof over her head, food in her belly, a provider of pleasure. He wanted her to share every aspect of her life: the things that brought her joy, the ones that made her weep, those that brought her comfort, those responsible for creating fear.

Odd that the things he admired most about her—her strength, determination, and courage— caused her not to need him. She provided sustenance to his soul, his life. But he couldn't provide the same to her.

After draining the glass, he poured more scotch. He should do the one thing she trusted him to do: build a fire and toss the packet into it. Sacrifice the opportunity she'd provided for him to learn something more about her. And he was desperate to know more.

In the carriage he'd been angry. Angry at Grenville for his threats, furious that he had the photographs and had looked at her, knew the intimate details of her. Incensed that she'd placed herself in the position of being extorted. If he were honest, he was upset she'd ever bared herself to another. But mostly, mostly he was upset because he wanted to be more than her employer, wanted to be as important to her as she had become to him. Which was ludicrous and made him an even bigger fool than he'd been with Lady Kathryn.

Because how could a man love a woman he knew to have such a scandalous past and perhaps more secrets?

HE AWOKE WITH stale scotch on his breath and aches in places that should not ache, his body protesting his falling asleep in the chair. An insistent hammering in his skull and a throbbing behind his eyes caused him to regret finishing off the bottle of scotch.

After stretching and contorting to loosen muscles, he shoved himself out of the chair. The mantel clock confirmed his suspicions. It was nearly noon. Much too late for breakfast. He was surprised Pettypeace hadn't sought him out by now to ensure he'd not forgotten to eat. Then his gaze fell on the packet still resting on his desk, and the memories from last night came rushing back. He needed to set matters between them back to rights, but damned if he knew where to begin.

He strode to his desk, tossed the packet into a drawer, and slammed it shut. Which did his head no favors. He needed to set himself to rights first.

He was grateful he didn't cross paths with her on the way to his bedchamber. The door to hers was open, and he cautiously peered in, inhaling and finding solace in the scent of jasmine permeating the room. Everything was neat and tidy. The chambermaid would have already seen to these rooms by now. Not that Pettypeace would leave the girl much to deal with.

An hour later, after a steaming-hot bath, a shave, and fresh clothes, he made his way back down the stairs and ambled along the hallway. As he neared the library, he gave a nod to the footman and continued on to Pettypeace's office, surprised to find the room absent of her presence. Odd that. Did she have errands to see to? He couldn't recall them having any meetings scheduled.

He wandered back to the library and addressed

the footman. "Do you know where Pettypeace has gone?"

"No, Your Grace. I've not seen her this morning."

"Huh." She was probably about somewhere or did indeed have errands to tend to. "Fetch me the blackest coffee you can find and a couple of slices of unbuttered toast." It was all his stomach could tolerate at the moment.

"Yes, sir."

Once he was sitting at his desk, he placed his elbows on it and began rubbing his temples. He hadn't imbibed to this degree since his Oxford days. He'd forgotten how miserable overindulging could make him and how the reason causing him to travel that path only loomed larger. Drinking never caused it to shrink or disappear.

"Your Grace?"

Squinting, he glanced up at Keating. His butler could move about as silently as a wraith. He was holding a silver salver. King could see a card resting on it.

"A Miss Taylor is here to see you, sir. She said Miss Pettypeace sent her."

He wasn't in the mood to converse with strangers. Hell, he wasn't in the mood to converse with acquaintances. "For what purpose?"

"I don't know, Your Grace. I suppose that's what she wishes to discuss with you."

He sat back in his chair. "Bring the woman in, then, and tell Pettypeace to join us here."

"I don't know where Miss Pettypeace is, sir. I've not seen her today."

A fissure of unease skittered through him, causing chilled bumps to surface. "What do you mean you've not seen her? She was at breakfast, was she not?"

Keating cleared his throat. "No, sir, she was not."

Shoving back his chair with such force that it nearly toppled over in spite of its sturdiness and heft, he came to his feet. "Take me to this woman."

In the foyer stood a dark-haired woman, dressed primly and properly in light blue. He judged her to be not much older than Penelope. "Miss Taylor, I'm Kingsland."

With a bright smile, she curtsied. "It's a pleasure, Your Grace."

"Miss Pettypeace sent you?"

"Yes, sir. My business is to arrange balls, you see, and I've been assisting her with the smaller details regarding yours. Securing the orchestra and such. She came by bright and early this morning and explained you were in need of someone to manage all of the event, and—"

"Why would I require someone to manage it?"

Miss Taylor's mouth was opened slightly, her eyes large, round, and blinking. A delicate clearing of her throat seemed to be needed for her to provide the answer. "Well, sir, it ensures you are free to enjoy the affair without worrying that something is being overlooked."

He shook his head. "I'm fully aware of why—Pettypeace is managing it."

Another series of blinks. "She's managing it, Your Grace, by hiring me. She paid me in full this morning and handed me this satchel"—she held up the soft leather portfolio he'd given Pettypeace for her birthday last year—"with all her organized notes and instructions. I've spent the past three hours studying them, and I must confess to being extremely impressed with her planning and preparedness. I've never seen the like. Every contingency considered. A solution already devised for anything that could possibly—"

The remainder of her praise for Pettypeace was lost to him as he tore up the stairs, taking three steps at a time, cursing his legs for not being long enough to take four. Barging into her bedchamber, he yanked open the doors on the wardrobe. Her clothes were there. The dark blue frocks, the gowns.

She wasn't gone. That no one had seen her and she'd hired a woman to manage his ball wasn't proof of anything. Glancing around, he saw the velvet case. He didn't have to open it to know he'd find the necklace nestled inside. Yet still he did. He slipped a finger beneath the teardrop, imagined he could feel the warmth from where it had rested just below her throat. A throat he'd kissed and licked.

He set the box back on the vanity and studied the remainder of the chamber. Where was the bloody cat? He dropped to the floor and looked beneath the bed. Not so much as a speck of dust. He shot to his feet, walked with purpose out of the room and down the stairs. Keating was talking quietly to Miss Taylor, probably striving to convince her that dukes commonly rushed out of rooms for no rational reason whatsoever. His butler went silent as King reached the foyer. "Assemble the staff immediately and have them begin a thorough search for Sir Purrcival."

"I beg your pardon? Sir Percival, Your Grace?"

"Her cat. Pettypeace's cat." She wouldn't have left without the cat.

His butler looked at him as though he was a madman, but he didn't attempt to reassure the man he was all right, that everything was all right, because he was beginning to doubt that anything would ever be all right again.

He strode into her office, up to her desk, searching for a clue that would confirm his worst fears. All the items he'd given her over the years were arranged neatly on top. Near the side where she should have been sitting rested an envelope. He picked it up and read the words she'd written with her perfect, elegant script.

Your future duchess.

She was gone. He knew it with a certainty that made him want to howl. The aches he'd felt upon waking this morning paled in comparison to the pain ratcheting through his chest now as the reality struck him hard.

Pettypeace had left him.

They weren't going to find the damned cat. She hadn't taken her clothing because the garments weren't suitable for whomever she intended to become. She would change her name, her occupation, the area of England in which she lived. She would disappear into her surroundings, become the chameleon he'd once likened her to. Impossible to find.

Turning the envelope over, he smiled wistfully

at the red wax she'd used to seal it. Etiquette dictated that only men use red. Women were to use any other color: blue, green, yellow. But Pettypeace had rebelled, always using red to signal that in her position as his secretary, she was on equal footing with any man. He wondered if she realized that she was superior to many of them.

Not wanting to risk marring a symbol of her rebellious spirit, he picked up the letter knife—the emerald marbled handle reminding him of her eyes, the reason he'd chosen it—and slit open the envelope. He removed the vellum and read the name she'd inscribed, and the truth hit him hard, nearly knocking him over with regret and remorse.

She'd chosen the wrong woman.

Chapter 22

That night was another for scotch. He'd opened a new bottle, dropped into the chair by the fireplace, and stared at his desk. Contemplating. Wondering if he should remove the ominous packet from the drawer taunting him and do as she'd suggested: open it.

Once he'd realized she'd left, he'd taken on the impossible task of trying to find her. He'd had a horse readied and ridden through London as though he might spy her walking the streets. He'd hired lads to watch over his gelding while he'd searched railway platforms. He'd explored the docks and looked inside coaches. He'd spoken with hansom drivers, describing her, striving to determine if they might have taken her somewhere, someplace where she was now waiting, someplace where he could convince her to return to him. Even as he knew that in his position, he shouldn't associate with a woman who had done what she had done. And he certainly

shouldn't have her taking care of his business or accompanying him to dinners and balls. The scandal
of her could lower his standing, bring him and his
family to ruin.

He couldn't risk having her back in his life, had
to convince himself to let her go. On the morrow,
he would place an advert in the appropriate peri-
odicals and, by the end of the week, have another
secretary hired. He didn't need Pettypeace.

But Christ, he needed Penelope.

Surging to his feet, he stalked to his desk and
yanked on the drawer so hard that it came out of
its cubbyhole. Too fast for him to catch the far end
and stop it from answering gravity's call and spilling everything onto the floor. After flinging the
drawer aside, he bent down and brushed items
away until he could snatch up the packet. Suddenly he was struck with how careless he'd been
not to secure it. Grenville had kept the photographs
locked in a beautiful rosewood box as though they
were a precious treasure.

He returned to the chair, placed his elbows on
his thighs, and held the packet between his hands,
studying the brown paper and the twine that
formed such a flimsy barrier for what was hidden
inside. He should probably start a fire and toss the
entire package onto it. Instead, he stroked the end
of the bow. Did he really want to see her doing
what Grenville had described? Exposing herself
to others? Was he jealous that men had looked
at her, still did so? Was he a hypocrite when he'd
been with other women? But that had been in
the privacy of a boudoir. He'd not posed for all

and sundry to view. Strangers. Anyone with the proper coin.

But to see her bold, brazen, and tempting was the only way to exorcise her, to ensure he didn't move heaven and earth to find her. He imagined her come-hither look, her sultry eyes, her pouting mouth. Her promise of wickedness. He tugged on the twine until the bow was no more and discarded the thin cord. He unfolded the paper—

And stared at the first image. Not at all what he'd expected. She looked so naive and frightened. How many years did she have on her? Fourteen, fifteen. Certainly not as many as sixteen.

It wasn't the body wrapped in some diaphanous cloth that hinted at what she was on the verge of revealing that captured the attention, the imagination. It was her face. Her lowered eyes, her unsmiling mouth. The shyness reflected there. His Penelope had once been shy and demure.

A pain struck his chest so fiercely and strongly that he thought he might die of the agony. It felt as though something was being broken apart in there and rebuilt.

The Fallen Angel, they called her. That's what Grenville had told her. King could certainly understand why. She was purity and wonder. Innocence and virtue. She exuded what became lost as one grew older, the ability to believe in goodness.

He brought the paper back over the portrait, unfolded his body, and took the necessary three steps to reach the hearth. After crouching down, he set the packet aside and went to work creating a fire. When the flames were dancing wildly, he carefully set the packet in the midst of them and watched it burn.

He'd always wondered about her past. Now he was torn between wishing he'd never learned anything at all and wanting to know the whole of it.

THE FOLLOWING NIGHT found him in a corner of Whitechapel the aristocracy tended not to visit, especially at midnight, which made it perfect for clandestine meetings upon which most would frown. As King strode into the mews, he saw leaning against the wall the silhouette of the man he was meeting. There was a loneliness to him, a forlornness. But then, the man had lost everything, been expelled from Society. None knew that King had maintained an association with him, but he found it valuable to know someone familiar with the darker aspects of London. "Stanwick."

"I've told you before. Refer to me as Wolf." He'd once been the heir apparent to the Dukedom of Wolfford until his father had committed treason and everything had been taken from Marcus Stanwick. His brother had recently married Lady Kathryn. His sister had married Benedict Trewlove. Yet Marcus still wandered, striving to discover the truth behind his father's fall from grace.

"Any closer to finding what you seek?" King asked.

"I'm beginning to fear it shall always remain elusive."

"Perhaps you should give up your quest and come out of the shadows."

"I find I like the shadows. You wouldn't have sent word to me if you didn't require something done within them. What do you need?"

"George Grenville."

"One of Viscount Grenville's younger sons. What of him?"

"I want him to decide he would be happier living elsewhere, in another part of the world. The Americas, Africa, Australia. I don't care. Just so he's not here."

"What did he do?"

"Threatened the peace of someone I care about."

"Your secretary, I assume."

His words were like a punch. "Why would you think that?"

"Because you have a very small circle of people you care about. And if it was one of the others, they'd be here with you."

He could offer no argument to that, so he just sighed. "I also need you to help me find her."

Two weeks until the Kingsland ball

LEANING OVER THE map of London he'd spread out over his desk, King studied it, striving to determine which area he would wander tonight. He was running out of places to look for her—even as he knew it was unlikely that she was still in London. He'd hired detectives to search nearby towns and sent others farther afield. No joy to be found anywhere, not even a hint that she'd ever existed.

She'd grown up learning how to start over, how

to disappear, how to avoid debt collectors. And later how to avoid those who knew of her past.

A few nights earlier he'd made a fool of himself by barging into the Fair and Spare to determine if anyone she might have met there—any gent she might have intrigued—had heard from her or had any inkling as to where she might have gone. Of course, no one had any information to share. His servants knew to alert him if they received any word of her whereabouts. A five-hundred-pound reward would be granted to anyone who betrayed her confidence. Even as he'd announced the offer, he'd recognized himself as being a cad for making it.

But he needed to speak with her. He wanted to know everything of her past. He needed to apologize for giving the impression he wouldn't have stood by her. He'd failed to earn her trust, and he couldn't forgive himself for that.

The clatter of rapid footsteps had his heart thumping before he recognized it wasn't her stride echoing down the hallway. Strange how he knew the smallest of details and yet so much about her was still a mystery. At the sight of his mother coming through the doorway, he straightened. "Mother, I wasn't expecting you for another week."

"Lawrence sent word that Miss Pettypeace has gone missing."

He sighed. "*Gone missing* has an ominous ring to it. She's left, and I don't know where she is."

"What did you do to make her leave?"

He didn't blame her for thinking the worst of him, for believing he was at fault. He was, and it grated knowing he was the reason Pettypeace had departed. "A scandal from her past came to light. I acted as an unmitigated arse and behaved in an unforgivable manner."

"Oh, Hugh."

"Don't ask for further details. I won't give them."

"You look dreadful."

"Thank you for that assessment."

"When Keating met me at the door, he informed me you're not eating, and those circles beneath your eyes tell me you're not sleeping."

What was the point of food or rest when the light had gone out of his life? Although Pettypeace would despise his morose musings, he didn't want to spend a single minute doing something that wouldn't lead to his finding her. He furrowed his brow. "Why would learning of her absence cause you to return from Italy before planned?"

"I've always liked that girl. I'm worried about her."

"She's resourceful and clever, with no shortage of funds, apparently." While the bank manager had not divulged the particulars, he had confessed to weeping when she'd withdrawn all her money and closed out her account. "She will see herself well situated."

"I am not concerned with a roof over her head or food in her belly. I worry about her heart and her very soul. I worry about how she will survive without you."

"She doesn't need me, Mother. She doesn't need anyone."

"Oh, Hugh." Shaking her head, she patted his cheek. "As clever as you are, my son, there are times when you are hopelessly foolish. How could you look at her and not see that she loves you? She might not need you, but I daresay she wants you."

Her words were a blow, doubling him over. Bracing his hands on the desk, he bowed his head. "If she loved me, she wouldn't have left." Even now, he knew if he found her, she was likely to tell him to rot in hell.

"Since scandal is involved, I would argue she left *because* she loves you."

Hope flaring, he jerked his head up. "You were playing matchmaker. The ball. The gown."

"You are both so frightfully stubborn, too afraid of getting hurt to open your heart. You wax on about risk and reward but have failed to take the greatest risk of all . . . on love. And yet it comes with the grandest of rewards."

"What know you of love, Mother? You didn't love my father."

"Not for want of trying. However, there was another . . . in my youth. But I was too young to recognize how precious what we had was, or how rare. I feared too much doing without to run off with him to America when he asked. Don't be afraid of the price you might have to pay to gain what you truly want."

"I will beggar my coffers to find her."

"Hugh, darling, giving up coins is easy. When you find her, what will you sacrifice of yourself to have and to hold her?"

CHAPTER 23

KNEELING, PENELOPE DUG the trowel into the dirt, loosening it, making it easier to pull the weeds from the garden. The day after she'd left Kingsland, in the room she'd secured at the Trewlove hotel, she'd scoured the *Times*' listing of advertisements for furnished homes for sale, visited a few of the more promising ones, and fallen in love with this small cottage on sight. She'd moved in a couple of days later.

Eventually she would replace the furniture with items more to her liking, but what had come with the residence served her needs for now. And Sir Purrcival had certainly made himself at home on the worn cushions. She had yet to venture out, her experience with Grenville serving as a reminder that her life could easily take a turn at any moment. However, she didn't intend to live as a recluse forever. She still wanted to assist women with investing, but was going to take a few more weeks to get settled before traveling down that path. She wanted to enjoy her freedom, relax, and put her garden to rights. The couple who had owned the cottage before her had let nature have its way so that presently everything looked quite wild and unorganized, but she had already mapped out her plans for the small lawn at the rear of her property. She knew exactly where she would plant the bulbs in autumn, and come spring—

"Tell me, Miss Hart—"

With a jolt at the familiar voice that visited her dreams, she swung around and stared up at the tall, broad, and beautiful man who had invaded her gardens. Why did the sight of him have to hurt so much, while at the same time send joy spiraling through her?

"—have you any idea how many cottages have recently been sold in the Cotswolds?"

"What are you doing here?"

"I should think that was obvious. I came for you."

With his words, her heart was desperately striving to break free of the iron box in which she'd recently stored it.

"You left a task unfinished. My ball. It is in three days hence, and you were to oversee it."

Closing her eyes, she fought off the disappointment. Of course he was here for Pettypeace. She shot to her feet. "I hired a woman to manage it."

"Miss Taylor. And she is working extremely hard, but she is not you, Penelope."

Oh God. He'd used her given name, and the

syllables rolled out so smoothly in his deep voice. The damned lock was straining to break, as her impractical heart wanted to have its way and freedom. "I left detailed instructions. I'm certain you'll find no fault with the evening."

"Why did you leave . . . without telling me? Without telling anyone?"

Because it was the way she was taught. Leave without goodbyes, without regrets. Before the temptation to hint where she could be found became too strong . . . or before acknowledging the loss of friendship would be so great that she might not leave at all. "Did you look at the photographs?"

"Only one. I set fire to it and the remainder of them, as well as the other twenty-one I've managed to find."

For several heartbeats, words deserted her. Twenty-one fewer. "How did you even know where to find that sort of . . . lewd offering?"

He gave her an indulgent look. "As you are very well aware, Penelope, I hire extremely capable investigators. They don't know specifically what I'm searching for, but they can locate the purveyors of obscene materials. Once they inform me which shops secretly sell illegal contraband, I visit, search through their stock, and purchase the items I find. How many are there, do you think?"

"Countless. I was unaware he could create as many as he wanted from one click of his camera. I thought one click, one photograph. I'm surprised none appeared sooner." She'd often been recognized after only a few months. "But that night at

Cremorne served as a reminder that they will always surface. And Grenville was correct. It would do your reputation no good for Society to learn you had in your employ a woman of such immoral character."

"You weren't a woman. You were a girl. I'd wager closer to twelve than twenty."

She glanced over at the crimson dahlias. "Fourteen." She peered up at him. "Old enough to know better. Or so my mum believed. She was horrified when she discovered how I'd come to have money."

"How did she learn of it?"

"The coins I earned allowed us to let a room in a common lodging house in St. Giles. The husband of one of the lodgers had obtained a photograph of me. His wife discovered it and wasn't half-livid. He could barely provide for her but had splurged on *filth*. She showed it to my mum. Showed it to everyone, actually. Held me responsible for corrupting her husband. I was tossed out—literally. But at least my mum and sister had the room for the remainder of the week."

"And then?"

If his voice hadn't contained such earnestness, such true interest, she would have walked away. She hated these memories. "I secured a room elsewhere. I was waiting for them when they left their lodging house for the last time. I urged them to come stay with me. Mum wouldn't even look at me. She just grabbed my sister's hand and dragged her away." The pain of the memory struck hard. She'd been cast aside like so much rubbish. "I tried to give her coins, but she wouldn't take them, said she was ashamed of having a sinner for a daughter. It was the last time I saw them."

"She couldn't have worked?"

"During my father's incarceration she withered away. I think his passing was the final blow. She became terribly ill. Had an awful cough. A couple of months after our final parting, I learned of her death. And my sister's." She met and held his gaze. "I wanted only to save them."

His arms came around her, and he pressed her head against his chest. "I know."

The tears came. After all this time, all these years, how could there still be tears? It had seemed wrong to let them die when she had the means to provide for them so they might live. What was removing her clothes when compared with the pain of losing them? But she'd lost them anyway.

"Your mother was wrong. There was no shame in what you did, Penelope."

"You felt differently the night you learned of it."

Leaning back, he tucked his forefinger beneath her chin. "I was wrong as well. I have no excuse for my behavior except to say that I am terribly sorry for any impression you may have had that I would not have stood at your side. I promise you that if it takes the remainder of my life and beyond, I will see every one of those photographs found and destroyed. They will no longer have any bearing on your life."

"They will always have a bearing. You can't know who owns them, who among your friends has looked at them and might at some point recognize me."

"But you have the power of my influence and support behind you. You will not be ruined, not by a photograph. I will not allow it. So come back to London with me. Manage my ball. And then we shall work out a retirement settlement for you, so when you are ready to leave, you are well cared for."

She was not an exception. He provided a generous pension for all his staff. After swiping at the lingering dampness on her cheeks, she stepped out of his embrace and angled her head slightly. "I'm really quite wealthy, you know."

"You mentioned before that you didn't need to work for me."

"I was once employed by a clever fellow who was very good at investing. I followed his lead."

"Smart woman. Now be even smarter and return with me."

She shook her head. "Your Grace—"

"Penelope, are you going to let your past dictate your future? It is going to be the most important night of my life thus far, because I opened the letter you left for me and fully intend to marry the woman whose name I call out."

Her stomach dropped to the ground, which was silly when he'd just confirmed that she had the right of things and had chosen correctly for him.

"While Miss Taylor is working diligently," he continued, "she is not you. I need everything perfect that night. I know your presence will make it so."

She sighed. Hearing him call out that name in his deep and resounding voice was going to be more difficult than removing her clothing for a stranger. But he was correct. She'd left before finishing this last task and had experienced a measure of guilt late at night when all grew quiet and the cottage settled in. "All right, but only to manage the ball. After that I return here."

"Splendid. Pack your things and grab your cat. My carriage awaits."

CHAPTER 24

I~T WAS THE~ ball to end all balls, the final event of the Season. An odd time, really, for the duke to select the woman he would begin courting when such an endeavor would be rather inconvenient. But after the embarrassment in June, he'd not wanted to wait another year. He'd rather people gossip about his impending courtship than his previous one.

Penelope hardly blamed him. If people weren't inclined to blather about the announcement he would soon make, she had ensured they would at least speak of the affair she'd arranged for the evening. It was befitting a king.

Liveried footmen were plentiful, offering every sort of spirit imaginable, as well as a lemon punch and a raspberry one. Platters of bite-sized morsels were also being carted around. In the room adjoining the grand parlor, a feast with enough meats, pies, vegetable dishes, and cakes to feed a small nation was waiting to be devoured. Anything that remained would be delivered to a shelter. Having once gone hungry, Penelope couldn't tolerate any food being wasted.

As she wandered through the ballroom ensuring everything was going smoothly, she acknowledged the Chessmen, as they were all in attendance. Whenever a hopeful lady caught her eye, she worked not to give anything away regarding the choice she'd made for Kingsland, but felt rather unkind doing so. She wanted to squeeze the hand of each unselected lady and reassure her that someone special was waiting for her. She just had to be patient.

Although she couldn't escape the irony that not everyone did end up with someone. Certainly, she would spend the remainder of her life as a spinster. But that was by choice. It was what she wanted. Although she might not marry, she would eventually seek out a companion. Surely the more years that separated her from the girl she'd been, the less recognizable she would become. Especially as she gained wrinkles and her hair turned silver.

"Miss Pettypeace."

She smiled at Lawrence. "My lord."

"Quite the crush this evening."

"It's to be expected, I think, when anything involves your brother."

"I should say so, yes. I would not like to have my every action commented on."

"He's accustomed to it."

Lawrence took a sip of his champagne and glanced around. "I'm sorry about Mr. Grenville."

Her heart nearly stuttered to a stop. Had Kingsland told his brother about the man? "Mr. Grenville?"

Lawrence studied her. "Yes. I saw you walking about with him at the Fair and Spare. I thought perhaps something might develop between the two of you. Although he'd certainly have to contend with an unhappy King if that were to happen. My brother wouldn't take kindly to losing you."

It seemed her secret was still safe. "Mr. Grenville was simply being polite, giving me a tour. I had no interest in him."

"All for the best since he left for Canada."

"He's gone to Canada?"

"Hmm. Odd that, really. Just packed a bag and went, from what I understand."

The relief washing over her was welcome. He'd never bother her again. "I hope he's happy there."

Lawrence leaned toward her. "Rumor is he was dallying with someone's wife. Fellow found out and broke his jaw."

"You can't believe everything you hear."

"True, but someone smashed a fist into his jaw. I can attest to that fact because I caught sight of him before he left." He looked past her. "Mother."

The duchess joined them. "Miss Pettypeace, I must say you have outdone yourself this evening."

"Thank you, Your Grace."

"My son is fortunate to have you." She placed a beringed finger to her lips. "Who did you choose for him?"

"You'll know in a few minutes, but I promise you will find her very much to your liking."

"But will he find her to his liking?"

"I shall be very surprised if he does not."

The gong sounded, the vibrations echoing through her, calling to her heart to remain strong, to her eyes not to weep, to her soul not to shatter. The orchestra went silent, but murmuring among the crowd increased in pitch. The footman struck the gong again. The mutterings continued.

Kingsland stepped through the doorway and onto the landing. And the crowd quieted. Such was his power, his commanding presence. He didn't have to use words to issue an order or to be obeyed. Dressed in his finery, he was so remarkably gorgeous, confidence brimming from every pore, surprising her that after all these years and knowing him as well as she did, he still took her breath.

Then his gaze landed on her at the edge of the ballroom and held for a moment, two, as though to acknowledge all she'd done for him, how she wanted this night to be one he and his future wife remembered. A night like no other. A good memory to see them through if doubts ever plagued them.

His attention drifted away from her and encompassed every single soul in the grand ballroom.

"My esteemed guests." His voice boomed, filling whatever space remained. "Last Season, I stood here and instructed you all to congratulate the woman I was honoring by calling her name. The man she would eventually marry informed me that I was searching for the wrong thing—it was not the woman upon whom the honor was bestowed. I should choose a woman whose presence in my life bestowed the honor upon me. That to have her at my side was the true blessing."

He held up the folded paper she'd left in an envelope for him, and then, slowly and deliberately, slipped it inside his jacket. "It does not seem right to announce the name of the lady chosen before knowing if she will even have me. Therefore, with your indulgence . . ."

He began descending the stairs. Penelope was slightly disappointed that he had so little faith in her judgment to think the lady she'd selected would turn him away. Of course she wouldn't. Lady Alice—

People began stepping aside. Rising up on her toes, she tried to see above the heads to find Kingsland. There he was. Daft man. Just as she feared. He was moving in the wrong direction. Lady Alice was on the other side of the room, at the back standing away from the gathering, which was the only reason Penelope could see her. Raising her arm, she pointed and waved, striving to signal that he was traveling the wrong course.

The crowd parted like the Red Sea, and Kingsland was suddenly clearly visible, all six feet of him. She shook her finger toward the far side. He paid her no heed. She would have to take his arm and lead him over. Finally, he was before her.

"The lady is over there," she whispered harshly.

"The one whose name you wrote out for me, yes. But not the one I want to marry." He lowered himself to a knee.

Through the thundering in her ears, she

barely heard the gasps and mumbles. "What are you doing?"

"For you, Penelope, I will go to a knee. I'll go down on both if you prefer." He took her hand, and she wondered if he could feel the trembling in it, the quaking that was coursing through her entire body. "I asked you to select a woman to be my duchess, and you chose wrong. But how can I blame you when even I didn't comprehend that she has been with me the entire time? I would willingly die for you. I will kill for you . . . I will live for you. Miss Penelope Pettypeace, you shall always be the love of my life, the echo of my soul. Will you grant me the greatest honor by becoming my wife, my duchess?"

She shook her head as tears began welling and rolling onto her cheeks. "Do not ask this of me." Because her answer would be no. It had to be no. A photograph could turn up at any time. She could be recognized at any moment. If the person recalled her face from photographs he no longer had, he could tell people where he'd seen her. Rumors without proof could be as devastating as rumors with. The shame it would bring Hugh, his family, his children—their children.

"I know what worries you, Penelope, but I give you my solemn oath that there is nothing we cannot face together and conquer. You are my strength, my rock. That it took me so long to realize the depth of my feelings for you is rather unconscionable. I always thought I had no heart, but you proved me wrong because when I realized you were gone, that I had wounded you so much that you would leave, it broke, shattered into a thousand pieces, each one with your name etched upon it. You own me, heart and soul. I shall devote the remainder of my life to ensuring you never have cause to doubt the depth of my love for you."

"Oh, Hugh." Her face would soon resemble a river. "Are you sure?"

Not even a thousand stars could compete with the brilliance of his smile as he pressed it against her hand and held her gaze. "I've never been more sure of anything in my entire life."

"I have loved you for so long. There was never anything you could ask of me that I would not do. I certainly won't say no now when what you are asking is something I dared not dream. Yes. Yes. Yes!"

Suddenly his arms were around her, his mouth on hers as though if he didn't kiss her at that precise moment he would cease to exist. Her toes barely touched the floor.

She was scarcely aware of the sighs, murmurs, clearing of throats. Since she'd returned to his residence, they'd been on their best behavior, and she'd assumed he'd relegated her to the permanent role of secretary. The two nights had been interminable, lonelier than ever before with him so near and yet beyond reach, beyond touch. She'd known then, with certainty, that she couldn't remain after he married. No, sooner than that. After tonight.

But now there would be no leaving, only staying. Here with him, with his arms tightly bound around her and his mouth doing terribly wicked things to hers. Forever.

It seemed her impractical heart had turned out to be not quite so impractical after all.

THE BALL WENT on and on. Midnight came and went and still people danced, and drank, and ate. Offered congratulations. The Chessmen, blast them, gloated, claiming to have known he loved her before he knew and not being at all surprised by his announcement. His mother had patted his cheek and told him, "It's about time you saw reason." Lawrence had looked smug, and King was relatively certain that somewhere his brother had made a wager regarding whose name would be revealed.

But all the well-wishers and attentiveness had prevented him from finding a single moment alone with her. While dancing with her had at least provided an opportunity to avoid all the attention from others, it hadn't truly given him a chance to lavish her with the devotion he wanted to bestow upon her.

So when the guests had finally departed, and his mother and Lawrence had settled into their respective guest chambers, he knocked lightly on the door leading into hers, grateful she answered so quickly. She was already in her nightdress with her hair flowing around her. Her brow creased ever so slightly.

"I thought I was always supposed to come to you."

"Ah, but tonight you are not my secretary. You are my betrothed. Although you may, naturally, deny me entry."

She gave him an impish smile. "Why would I do that when I was on the cusp of crossing the hallway to be with you?"

When she stepped back, he stepped over the threshold, closed the door quietly when it took everything within him not to slam it, drew her into his arms, and claimed her mouth with a fierceness that might have been unnerving if she hadn't welcomed him with a hunger as strong as his own. What a fool he'd been not to have recognized what was between them sooner. He dragged his lips along her throat. "It nearly killed me not to come to you before tonight."

"Nearly killed me not to go to you—but I knew having you for a while when I couldn't have you forever would hurt too much. As wonderful as the pleasure was, I always had an ache in my heart afterward."

He lifted her into his arms. "From this night forward, Penelope, you are mine forever. To have and to hold. To love and to cherish."

"Those are vows we've not yet made."

"The ceremony is only a formality. In my heart they are already written, never to be erased."

"Hugh, have you a poetic bent I've never known about?"

"Hardly." He tossed her on the bed, tore off his clothes, and watched as she shed her nightdress. When it joined the pile, he leapt on her, capturing her screech of surprise, kissing her as though she provided sustenance. And she did.

"God, I missed you," he growled, lowering his

head to pepper kisses over her breast before suckling gently.

She scraped her fingers through his hair and held him close. "But I've been here for three days now."

"Not like this you haven't."

"I can think of so many reasons why you shouldn't have asked, why I shouldn't have accepted. I'm eight-and-twenty."

"Seasoned." He moved to her other breast.

"I am not quiet."

"But I have always enjoyed hearing what you have to say. My favorite part of investigating any potential business venture involved asking your opinion."

"It always made me feel you valued my mind."

"I do." He left a trail of kisses along her ribs. "I value every aspect of you. The silk of your hair through my fingers. The satin of your skin against my palm." He shoved himself farther down and spread her open. "The taste of you against my tongue."

Her throaty sigh as he stroked her intimately nearly caused him to spill his seed then and there. He loved the sound of her mewls and moans, the way she squirmed beneath him, tugged on his hair, dug her fingers into his shoulders. There was no aspect of her that he didn't love. While he wished the past that had shaped and defined her had been kinder, it had molded her into an intricate, complex, multifaceted woman he admired as he did no other of his acquaintance.

Her thighs began quivering, and he intensified his ministrations. Her back bowed, and she cut off her cries with her hand pressed against her mouth. Moving up, he thrust into her, taking satisfaction in the throbs that had yet to dissipate and the velvety heat that no sheath prevented him from relishing. Brushing her hand aside, he blanketed her mouth with his and smiled inwardly as her tongue met his. Bold as brass, his Penelope. How could he have ever thought he needed to hunt for the perfect duchess when she had been with him for so very long?

Perfect for his soul, his heart, his body. Perfect as his wife, his lover, his partner. In all things, he'd never find a better match.

What an absolute numbskull he'd been.

Then he was pounding into her with all the fervor of his love, claiming her, making her his own. It was only fair. Without realizing it, he had become hers. She was the reason last Season's choice for duchess had proved a debacle, the reason he'd chosen Lady Kathryn Lambert, knowing he was likely to lose her to another. She was the reason he'd been unable to retain his ardor for Margaret. And damned if Margaret hadn't been able to figure it out.

He who was so skilled at identifying opportunity had nearly missed the treasure that was Penelope Pettypeace.

Lifting himself up, as he rocked against her, he gazed into her beautiful green eyes, made all the more so by the love for him reflected in them. "I love you, Penelope, so damned much."

Tears glistened in her eyes. "I love you, Hugh, so damned much that sometimes I thought I would die of it."

"Never leave me again."

"I won't."

The rough conviction in her voice caused him to shatter, inside and out, as his seed poured into her, and he collapsed on top of her, breathing heavily, harshly.

She wound her legs tightly around his hips. "I love you."

"Good. Because we'll be married within the week."

Her laughter floated around him. "I can't arrange a proper wedding for a duke in only a week."

"Miss Taylor can."

"She is skilled, but not that skilled."

Rising up, he held her gaze once more. "She can if she's been planning it since the day you hired her. A few days after she arrived here, I set her to the task of organizing our wedding so all could be prepared with a minimum amount of fuss with a short notice. All she needs is for you to approve what she has arranged."

"That was rather checky of you. What if you'd never found me?"

He was slightly insulted. "Knowing me as you do, do you honestly believe that would have happened, that I would have ceased searching for what I sought?"

Her smile could have toppled empires, would have dropped him to his knees if he'd been standing. "Knowing me as you do, do you honestly believe I would have been found if I didn't want to be?"

"What I believe, my future duchess, is that we were made for each other."

Epilogue

Kingsland Ancestral Estate
Six years and four months after the Kingsland ball

IF THERE EXISTED a more pleasant task in the world than waking up next to the man you loved, Penelope Brinsley-Norton, Duchess of Kingsland, certainly couldn't imagine what it might be. Unless it was rocking your children to sleep, or reading them a story, or watching them play with their father.

Within the first three years of their marriage, she'd given Hugh his heir, his spare, and then a daughter. Her husband had teasingly praised her for her efficiency. They were increasingly lighter of mood as the years progressed, and neither of their secrets returned to haunt them.

Shortly after they were married, he'd hired Miss Taylor to serve as his secretary. She'd passed the ball-arranging business off to her sister. One of the things Penelope had always loved about him was his willingness to view a woman as capable as a man. They'd also hired Lucy to serve as Penelope's lady's maid, elevating her status in the household and allowing their friendship to continue. And when she'd married Harry the footman, who now served as underbutler, they'd moved into a small cottage on the estate and shared a larger room at the London residence.

Penelope had set aside her plans to go into business for herself and instead had established a charity devoted to the betterment of women through investment opportunities. While her focus was on women, she never turned away any man who needed to learn how to effectively manage his earnings.

After experiencing the thrill of success when the wake-up clock was well received, Lawrence had invested in other manufacturing opportunities. He seemed to have a gift for identifying the sort of merchandise people would purchase. He was wholly independent of his brother now and it suited him.

Her husband's eyes fluttered open, and he smiled. "Good morning. How long have you been awake?"

"A while."

"It's Christmas. We're supposed to sleep late, aren't we?"

"The children will be knocking on the door soon, anxious to go down to the parlor to see what Father Christmas brought them."

"Tell them to wake their grandmother or Uncle Lawrence." They always visited at Christmas. "I'm in the mood to ravish their mother."

He rolled onto her and began nibbling on her neck. Still finding it difficult to believe she had this wonderful, gorgeous, generous man to herself every morning, she wrapped her arms and legs around him, squeezing tightly, holding him close, absorbing the warmth of a body just beginning to fully awaken. "You're always in the mood to ravish their mother."

"Lucky you."

"Indeed."

After lifting himself up to his elbows, he skimmed his knuckles over her cheeks. "I hear the patter of their feet. They are as determined as their mother, so we're not going to get out of this, are we?"

"Would you want to? Truly?"

"No. It will be said of the ninth duke that his residence was always filled with laughter and joy."

"What will be said of the ninth duchess?"

"That she was well loved by her duke—and once the children tire out and retreat for a nap, I'm going to prove that statement true."

Later that afternoon he did exactly that. And every day and night afterward.

¶In the summer of 2021, locked away in a Victorian-era mahogany cigar box, was discovered what was believed to be the last remaining photograph of a young girl who was known only as the Fallen

Angel. The rare find was offered by Sotheby's in an online auction and sold for fifty thousand pounds to an anonymous bidder. When it was inconspicuously delivered to his residence, Brandon Brinsley-Norton, fifteenth Duke of Kingsland, as the others who came before him had done, kept the vow made by his too-many-greats-to-count grandfather. He built a fire in the hearth in his library and pitched the recently received package, without opening it, onto the flames.

Author's Note

$\mathcal{I}$ MUST START BY thanking Alexandra Hawkins, longtime friend, confidant, and sounding board, who shared a realty advertisement page from a Victorian-era issue of the *Times* so I could determine how my heroine might manage to secure a cottage in a relatively short period of time. The number of properties for sale or let, many of them fully furnished, was astounding.

The first alarm clock was invented in France in 1847, but it only allowed one to set the particular hour to be awakened. One invented in America in 1876 did allow for the setting of the hour and the minute when one wished to be disturbed from slumber. While it was the American one that eventually made its way to England's shores, I thought it possible for an English-made one to be produced before that.

Pornography was a term first used in 1864 and

applied to the erotic materials banned by the Obscene Publications Act of 1857. The act resulted in an underground system devoted to creating and distributing salacious writings and images. Photography was partially responsible for making such materials more widely available, especially after 1841, when the development of the calotype process allowed for a photograph to be repeatedly printed.

As for Penelope's investments: since at least Regency times, unmarried women—in particular widows—invested their inheritances in various ways as a means to ensure a steady yearly income. The downside was that if they married, the shares and income became the property of their husbands. In 1870, the Married Women's Property Act gave women the right to remain the legal owners of their investment shares. As a result, women were encouraged to invest. Recent studies have shown that women investors played a far greater role in cultural, societal, and financial changes than originally believed. (Sources: *Women Writing about Money 1790–1820* by Edward Copeland and *Women, Literature, and Finance in Victorian Britain* by Nancy Henry.)

CHECK OUT THE FIRST BOOK IN THE
ONCE UPON A DUKEDOM
DUOLOGY

SCOUNDREL OF MY HEART

The second son of a duke,
Griffith Stanwick was the spoiled
spare for whom everything came
easily. Until his family lost everything,
and he lost the woman he loved. Now
he will pay any price to have her
back in his arms.

Next month, don't miss these exciting new love stories only from Avon Books

Holiday Ever After by Jill Shalvis

Three fan-favorite Jill Shalvis novellas are together for the first time in this holiday anthology! Dive into the romances in *One Snowy Night*, *Holiday Wishes*, and *Mistletoe in Paradise*.

Second Chance Christmas by Lori Wilde

Best friends Joel and Jana discover a shocking surprise while organizing the living Nativity. They find a sweet little baby in the manger with a note saying the mother will return . . . soon. They plan to care for the baby until New Year's, when the mother will hopefully come back. But as the days pass, they're forced to face facts: their relationship goes far deeper than friendship . . .

The Lady Gets Lucky by Joanna Shupe

Shy heiress Alice Lusk is tired of being overlooked by every bachelor. Something has to change, or else she'll be forced to marry a man whose only desire is her fortune. She needs to become a siren, a woman who causes a man's blood to run hot . . . and she's just met Christopher "Kit" Ward, the perfect rogue to help teach her.

REL 10 21